NATURAL FORCES II

JEAN GILL

From award-winning author Jean Gill, author of *The Troubadours Quartet*
Winner of the *Global Ebooks Award for Best Historical Fiction*
Finalist in *the Kindle Book Awards, Cinnamon Press Novella Award, the Wishing Shelf Awards and the Chaucer Awards*

Praise for *Queen of the Warrior Bees*
'Gill's work stands apart through its strikingly inventive concept, distinctive sense of place, and masterful use of imagery.' *Booklife Prize Quarterfinalist*

'An epic fight for nature...With more backstabbing that the Roman Senate, more deceit than *Game of Thrones* and more paranoia than *The Handmaid's Tale*.' Deb McEwan, the *Afterlife* series

'Spellbinding! If you liked *The Bees* you'll love this. A brilliantly imagined fantasy with a strong environmental message. Jean Gill writes with a beekeeper's clarity about hive structure, and of 'hive mind' with the heart and passion of a talented author and poet.' Ashley Dyer, *Splinter in the Blood*

'The most original book I've read this year.' Anna Castle, *the Francis Bacon mysteries*

'The perfect gift for young environmental campaigners raised on Harry Potter.' Debbie Young, the *Sophie Sayers Village mysteries*

'The climactic conclusion of this vibrant tale took my breath away.' Elizabeth Horton Newton, *Between the Beats* blog

'Dazzles, varies and enchants... A great read, to be done in one sitting to find out what happens, then once again to fully savour the marvels of this book.' Laurette Long, *the French Summer novels*

© Jean Gill 2020
The 13th Sign
ISBN 979-10-96459-12-4

First published in 2020

All rights reserved. No part of this publication may be reproduced, stored in a retrieval system, or transmitted in any form without prior permission from the publisher.

This is a work of fiction. Names, characters, organisations, places and events are either products of the author's imagination or are used fictitiously.

*For Sigourney
with love*

*'When you shoot an arrow of truth,
dip its point in honey.'
Arab proverb*

CHAPTER ONE

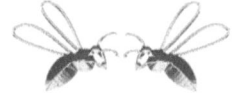

'Chief Mage Rinduran was attacked by the nightmare creatures of the Forest, drained his magecraft to protect the Citadel. Until all he had left was his last drop of blood.' Bastien choked on a sob, his voice quavering as he continued, 'But that was enough. His giant sacrifice was greater than the Forest could fight and the Citadel is safe. The war is over!'

He paused to allow his audience to show its enthusiasm. When the roars had died down, he announced, 'I've been asked to take on the role of Chief Mage.'

Here, Bastien cast a sideways look at Hamel, who might have hidden a sceptical twitch of an eyebrow before he squeaked, 'Quite right, quite right.' It was hard to tell what Hamel thought. His expressions were as alien as his appearance, from his pointed head and greenish skin to the claws he tapped impatiently on the High Table.

'So,' Bastien resumed, 'I must try to fill my father's shoes. We need time to mourn and time to choose new Councillors but, rest assured, the Forest is defeated! Our Perfect society is safe once more! And we shall celebrate with the Courtship Dance that was postponed because of the war. Our Perfect Society has overcome those who would destroy it!'

Cheering was clearly required again at this point so hearty hoorays ensued. A dance would allow new adults to pair up and weddings would follow, as sure as light was grey; undoubtedly a good thing.

This time when he paused, Bastien looked towards the slight figure beside him. He took her hand, kissed it. 'My sister Verity will be with me at the dance as she is with me in mourning our father.' His voice broke and the white-faced girl squeezed his hand.

Sister? Verity? There had been rumours that Rinduran had another child, hidden away because she suffered from allergy, and now here she was, thin and pasty-faced but sitting at the High Table all the same. What to make of that?

Not only was the girl sitting with the Council of Ten but she even presumed to speak, in a sweet whisper amplified by speech magic. Her magecraft? Or Bastien's?

'I...' she began and quickly corrected herself. '*We* want to commemorate Daddy...' A child's slip. 'Our father. If you have any suggestions for how we should do so, please let Hamel know. We'll say goodbye to our beloved Chief Mage before we hold the dance.' Her voice trembled.

Hamel's face darkened to bilious green. He was clearly not impressed by the role he'd been given. He was one of only four Councillors who'd returned from the battle, out of the ten who'd fought. Wasn't he a hero too?

Nobody challenged the triumphant speech made by the new Chief Mage from the High Table but, later, rumours spread like a virus around the Citadel and the forbidden word 'Forest' was on everybody's lips.

The most hushed question concerned what had happened to the freak, the girl who'd infested the Citadel with Forest. The one they called – barely mouth the dangerous words – Queen of the Warrior Bees. Those unfortunates who'd seen her, wreathed in a cloud of her vile familiars, still had nightmares. Was she dead? If the Citadel had won the war, and they were all safe, she must be. But why did none of the mages say so? Who knew the truth?

One person did know but he was not in the Great Hall or his *harrumph* of disbelief at Bastien's speech would have been the focus of attention. Instead, the absence of Kermon, the new Mage-Smith, went unnoticed amid the hubbub after the speeches.

Had he been missed by the other mages, they'd have merely concluded he was mourning his dead master and preparing for his new role in the Citadel.

If the servants noticed the blue fires that leaked raw power from the smithy, through every crack in the stone, none of them was foolish enough to say so. Nor to comment on the food and drink left untouched for three days outside the closed door to the forge.

On the fourth day, the Mage-Smith emerged and sent for sustenance, another indication that the Citadel was returning to normal after the war. But Kermon was not the man he'd been when he entered the forge. And the Citadel rippled with unease.

CHAPTER TWO

Kermon's self-sacrifice was not a glorious death in battle but the harder choice of living his mission every day. Confined in a place he hated, with people he despised. Alone.

Somewhere in the Forest, Mielitta was soaring free with her bees or sharing a camp-fire with her two human friends. He could have been at her side, his senses exploding in the sunlit bounty of the Forest, if he hadn't volunteered to return to the Citadel. To serve Mielitta in her enemies' grey lair.

Kermon couldn't get used to thinking of the girl he'd known from childhood under her new title but he was here in her service – and for the sake of all who lived here. Somebody had to return with the Citadel children and nurture the future they could shape, remind them of the taste of honey. He could taste it still, a sweetness of trees and stars bursting on his tongue. He had not known how impoverished his diet was until his mouth awoke. And now the craving gnawed at him. How could he settle for the tasteless sustenance of the Citadel? How could he pretend that he preferred purity and security to being fully alive?

Thanks to the Queen of the Warrior Bees, the Citadel children had known the Forest and tasted honey, brought to them by the bees who made it. Surely, like him, they would never forget, even without his help. Perhaps he was not needed here after all. He could escape, now, before he was found out and failed Mielitta anyway.

The mages had sealed the water gate but there must be some weak spot in their wards. If not, Kermon could go into the walls to seek a new way out. The wise ones who dwelled in the walls would help him and now was his only chance, while the mages were distracted by their own tangle of outrageous lies in the aftermath of the war.

He tried to imagine Mielitta's welcoming smile at their reunion but instead he saw the warrior Jannlou's contempt and the Forest Mage Drianne's disappointment. Each of them had volunteered to return with the children, been prepared to shoulder the burden Kermon now carried. Each of them would despise him if he gave up on his task without even trying.

So Kermon must see it through, for as long as it took. He had no idea how he would know if he'd succeeded but he had promised to be Mielitta's eyes and ears in the Citadel, to make sure the honey did its work. She believed that this generation of children would challenge Perfection, allow the Forest into the Citadel once more. Then they would all be reunited in a world where Nature's rich variety was celebrated. Where Mielitta and those like her were not sentenced to death. He must believe that too, stay alive and do his work, whatever that might be. Death in battle would have been so much easier.

Heavy-hearted, he set to his first impossible task: to communicate with Mielitta. He'd promised to make a twin to Steelwing, the arrowhead he'd forged for her. They would connect through the arrowheads. What he hadn't told her was that he had no idea whether it would work.

As he'd done a thousand times, first as assistant, then as apprentice to Declan, he lit the fire and arranged his tools while he waited for the heat to intensify. Then he donned his leatherette gauntlets and made a metal sandwich: five layers of two different kinds of steel. Pinching the raw block tightly in long tongs, he thrust it into the white-hot heart of the flames.

As he'd done a thousand times, Kermon readied himself for the surrender to fire and darkness, the smith's partners in creation. But this time, his old master's face smiled back at him from the blazing heart, a demonic vision haloed in flames.

'You'll need help with this,' the black semblance of a mouth breathed, before clamping down on the tongs, which Kermon jerked backwards in instinctive recoil.

The raw steel was pulled deeper into the inferno and Kermon took refuge in his craft, concentrated on the making.

'Declan,' he greeted the fire demon as if they'd last met over a jug of Citadel ale, not on opposing sides in the Battle of the Forest.

'You killed me, boy.'

It was true and not true. Declan had awoken Steelwing's vengeance but it was indeed Kermon's double-edged magecraft in the arrowhead.

'You killed yourself,' Kermon replied, remembering the smell of blood and treachery, acrid on the arrowhead he pulled from Declan's corpse. He could not have returned it to Mielitta like that, the beauty of its patterned waves defiled, so he'd cleaned it, in the same way mages on the Council of Ten cleaned the minds of servants, to keep their secrets safe. But Kermon had never used his powers in such a manner and was untrained. In cleaning the arrowhead, he'd taken into himself the dead man's dark history, written into his blood.

Darkness and fire played over the metal, bonding the different layers, just as Declan's duplicity was welded to Kermon's own soul. If Steelwing was now untarnished, the same could not be said of the new Mage-Smith. But such knowledge could be used.

Kermon would read the depths of this soul so he could understand the black heart of the Citadel, the forging of its citizens.

'You would have killed Mielitta,' he said. The pressure on the tongs relaxed at the name, as Kermon had expected. He pulled them out quickly and set about his work, hammering and folding, ignoring the flames behind him.

When he was ready, he thrust the tongs into the forge once more, prepared for a struggle this time. He gazed into the fire as it flamed defiance and he let his magecraft reach for the demon's thoughts, as he did with living people. For this, they called him soul-reader.

'Declan,' Kermon acknowledged again, with no words of welcome or of judgement, though his stomach clenched with loss. This man had been his mentor, his role model, his surrogate father. His gut posed the first question.

'How could you?' he asked. 'How could you do it, to me, to Mielitta? You'd have killed us in the Forest.'

'It hurt me too, boy.' Declan's voice still held the gruff warmth Kermon remembered. 'You shouldn't be doing this. Playing with fire.'

'Why?' Kermon insisted, coldly, forcing an answer.

'For Perfection. The greater good. Same as you're doing now but you're on the wrong side, aren't you. I expect you'll betray everyone in the Citadel. Again.' The fiery mouth spat sparks but couldn't reach Kermon.

He mustn't waste his questions. *Did you ever love us?* his heart screamed but, aloud, he demanded, 'What am I supposed to do in the Maturity Test?' The question sounded straightforward enough but Kermon suspected Declan had no knowledge of the terms Mielitta had imposed when she'd won the battle. There would no longer be a Maturity Test. Kermon's work as a spy had begun.

'I don't know whether your magecraft is up to it, boy,' the soot-black mouth sneered from the flames. 'You're a soul-reader, not a proper mage. But you were so good at the work and I didn't have other choices lining up... except the girl of course, Mielitta.' Her name came out in spit and angry sparks. 'Who'd think a baby could curl her fingers round your heart then rip out everything you care about? My fault for forgetting where she came from; for not seeing she was riddled with Forest. So I chose you and you'll have to do the job the best you can.'

Kermon kept the emotion out of his voice. 'What's the job?'

'The Maturity Mages will tell you when there's to be a Ceremony so you can prepare. Give the assistants the day off.'

'And the apprentice.' Kermon was bitter.

'Yes, and the apprentice. You'll have to choose one of the assistants to be your apprentice now you've had your big promotion.'

Kermon ignored the jeer, kept his eye on the shaping of the steel.

Heat, remove, fold, hammer. Repeat. Cut off the section he wanted. Shape.

He visualised Mielitta's pattern, which he had read in her mind, which she'd wanted to create for herself had she not been a girl. Waves like bees' wings, shining and flying through the folded steel of her arrowhead. He'd made it for her, his smith-piece to prove himself, and now he must make its twin.

Heat again.

Kermon reminisced, hoping to draw out all the information he could from his ancient master. 'I used to watch her, when I was an assistant. She was so miserable at never being chosen, never getting her Ceremony. Why wasn't she ever chosen? Why didn't you just forge her like the others? Let her fit in?'

'I used to let her look through the window until it was time for me to do my work. She liked to watch the procession cross the greensward to the Barn.'

The greensward. A fancy name for the grassette which was the Citadel's pretence at lawn underfoot. Fake, like everything in the Citadel. Kermon ached for the Forest, for real grass and real trees, sighing leaves and whistling birds. Everything he'd lost because of mages like this one.

He repeated his question. 'Why was Mielitta never chosen?'

'I don't know how the Council say who's ready and who's not but them as reach fourteen and aren't ready, they're suppressed. Perfection's way.'

Kermon kept a tight grip on the tongs, made a guess. 'No doubt the Council says they've died of allergy.'

'That'd be the way of it. But I kept her too long, cared for her, so I told the Council she must have some purpose, something good that the walls meant for us when they sent her.' The face spat flame. 'Forest-infested! Not fit to forge! See that window?' The fiery head jerked sideways. 'That's where she watched. But *we* can see the Test in our minds and that's the important bit, not the ceremony and fuss.

'You need the fires going and the welding rod hot, ready. When the candidates have proceeded through the forge, speechifying is done and they're in the Barn, you'll know the moment because the Maturity Mage will mind-call you. They can only do it when they're in the Barn. That means they've done their job and now it's your turn.

'You follow their link to see each candidate's mind – you'll find that bit easy. Than you take the hot rod and close off the deep thinking in each candidate, neat as a weld, cauterised. They can't feel a thing and they're happy after. But there's one special thing I do, though I doubt you're good enough.'

Kermon felt sick. 'Tell me anyway.'

'I leave just a blade-space open in the boys – you can tell boys from girls because their minds are coloured by the drinks. And the Maturity Mage does all that. She sorts them.'

'What about young mages?' asked Kermon, remembering his own ceremony.

'Green,' said Declan.

'I don't understand.'

'Their minds are green from the magecraft reacting to the drinks, so you know to leave them unforged. Until Puggy that is. She was a pleasure to seal, so easy and neat her mind closed over. Rinduran was right. It's for the best. Female mages just cause trouble. A distraction from our work, sure enough.'

'Green,' repeated Kermon stupidly, picturing Mage Puggy. Once a powerful opponent to Hamel on the Council, she was now reduced to Lady Puggy, beautiful and brainless. Thank the stones that Mielitta had demanded an end to forging, with Bastien's blood oath sealing the compact. This wraith of Declan seemed ignorant of all that had happened after his body's end and Kermon had no intention of enlightening him.

'Did you never wonder why Hamel is greenish?' asked Declan, as if they were sharing a joke, convivial at High Table together. 'Sure and he had an overdose of the green drink from a new Maturity Mage not in control of her magic. Strange side effects but no damage to his mind – thanks to the Master Smith.'

The fire visage narrowed his eyes, seemed closer and when he spat sparks again, he nearly reached Kermon.

'You're not strong enough to replace me,' Declan jeered.

Kermon suddenly realised how drained he felt, his feet glued to the stone cobblette, the Citadel's power drawing from his own through the fake stone.

'I'll do my best,' he said feebly and tried to break the link. The jeering flames still mocked him.

'Where's Mielitta? Is she alive? I want to see her,' demanded Declan, looming larger, billowing towards Kermon, drawing on his magecraft. In a gust of fiery breath, he spoke in words of power. 'I name this arrowhead Perfection. Find Mielitta and–'

Mielitta. The name gave Kermon a surge of energy, freed him from the cobblette and he pulled the rod from the fire, letting the face hiss and writhe, spitting into an ordinary forge once more.

Kermon plunged the arrowhead into the waiting bucket of oil, which boiled and flamed in a rainbow of bubbles as it tempered both the steel and the Smith Master. They both held true against the gobble of oil and flame, a last hint of flickering rage from a dead master. Then the oil calmed and Kermon placed the arrowhead on the stone anvil to cool and harden.

He sat in a daze for some time before returning to whatever senses he retained. Through careful questions to different servants, he'd ascertained that – unbelievably! – three days had gone by. He needed to eat and regain his strength before he tried using the arrowhead to reach its twin. Steelwing had been forged by Kermon with love, tears and a whispered protection spell that had saved Mielitta's life.

This arrowhead bore an unfinished curse and its name was Perfection. These things could not be changed.

CHAPTER THREE

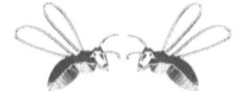

Bastien felt claws shredding his skin, smelled the bear's reek and woke in a panic, his pillow soaked in what must be sweat. Not even for his father would he give way to night tears. The nightmares, however, were beyond his control, bursting through every barrier of magecraft, defeating every potion that could be devised by his own skill or that of his physician. It seemed he was doomed to relive the Battle of the Forest night after night, without relief. Instead of recovering, he grew ever more exhausted from lack of sleep, unable to distinguish reality from the fictions spun by his subconscious. For the bear had done him no harm. Or rather, no direct harm.

His indomitable, peerless father lay crushed on the ground and Bastien charged at the bear, hurling power and words with equal futility against the merciless eyes, the stone-hard muscles, arms closing in a vice, squeezing out thought and breath–

Bastien jerked awake again. *Jannlou*, he thought, then told himself not to think. As Citadel darkness was followed by the reassuring greylight of daytime, his remembered fight with the bear led to the memory of betrayal. Jannlou, his blood-brother, not by his side but at *hers*, the freak's, dictating *her* terms to the Citadel, while the Chief Mage's body was still warm!

Chief Mage Rinduran. *Yes,* thought Bastien. *Better I think of him as Chief Mage Rinduran, murdered heroically in a battle, than as my father, ripped apart by an animal. What would he want me to do in his memory?*

So far, the commemorative suggestions made by the citizens had been predictably dull. His picture in the Great Hall. A statue. An award for a scholar. But the people did enjoy such dull tributes. And it was important to give the people what they wanted, while the Council returned to its former glory, in fact as well as in appearance.

The Council of Ten was currently the Council of Five, emasculated by their contract with the freak – he refused to think of her as Queen of the Warrior Bees! A contract he'd signed with a blood oath so must keep in spirit, not just in name. They'd have to appoint five mages, even include women. After all his father's work towards Perfection, they were forced to take this backward step.

But Chief Mage Rinduran *would* be honoured, the people would be given what they wanted and the Council would benefit. There would be an award... but not for some fresh-faced schoolboy. For a mage. Rinduran had specialised in the Citadel's history, had ventured deeper into the walls than any other mage had ever done. So the award would be for fresh research into the walls, with a contest and an achievement worthy of a place on the Council. That would give the mages something to think about.

He dressed carelessly, throwing on his knight's protective leatherette jerkin and britches, then his new black gown. The Seamstress Mage, Fabrisse, had taken his grey Apprentice Mage gown and brought out a black one, without comment. But he'd noted her lips purse as she added the gold braid of a Chief Mage and he knew she was not the only one with seditious thoughts at such a promotion.

He must exert his authority quickly. He would call a meeting and present his plan to honour Rinduran to the other Councillors, who needed something to keep their minds fully occupied.

Bastien was his father's son and knew full well that the other four Councillors would be watching his back carefully – and planning where to stick a knife.

A soft knock on his chamber door was followed by his name, softly spoken. Verity. He bade the door open and let his sister in. How strange that *she* could visit *him* now, after so many years confined to her sterile chamber, struggling with the allergy that had killed their mother. Although still greylight-pale, her face was no longer ghostly. In truth, he probably looked worse than she ever had. Her pastel pink gown suited her.

'I haven't heard you coughing.' He spoke the thought aloud.

'I haven't coughed.' Her brown-eyed gaze confirmed how monumental this statement was. Bastien's childhood had been racked by his sister's coughing fits whenever he visited her sterile sick-room. Not sweat on her pillow but blood.

He looked at her sharply and she rubbed her hand, self-conscious. 'What if it comes back?'

They'd argued over this. 'I haven't coughed,' she repeated stubbornly, her eyes challenging her brother's, as if she were the elder. 'I have work to do if I'm to find the freak that killed Daddy.'

He looked away, unable to meet her eyes, remembering the pact they'd made with the Forest. He found it hard to accept that Verity had been named his equal, a fellow Chief Mage, by the freak herself. As if there could be two Chief Mages. As if any girl was capable of such a role. But he had sworn by blood oath and he must humour his little sister, while protecting her.

'I know, Vivi.' He smiled at her. 'I just don't want you doing too much too soon. Nobody will be happier than me if your– if your health is improved.' He couldn't say 'allergy', not having watched his mother die. He dared not hope for Verity and yet he could not stop her testing her boundaries, exploring further from the safety of her room each day.

'Something happened, changed. We'll speak no more of it.' Her tone brooked no contradiction – a change as big as her health. 'We will need a Council meeting?'

At least she'd posed it as a question, he thought ruefully, as he explained his idea for a tribute to their father. *We can only appoint four*, he realised as he spoke. *There are already six of us. I must take Verity into account.*

'Good idea,' she approved. 'And I've been thinking about what happened.'

Again her gaze was too direct. Could she see his nightmares? Did she have them too? He did not want to talk about them but if it would help her... No, he couldn't. Did he blench?

'Kermon, the Mage-Smith,' she began and he tried to concentrate.

Not the bear. Not the bear, pounded his heart.

'He carried me out of my room. He's the one who abducted me.'

'We've been through this.' Bastien was impatient. 'He was under the influence of the other one.' Another word he didn't like to say, the name of his erstwhile fiancée, now a scarred fiend possessing magecraft.

'Drianne. Yes. She was strange and she did have powers,' admitted Verity. 'It's hard to know the truth because she didn't speak. Well, not with words anyway.'

'And she was with the freak.'

'Yes, the three of them were there. But the Mage-Smith didn't seem bound. He behaved like he did when he read Drianne's thoughts in the Great Hall.'

'He's a soul-reader. That's what he does.' He hesitated but forced himself to say her name. What kind of leader would he be if he couldn't name their enemies? 'Drianne *could* have made him kidnap you, as he says. And nobody saw him take part in the battle so he wasn't on their side.'

'Maybe,' she conceded. 'But don't trust him. I'm sure ... I think he has feelings for Mielitta.'

Bastien laughed. 'How could anybody have *feelings*,' he turned the word into a big brother's mockery of matters a little sister was too young to know about, 'for the freak?' He pictured Jannlou at Mielitta's side, laughed louder.

Verity was looking at his black robe. 'When do I get a robe like yours?'

Bastien hoped she would attribute his fresh outburst of laughter to the thought of anybody feeling something for the freak. Verity would soon realise that her position as Chief Mage was purely titular. One session of the masculine cut and thrust required in robust debate would teach her how unsuited she was for political responsibility. Meanwhile, he had made an oath to the freak and must keep it. Let Verity dress up. Without power, the clothes meant nothing.

'I shall order one for you today from the Seamstress Mage. It will need to be made specially for you, Vivi, as there are none your size, obviously.'

Verity just looked at him.

'Let's set up a Council meeting,' he told his little sister.

She nodded, smiled and summoned a messenger.

CHAPTER FOUR

'You're there,' stated Kermon stupidly, clutching the arrowhead he wore round his neck. His daytime sleep had taunted him with fire demons, left him befuddled rather than refreshed, but he'd rushed back to the forge to test this twin to Steelwing. He refused the name given by Declan. He would not call this masterwork of silk patterns in steel after the Citadel's credo. He refused any input by Declan into the making of the arrowhead, into the making of him, Kermon. He was no longer an Apprentice Mage-Smith but the master, clutching an arrowhead and gazing into a vision, who stared right back at him.

No vision of fire but of green light in the black of the forge. Eyes black as darklight, a halo of bees dancing around her long red hair, Mielitta looked every inch the Queen of the Forest, a stranger to him. *For years, she didn't even know you existed*, whispered some shred of filth that had wriggled into Kermon's gut when he'd purified Steelwing and sullied himself.

Why should she? his better self replied. *Look at her.* Around Mielitta, the bee-stripes danced amber and black amid the greens and golds of dappled sunlight through a canopy of leaves.

Bees. Sunlight. Trees. Mielitta was queen of this dancing world while Kermon was stuck in the Citadel with greylight in daytime and darklight at night, when he went to bed in his sterile chamber. In what passed for daytime, he could work in the forge and eat in the Great Hall, surrounded by enemies, consuming tasteless sustenance which varied in name only. Mielitta was as far above his reach as the Forest surpassed the Citadel and he would die in her cause, however little she valued him.

He was immediately annoyed with himself for having such a thought. That was Declan's foul work. Kermon *knew* he was more important to her now she had come into her powers than when he yearned after the misfit girl in the forge, who'd never noticed him. Or at least not until he took her job, become her father's Apprentice. And then she'd hated him, for a while.

Since then she'd called him friend and brother, although that was not what she called him now. 'You torturer! I've been waiting for weeks! I thought I'd never speak to you again! We've all been waiting to know if you're all right. What's happened? Has Bastien kept his word? Who are the new Council Members? Are some of them women? Have they stopped the Maturity Test? Have you seen the children?'

'Weeks? I don't think...' Kermon stammered. 'It took me a couple of days. I had–' But no, he couldn't tell her about Declan. Not this time. 'I had some problems,' he finished lamely.

'Days?' As Mielitta calmed, her bees ceased buzzing and disappeared from view. Kermon didn't think he'd ever grow accustomed to her companions. Mielitta's eyes glazed as she focused on the invisible bees, lost in some interior communication.

'I'd forgotten!' she told Kermon. 'Time here is different. And I've been so worried about you. We all have.'

This was as close to an apology as Mielitta was likely to come and Kermon was not going to waste his limited strength and time on his own feelings. He had a report to make.

'What matters is that it works, the arrowhead,' he told her. 'I can sense Steelwing, know whether you are open to me.' He used the formal words by which soul-readers gained permission from the subjects whose minds they entered.

'Of course. Steelwing's twin.' She made it sound so easy. If only she knew what had gone into the making. 'What is its name?'

He was silent. He would not be mastered in this. He conjured up the essence of the arrowhead in his heart and his magecraft, choosing carefully so that the steel would hear truth in its new name. Then he made his lips over-write Declan's curse. 'Unfinished,' he pronounced and he felt the power welding new name to old in the folds of steel. *Perfection Unfinished.*'

Mielitta's face wrinkled, then smoothed in acceptance of mages' strange ways.

'It doesn't matter whether our times align,' he told her. 'I need to choose moments carefully.'

He wondered what she saw when she looked at him. If she could read his soul, she'd see fire and darkness, blood and tears. Wounds unhealed.

'I know what you did for me in the Battle of the Forest,' Mielitta said. 'And I will never forget it. I know this must be tiring for you and I must be quick but you are not alone. You mustn't feel alone.'

He coughed to cover up the sob that rose in his throat. 'Nothing has happened here yet.' There was no point enraging her with the version of the Battle being publicised in the Citadel. 'Bastien and Verity have taken their places and I'm sure there will be a Council meeting soon. I'll let you know what I hear about it. What about you? Tell me about the Forest.' *Remind me why I'm doing this.*

Her eyes softened. 'Every day, we learn its ways. The more softly we tread, the more we are accepted. We have two sleep trees, where we spend our nights. Drianne woke this morning draped in a snake and she sang it uncoiled until it eased down the trunk. I don't think any creature would hurt her. When we seek food, Jannlou and I hunt, each in our own way...'

Mielitta's way was familiar to Kermon and as usual, she wore her bow on her shoulder and her quiver at her waist. He wondered what Jannlou's method was. *He probably wrestles deer to death with his bare hands, ten at a time,* he thought, then felt ashamed. Their purpose was more important than his petty jealousy.

'But the lessons aren't working.' Mielitta's account had moved on to Drianne's magecraft.

'Jannlou tries to pass on what was taught to him in magecraft lessons but he never had any magecraft so he doesn't know what it feels like and he's forgotten most of what he was told anyway. And Drianne just gets blocked. Either her magecraft comes naturally and then she exhausts it on whatever takes her fancy. She wished for eggs to eat and we had birds appearing all day offering us enough eggs to feed the population of the Citadel! Or she thinks about how her magecraft works so she can control it and then – nothing happens.'

'It's not easy, starting at her age.' Drianne's magecraft had come to her late so she'd had none of the training given to him and his gifted schoolmates. He allowed himself one heartbeat's smugness that Jannlou could not teach magecraft, having relied on Bastien's all his growing-up years. Then his better nature prevailed.

'Maybe I can help them both,' he said. 'Even without magecraft, Jannlou can support Drianne, if I give a lesson, if I can communicate through the arrowhead.'

'That would help so much! We need all our skills here.' There was a flutter like tiny wings across her eyes and Kermon could sense the mutual support she and her bees gave each other.

'The children,' Kermon said slowly. 'You've given me an idea, a way I can see them without it seeming suspicious. And help Drianne at the same time.'

At that moment, the three-beat knock of a messenger came at the door and the high voice of a young boy piped in one breath, 'Chief Mage Bastien summons Mage-Smith Kermon to a Council meeting after evening meal which you should attend now please confirm that you have received the message and will attend both.'

'Oh, stones,' breathed Mielitta. 'That doesn't sound too friendly.'

'I'll have to go,' muttered Kermon. 'And at least I'll be able to report back on the meeting.'

'Take care. You look so strange surrounded in fire.' She hesitated and he knew what she was about to say. He knew how she saw him.

'Like Declan.' She stumbled over her foster-father's name.

'Wait! I–' he began but she was fading from sight, their connection broken.

Kermon opened the door.

'Message received,' he told the page boy. 'I'm on my way to the Great Hall now.' He had no need to tamp down the fires. The forge was black, lit by neither fire nor candle. The flames Mielitta had seen were those Kermon wore for penance. He hoped Steelwing saw nothing else that was invisible to others.

CHAPTER FIVE

The day after the Battle of the Forest, the Queen of the Warrior Bees woke up, wondering what exactly she had won and what she should do. She'd preserved the Forest against the mages, sent their children back to the Citadel with honeyed memories and now she must wait for time and Kermon to work for change to that society they called Perfection. She'd got everything she wanted. But no books in the Citadel library had told her what a person should do the day *after* she got everything she wanted.

What sort of life lay in store for her and her companions now? What had she led them into? She looked at them as they lay sleeping on the ground. Their first night under the stars had dazzled them but now morning had come.

Drianne's bright golden hair splayed across her face, strands shifting gently as she breathed. In. Out. The rhythm of life, of healing sleep. Although made a woman by the Citadel's vile forging rites, the twelve-year-old slept like a child, curled in an invisible womb.

Jannlou lay sprawled half in, half out of his mage's black robe, his head resting on Kermon's backpack, a last gift from their friend. She wanted to ease herself down beside him, draw from his strength, take shelter. She'd fought so long and so hard. Would it be wrong to seek comfort, just once?

Not mating time! her scandalised bees admonished.

'I just wanted a cuddle,' she told them and then the blocked memories of the battle flooded her. They'd won but she'd killed and watched men die, among them the only person who'd ever cuddled her. Declan was gone, had never been the father he pretended to be. He'd tried to kill her with her own arrowhead but the unhealed wounds were from his words.

Unwanted child, friend to no-one, traitor, riddled and contagious.

She would never be cuddled again. She had no home, no family. The insults stung because they were true. Whoever they'd been, her parents hadn't wanted her and her stepfather had merely been her gaoler until the time came to kill her.

Not alone. One hive, her bees chastised her.

What did bees do to salve wounds? *Propolis,* she remembered. And she imagined a thick sticky smear of antiseptic orange goo wrapping all her pain inside a shell that hardened until she could feel nothing. Better to be self-sufficient, with her bees. Treat both her friends the same, remember that they were her followers too.

Cuddled? the bees queried.

'Touched, stroked, physical affection...' How did you explain cuddling? She pictured two bees rubbing pollen from each other.

This caused further confusion. *Not two! Many bees. Not with a drone! Only with worker bees! Drones are for mating.*

Mielitta understood the bee point of view. Jannlou was male so he was a drone. And a drone's only purpose was mating. She looked at her drone, the warrior's muscles gleaming in his brown shoulders as he moved restlessly, lashing out at an unseen enemy. His battle had been violent, like her own.

His legs twitched again and he jerked awake, his startling blue eyes losing the battle vision and gradually recognising who she was, where he was and why. So vulnerable in that moment between sleep and wake.

Directions. Food. Work. Home. The bees buzzed in her head, insistent on what should be her priorities. *Not mating.*

'Not mating,' she agreed wholeheartedly, in silent communication.

Aloud, she said to Jannlou, 'Good morning.'

He just looked at her, eyes soft as blue velvet.

Before the pause shimmered too long between them, Drianne too stirred, greeted Jannlou with a wave of her hand and murmured *Morning*, in Mielitta's mind.

As Drianne rose to her feet, the early sunlight caught the silver marks she'd carved on her own face in a puckered spiderweb. Her features were distorted so that her right eye was higher than the other, her nose tipped sideways and her mouth skewed, one half expressive, smiling now, and the other half permanently sour.

'I don't know what they're saying unless you tell me.' Jannlou's words interrupted Mielitta's thoughts and she had to force herself to speak aloud.

'I forget that you can't hear the bees or Drianne.' Yet again she was trying to explain something which seemed obvious to her. Only this time it was to a human.

Drone, corrected a bee and she hushed it.

'I need to concentrate!' she told the bees, irritated. And Drianne. And Jannlou because she'd said it aloud by accident.

Jannlou watched her as if she were about to bite him. Which was understandable.

Drone, persisted one cheeky bee. Mielitta ignored her.

'When we were in school, do you remember passing notes to Bastien?'

Jannlou's dark skin hid any blushes but if you knew him, you could see he was embarrassed. 'I'm sorry,' he said awkwardly. 'About–'

'No, not that,' she interrupted him hastily. The last thing she wanted to talk about was the way Jannlou and Bastien had treated her in the Citadel.

She rushed on. 'I'm trying to explain about what I hear.

Remember when you passed notes and you had to listen to the teacher at the same time, in case a question came your way. And if somebody, a girl you liked, talked to her friend and mentioned you, then you'd listen in to that conversation too. It's a bit like that. I hear you all differently but it's a bit tiring if you're all talking at once!'

'And I hear nothing. So I feel left out.'

'Then you know how I used to feel.' The words were out before she could take them back.

He nodded. As if one of his sparring partners had landed a punch and he was telling himself it was his own fault, that he wouldn't leave such an opening again.

'I'll try,' she said. 'To tell you what they say.'

'I'll try too,' he replied and turned away from her to pick up his clothes.

And so began their first day as Forest dwellers. Morning brought renewed energy and the rumbling of empty stomachs. Water was plentiful and they filled up the two leatherette bottles they carried. An inventory of their possessions was not encouraging but they discovered enough bits of crumbly sustenance to take the edge off their hunger. Along with a snood, a knife, a mage's robe and two ladies' gowns.

The three of them combined clothes so that all wore more practical combinations of britches, shirts and jerkins, using some basic magecraft stitchery from Drianne to hold the outfits together. The robe and gowns would be useful for wrappings, pillows, rags and bandages, so they were stuffed into Kermon's backpack, along with the snood, that Drianne instructed to grow into a larger net. She looked even paler than usual after using magecraft and Mielitta warned her she'd have to be careful. They'd all reached their limits the previous day and needed time to recover.

Directions. Forage. Home. The bees nagged Mielitta with their priorities and wouldn't quieten down until she shared their views.

'The bees think we should all have a sort of mind map of the Forest, like they've given me, so that we don't get lost and can meet up again when we want. And that we should each find some food, then figure out some kind of home base.'

'That makes sense,' Jannlou agreed. 'I think I can find my way all right and we already have the beehive glade and the beech tree at the edge of the Forest as two landmarks. We should find some more and mark them out on a written map.'

I can find my way too. I won't get lost, Drianne added.

'I don't suppose you can magic up some food for us?' Mielitta asked hopefully. 'Later, after you've rested.'

I don't think so. It would have no substance and I don't think Citadel sustenance can be made in the Forest.

'What's she saying?' asked Jannlou, looking from one to the other.

Mielitta translated, knowing it wouldn't be the last time she missed Kermon.

'Good riddance to sustenance! I'd rather hunt for food and eat something that you can taste!' Jannlou's enthusiasm caught Mielitta by surprise and reminded her of the conversation she needed to have with him, in private.

She eyed him narrowly. 'I suppose each of us has different skills when it comes to gathering food.'

'You have your weapons,' he pointed out but he didn't meet her eyes.

Neither did Drianne. *Too many secrets.* Mielitta sighed. 'Right, each of us takes a bottle of water and forages. We'll meet back here with whatever food we catch or gather. We can make a cook-fire here without any risk, and there's less cover for predators who might come after us.'

'Isn't it too close to the Citadel?'

'I don't think anyone will come out of the Citadel for some time! The bees are right. We do need to find a better home but there's no rush. This will do for now. If we go in different directions, we can explore further and keep an eye open for somewhere that we can turn into a den.'

We only have two water bottles, Drianne pointed out. *But I don't need one. I can open the ground and ask water to come up. There is always water underground.*

'And I can scent water,' said Mielitta. 'So we can take turns with the water bottle. You have it today and save your magecraft.'

'I might be able to help Drianne, with conserving magecraft,' offered Jannlou. 'I did the training, even if I can't practise any of it myself. I know what it looks like and how Bastien said it felt. I can pass on what I know to Drianne.'

Thank him for me.

Mielitta complied, feeling more like a servant than a queen. She was supposed to be a leader!

'Priorities!' she reminded them. 'Forage. Food. Home! And you need to know what the bees taught me about directions.' She taught them to orient themselves by the sun, and the way the sun would move during the day so they could adapt their direction accordingly.

'The Citadel is due south. Drianne, you go north-west, Jannlou north and I'll go north-east.' They each turned resolutely in their allocated direction, shouldering their small stock of belongings. When the last snapping twig was out of earshot, Mielitta felt a wave of nausea. Alone. Completely alone.

Not alone, the bees objected. *Foraging. Then join hive. Home.*

Three people did not make for a very strong hive, thought Mielitta, but they must build one cell at a time.

Work! the bees encouraged.

CHAPTER SIX

In her long and tedious childhood, waiting to be declared ready for the Maturity Test, Mielitta had found solace in archery lessons when her teacher Tannlei was still alive, then in practice after Tannlei's death. She'd had plenty of time to hone her skills for her own pleasure and for the entertainment of her little follower, Drianne. Now, for the first time, she must use her bow and arrows to hunt in the Forest.

What's your target? she asked herself, using Tannlei's perennial question to focus her mind. *Food,* was the answer. Today, she was going to kill so she and her friends could eat. And if she was going to kill, she should do so with precision, with respect.

Mielitta had learned how to become invisible, hiding from Bastien and Jannlou in the passages of the Citadel. Now she merged with the trees and waited, bow strung. Time changed as she settled into stillness, a Forest creature among other Forest creatures, aware of every tiny movement. A flicker betrayed a lizard's forked tongue as it basked on a hot stone. Ants in a procession carried their giant burdens, marching over her foot in a determined black column.

The thump of a heavy-feathered landing among rustling leaves was followed by cooing. Wood pigeons. Mielitta aimed and fired at the movement, noted where the bird fell and nocked a new arrow so rapidly she caught its mate in flight. She smelled their landing-places, the purple of death and new blood, prey. She was a predator among predators and she had to retrieve the dead birds quickly before another animal scented food.

Without her acute sense of smell, she might not have found the second pigeon, grey and purple on dappled pine needles and rocks, the white ring around its neck dulled in the shadows. She extracted her arrows, wiped them on the ground and looked around for something to tie the birds together to make them easier to carry.

Long trailing plants looped around the trees, refusing to break when she pulled at one.

Liana, she named the creeper. As always, book-words came to her when needed, showing she'd not wasted her time as the Citadel's Assistant Librarian.

She drew the knife she kept for trimming flights, cut a length of creeper and secured the birds' legs with the green twine. She attached this to one of her headless shafts and carried the makeshift pole from her shoulder, the birds' heads dangling. She needed a game bag but, for today, this would do. What she wanted now was water, to drink and to clean her arrows properly.

Head north-west, her mind map and her bees told her. *Water.* She no longer troubled to hide her presence and as she walked, birds warned each other of her presence. The *screak* of a diamond firetail and the clatter of wagtails sent the alert ahead. A woodpecker stopped its hammering against a trunk as she drew near.

Danger complained the bees, which had been silent during her hunt, an activity too human for their liking. *Breaks into home. Eats bees.*

'No danger for me,' Mielitta told them, as the woodpecker flashed green and red, in its looping flight from one tree to another, hammering its message in the bark. A bob of white tail, spotted brown flanks, black and white stripes, hinted at the various creatures that skipped or slipped between the trees when they heard her coming. She had enough food for today, so she watched and learned, sniffing, identifying.

A scent she knew tickled her nose. Brown, earthy. She followed the scent as bees do, visualising the path that led – as she knew it would – to the bear. Not just any bear but the one she'd last seen wielding his death grip against Rinduran's limp body. Now, he was rubbing his back against a tree-trunk, crooning in pleasure as he too sniffed the air.

Mielitta was downwind so she could safely watch. Besides, she knew this bear and he would not hurt her. Even if Jannlou refused to talk about her suspicions, she knew she was right.

Having finished his toilette, the bear sniffed again, then followed his nose to another pine tree. Bark hung like festive ribbons from deep fissures as the bear ripped an experimental strip downwards. Claws long as arrowheads worked under the damp wood, levering and shredding whole plants to get into the decaying heart of the tree. Thousands of insects scurried about, squirting tiny jets at the invader, which made him pause to wipe his face, before he renewed his attack.

Ants, Mielitta realised.

Ignoring the ants' defence of their nest and the piled debris around him, the bear reached into the exposed wood, extended his claws and scooped out a lip-smacking maw-ful of ant eggs. Soon he was scooping with both paws and gorging on ants. When he'd had his fill, he dropped to all fours, went back to his scratching post and rubbed against it, crooning again.

No wonder he needed to rub that thick pelt! Mielitta's skin itched at the very thought of ants all over her.

Danger! panicked the bees ten times louder than for the woodpecker. *Breaks into home. Eats bees. Eats brood. Enemy! Fly now!*

'Not my enemy,' Mielitta told them firmly, exasperated at the bees' obsession with flight when she wanted a closer look at all the creatures in the Forest, especially this bear. She needed to know everything about him. She flared her nostrils again, confirmed the scent. Yes, that was him all right.

She'd had enough of secrets and she moved resolutely out from behind the tree and stood in full view.

The bear's ears pricked alert. His stony brown eyes fixed on her and he dropped to all fours once more, ready to run. At her, not away. He plodded a few paces in her direction.

She stood still, waited.

The bear grunted but whether in greeting or warning she had no idea. He came close enough for her to smell the ant acid on his breath, then he reared up on two legs in front of her, above her. He was much taller than she was, taller even than Jannlou and bulkier than any human.

Then cries of *Help! Help!* shook her in a furious vibration. The bee sigil on her thigh throbbed with power and she whirled against her will into bee-shape and was transported across the Forest into the beehive.

'Not now!' she protested, then saved her voice to breathe.

She was the epicentre of a ball of bees that grew every second so she could see nothing but bodies, whirring fast wings, creating an inferno of heat.

Surrounded by a black vibrating fireball, she was suffocating in fine hairs, burning up, desperately begging her inner queen to do something. Her people were killing her. Why? What had she done?

CHAPTER SEVEN

Just as she felt her body about to explode and her senses slipping away, she heard an anguished squeak in a voice she recognised.

Stop! You're killing the Queen Mother!' The Young Queen exuded a calming scent, covering Mielitta in right-smell to reinforce the colony's acceptance of this newcomer. The wings slowed to fan beats, the outer rings of bees peeled off and Mielitta was left with a circle of apologetic attendants trying to revive her.

A tongue down her throat fed her with nectar amid the anxious queries of bees crowding around. Still dizzy, she took even longer to adjust to her bee sight: blues and ultra-violets instead of yellows and greens. No red at all.

Bees have no sense of personal space, thought Mielitta as she staggered to her feet and glared at them.

'You nearly killed me!'

We've had robbers, explained the Young Queen, *because there is so much honey and our riches attract thieves.*

Now she could breathe properly, Mielitta inhaled the woody notes and heavy sweetness of the upper hive, food wealth in a greedy forest. She thought of the bear and shivered, hoping he was far away.

A hornet was sniffing around earlier. If she entered and escaped back out, then reported to her nest, we would be in trouble, so the workers were ready to hotball any invader.

'To the death.' Mielitta understood.

Yes. They were so tense and you didn't smell quite right. You've been away a while and my scent has changed as I've grown older, no longer the same as yours. The Young Queen excused her people's mistake. *But you are welcome here for whatever reason.*

Now Mielitta was confused. 'But you summoned me.'

Oh no, I don't think so.

'Do you need help against the hornets?'

No. You are no hornet. A tinkle of bee laughter. *Which means they haven't come back. It looks like they found easier pickings elsewhere. We need time to regain our strength but we are working hard.*

Mielitta remembered the damage done by Rinduran during the battle. Worse than bear.

Maybe that was why she'd been called? Would she have to perform a queen bee's duties again? Lay eggs day in, day out; maintain morale and survive the occasional fight to the death with invaders or would-be usurpers? Selfishly, she hoped not.

'Do you need help rebuilding the hive?' she asked cautiously, not wanting to offer too much.

No, the Young Queen was adamant. *But thank you. The entrance is reduced in size so we can defend the hive more easily and honey season will be over soon so the robbers will lose interest. We need more people so we are prepared for winter but I can manage that. If you'll excuse me, I must lay eggs now. Work, you know.* Her pride sent happy vibrations buzzing around the whole hive.

Mielitta did know and she could still remember the fullness in her abdomen, the compulsion to lay a thousand eggs a day. She watched the Young Queen waddle up to the exact cell where she'd been interrupted in her laying by the commotion over Mielitta's arrival. She laid an egg like a grain of rice in the next empty cell and the next, moving outwards in a neat spiral on the waxed frame.

As the work of the beehive made its contented hum around her, Mielitta demanded, 'Why did you call for help if you don't need me?'

The sigil on her thigh glowed and her inner queen tinkled with laughter. *The help is for you, Mielitta, not for us. We are recovering well from the battle but you are not.*

A bee's body did not allow for balling up fists or frowning but Mielitta thrummed with tension and her stinger pulsed with venom. 'I don't have nightmares. I'm fine.'

The spirit bees who kept Mielitta company politely ignored the lie, telling her, *Work!* which was as unhelpful as it was enigmatic.

You can take a worker bee's form, explained her inner queen. *Fly, find flowers and gather pollen. This bee is on pollen duty and will show you how.*

The only word Mielitta took in was *Fly!* She loved flying. Maybe there was no harm in laying down her leadership for one afternoon in the sunshine, flying. She'd seen worker bees gather pollen and it looked easy enough.

Her body morphed from queen to worker, more compact in body, with stronger jaws, different glands and some added weights on the hind pair of her six legs – pollen baskets!

Prepare your tools! ordered her co-worker, smoothing her forelegs and showing the clumps of hair on the lower parts. *These are our basitarsal brushes – make sure they're clean! You have more brushes on the middle and hindlegs so groom them too.'*

So that was another difference from a queen's body, thought Mielitta. *I have tools!*

Follow! ordered her co-worker and Mielitta followed, scuttling to the queue at the bee-sized doorways in the entrance portcullis. As the Young Queen had explained, the other doorways were blocked to make the hive more defensible while its inhabitants recovered.

Blocked with what? wondered Mielitta, glancing sideways as she reached the doorway. She had a glimpse of what looked like crumpled parchment before she was pushed from behind by workers eager to get going. She barely had time to think *Fly* when she was airborne, tilted a little in the tiny breeze, then zooming after her designated tutor.

I know a place. We'll go back there. Directions here. The bee shared directions with Mielitta in a mind map, a dance of compass points that took her with the other worker, and no doubt many more, through the trees to a meadow beyond, a prairie of yellow-striped purple flowers and the sparkle of a wide river.

Water! warned her companion, carefully alighting on a large rock so they could sip from a shallow puddle. *Deep! Drown!*

Mielitta was careful, spreading the soft pads of her feet to adhere to the stone surface as she too drank puddle water. A mix of rain and river overlaid its limestone tang. She knew this place well. To human sight, the river was just a stream and the huge rock a pebble. The flowers were really all-gold sunflowers and the beauty of their ultra-violet centres and exterior rings was invisible. But why did she think that was reality? Surely what the bees could see – what she saw as a bee – was real too? A better reality, even, if the invisible became visible?

This is our flower, instructed the bee, looping along the sunflower's landing guides.

'Why this one?' asked Mielitta.

Bee laughter at her ignorance. *Because a sunflower was my first flower. We must harvest only those like our first one.*

Her first flower. And from now on she could know only sunflowers. Mielitta could see the circles, like her archery target, drawing her like an arrow to the bull's eye, where long stalks waved their dark blue fluff. She sneezed as pollen hit her face, disturbed by the other bee's landing.

Pollen Bee, Mielitta decided to name her, in defiance of the bees' insistence that they were all called worker bee and had no use for individual names.

Pollen Bee laughed and pulled on the long stalks, shaking the blue fluff loose to dance around them in the tiny breeze they created. Mielitta retaliated, stirring up more pollen and vibrating her wings to send it towards the other bee, who giggled. By now, they were both covered in pollen, stuck to their furry bodies and dusting their heads. Mielitta could barely see through pollen-spotted eyes.

Brush it off your eyes first. Pollen Bee used her front legs to groom her eyes. Then she set to work, brushing the pollen off her body into clumps. She passed these from front to middle to back legs, rolling them together to place in the pollen baskets on her back legs. Mielitta did likewise, glad she'd cleaned her basitarsal brushes before setting out.

Fun, she thought.

After twenty thousand flowers, Mielitta had lost her sense of fun and was carrying three times her weight in her pollen baskets. Pollen Bee showed no signs of tiring but she must have sensed how tired the novice was.

Let's sleep, she suggested, landing on a big-hearted sunflower whose ultra-violet centre looked to Mielitta like a soft double mattress with pillows ready plumped. An irresistible invitation. And they had both worked so hard. Pollen Bee curled herself into a neat arc at the flower's centre and her wings instantly settled to a sleep flutter.

Mielitta lay down too, leaving a polite space as she had with Drianne and Jannlou. Without waking, Pollen Bee instantly closed the gap, rolling her body so its length curled against Mielitta's in furry warmth.

Living sunshine thought Mielitta as the hum of a sleeping bee reached deep into the hurt she dared not prod. Bees did not care about words, nor about a father's hatred for his adopted child. They did not care about loss or death beyond the moment either happened. They lived and buzzed for each other and the hive.

Cuddle, thought Mielitta as she drifted off, breathing sunflower freshness and the home hive scent of her companion. *Cuddle Bee.*

No need for the bear, her voices commented, but she was too deeply asleep to disagree, warmed by more than sunshine. She belonged.

Time!

Mielitta felt the insistent antenna shaking her awake.

'Cuddle Bee,' she murmured.

Her companion giggled but her own bees rebuked her.

We're all cuddle bees, they commented. *We're all bees. Work!*

Mielitta sighed. Work, it was. She struggled to lift off from the flower, weighed down by her pollen baskets and the flight through the forest seemed ten times as long as her joyful outward voyage.

Despite the dire warnings from her bees – *Eats bees! Traps bees!* – no evil befell them on their flight and at last they reached the clearing and the hive.

She staggered onto the landing platform, tilted a bit and was instantly supported by four of the hive guards who rushed out to help her. They half-carried her inside, complimenting her on her trawl, and they took her to the stores of bee bread to carry out her last task for the day.

In an empty cell of the store, she unloaded one pollen ball. The workers added a soupçon of nectar and of honey, then tamped the mix down to form bee bread. The process was repeated for her second ball of pollen. And her body felt so light she could fly again, as if the pain she had balled up after the battle went into the hive with her crop of pollen, disgorged.

Food, the workers told her. *To feed the babies, make the hive strong.*

Mielitta could barely stand after the day's work.

Come with me tomorrow? asked Cuddle Bee.

Before Mielitta could find a tactful way to say, 'I'd rather a bear ate my insides,' the familiar whirling nausea began and she found herself in human form, clutching Steelwing and looking at a blacksmith. He wavered, a vision born of magecraft; as she recognised Kermon, her heart calmed. He had finally managed to reach her so must have made the twin arrowhead. Whatever he had to report from the Citadel, she was now a two-basket pollen-carrying worker bee and she was ready for anything.

CHAPTER EIGHT

'You can communicate with her, can't you,' Verity accused Kermon, who stood meekly in the Council Chamber.

He raised his eyes from the woodette floor to the girl's face. She was still sickly-pale, brown eyes over-large but tranquil, whatever the emotions beneath. Her hands were more expressive, fluttering beneath the new striped mage's robe, slightly too big for her – Councillor's robe, he amended. A new uniform, for this new order of Councillor. A girl without magecraft, equal leader of the Council, thanks to the Queen of the Warrior Bees.

Verity's hands stilled and Kermon observed a feverish red circle with a dark centre on her right palm. He remembered her sitting sullen in the Forest before the Battle, a hostage, refusing the honey offered. She'd swatted the bee who'd made her sweet offering, killed her. Perhaps she'd been stung, with who knew what consequences, given Verity's history of allergy. And yet she seemed healthier.

'Does that hurt?' he asked Verity, who flushed and hid the telltale mark, palm against her robe.

Bastien frowned, snapped, 'Well, can you communicate with her?' His magecraft sizzled in the air, a yellow-grey aura, making

Kermon wonder how he would fare in a duel. He swallowed, hard.

'I can try if you wish me to,' replied Kermon, not lying.

'It would be useful.' Bastien had already learned to measure his words.

Not so, his sister. 'Tell her she'll die at my hand for my father's death! I swore by the stones and I want her reminded!'

'My sister doubts you.' The sulphurous aura around Bastien fizzed with power as he stated the case against Kermon 'You took instructions from – *her*. You carried Verity out of the Citadel, knowing she'd been protected all her life, could *die* outside her chamber. You were an accessory to her attempted murder.'

Kermon kept his voice strong, reliable as Citadel stone. 'I had no choice. My soul-reading creates a link and the new mage, Drianne, wielded great power.'

Bastien winced at the mention of his erstwhile fiancée. *Good. That will shake his objectivity. And it was all true. Just not in the way they might think. Drianne did wield great power but never against me.*

'I was compelled to take Lady Verity–' Kermon continued.

'Councillor Verity,' the girl interrupted. Her narrowed eyes suggested her suspicions were not allayed.

'Councillor Verity.' Kermon bowed his head respectfully. 'I did so as gently as I could.'

Bastien looked a question at his sister, who gave a curt nod.

Kermon remembered carrying her through the Citadel and out into the Forest, barely a robe's weight in his arms so thin she was. Did he imagine it or was she rounder in face and form than when he'd set her on the roots of a great tree, there to set her sullen face against all the wonder on offer? A tiny girl but on the cusp of womanhood, raised as a jewel in a glass case, hardly touched until he'd picked her up like a bale of cloth. To convince such a girl he was no traitor would not be easy. Especially when he *was* one.

He continued, 'My magecraft is not sufficient to fight those with greater powers. When the Queen of the Warrior Bees–'

'Don't call her that!' interrupted Verity.

Kermon looked at Bastien, waited.

'Call her the Freak,' was the decision.

In his own mind, Kermon made *Freak* a title he respected but it still felt like betrayal to name Mielitta so. 'When she,' he hesitated and felt the weight of suspicion growing heavier at his evasion.

He started again. 'When the Freak deceived the teachers and stole the children, I made it my work to protect the Lady – Councillor Verity – and the other children, whatever might happen. But I could not prevent their experiences.' He remembered the children playing, their joy in water, sunlight, trees and honey. The bees alighting, each on its designated child, offering sweetness. The children's openness to the Forest. While Verity sat in the glass case of her own mind. 'I could not prevent the battle.'

'In which nobody saw you,' pointed out Bastien. 'You did not fight alongside the mages. You could have been supporting the Freak.'

'I am no fighter. I could not help the mages.' Especially not the three mages he'd stalked in the confusion of shadows and bound to three trees by magecraft. 'I did not expect anyone to die.' Especially not those same three mages, who'd been swallowed by the enraged trees. They would not bear witness against him.

'So you are loyal to the Citadel.' Bastien's statement was the one Kermon had been dreading and it required assent.

'I would give my life for the future of the Citadel and for its children.' Steady, reliable, honest Kermon. He must not lose himself in this game of double-speak. He clenched his fists to stop his hands shaking, slipped them out of sight through the slits in his robe, into the pockets of his britches.

'Hmph.' Bastien was noncommittal but his power was no longer manifest. He'd been lulled, for the moment.

Kermon relaxed his guard. As he rubbed his sweaty palms against the pocket linings, he felt several tiny pellets trickling through his fingers. Like solid raindrops. He racked his brains for what they could be, whether some debris from the forge or from the Forest, whether Perfectly normal or evidence of treachery. He couldn't check now.

He was wearing work britches, the same he always wore, so that didn't help identify the objects. Flakes of metal wouldn't be as regular. Nor would hard crumbs of sustenance. But if from the Forest, what were they? Grubs? Was he going to hatch bees right in front of the Leaders of the Citadel? *Stones forbid!* He wiped the pellets off carefully on the lining so as not to withdraw one by mistake.

'All right,' Verity told her brother, nodding acceptance, also for the moment. 'Tell him,' she urged, 'before the others get here.'

'We need a soul-reader to replace Mage Shenagra on the Council, to test children, to seek out traitors, to suppress them. You'll be asked in the meeting and you'll agree. And there's one other thing–'

Bastien stopped speaking as the door opened and Hamel slunk through, his long toe-nails hanging over the edge of his sandals and clicking on the woodette floor.

'I hope I'm not interrupting anything?' asked the mage, overplaying hesitation, offering to retreat, making it impossible for Bastien to ask for privacy without seeming conspiratorial. Which of course he was, as everyone there suspected.

'No, indeed.' Bastien's laugh sounded as genuine as grassette. Pure Perfection. 'I'm warning our new Mage-Smith that he might receive an invitation today but that is for discussion when all are gathered.'

'Meanwhile, we can allow him to sit,' suggested Hamel, pointedly taking his seat at the table and nodding to some chairs against the back wall, presumably for non-Councillors. 'It shouldn't take long for *all* the others to arrive.'

Kermon was happy to remove himself from interrogation to the back of the Council Chamber and watch the members arrive. He was under no illusions about his own status. He was on trial.

Hamel's barbed comment was accurate. The Council had been decimated by the battle of the Forest. Who else had been invited, like himself, a mismatched scrap of magecraft to patch a hole?

CHAPTER NINE

Kermon had only missed four days of Citadel politics but that was enough time for post-battle changes to have lost their novelty. He watched the incomers nod at Bastien and Verity, with perhaps a widening of their eyes at her striped robe but no other sign of surprise as they took their places.

At the Council table, the five battle survivors: Bastien, Verity, Hamel, Veebo the gatekeeper and Garth, the Archery Mage. People still referred to him as the new archery tutor because those taught by Tannlei never forgot her, but he had been in place for years now and was the best qualified of those there.

Shifting nervously on their seats at the back with Kermon, potential Councillors avoided any contact, all except one. Bastien's stepmother.

Mage Puggy had been one of the Ten, until Rinduran barred women mages and subjected Puggy to forging by the Mage-Smith in the very Ceremony she'd presided over for years. Then he'd married what remained as Lady Puggy: a limp brain in the curves of a goddess. Kermon was not the only one in that room who remembered Puggy in her chosen avatar, dumpy and plain, a misglamour that allowed her power rather than her sensual beauty to affect others.

There was no trace now of either power or misglamour in Rinduran's widow. She spoke softly to Kermon as she sat down beside him.

'May the stones be with you, beautiful man,' she breathed, her words honeyed arrows.

Kermon could not help but notice her peach-soft skin, flushed at the delicate edge of the blue gown framing her breasts, which rose and fell, rose and fell as she breathed. His own breathing instinctively echoed her rhythm. An arc of eyebrow, fringe of dark eyelashes; crimson bow mouth slightly parted, glistening; silky golden hair begging to be freed from its braids and wound in a man's hand, drawing such a woman into his arms.

He shook off the effect Puggy had on him, noted that she showed no trace of a widow's grief and then concentrated on more important matters. Business had begun.

'We drove a hard bargain to enforce our sovereignty and banish the Forest forever from our walls,' began Bastien. 'And I gave my blood oath that bargain would be kept so we must honour it.'

The price of peace with Mielitta was being implemented. Kermon knew Bastien had no choice about *whether* he did so, only in *how*. Even in that, the blood oath bound him to the spirit of the agreement, not just the words, repeated now by Bastien.

'One. My sister and I are to be leaders of the Council. Done.' He ticked off this demand on a finger. 'Although I know some of you are unhappy that she is neither a man nor a mage, I believe Councillor Verity will prove her worth.'

Hamel drummed his clawed fingernails on the table but said nothing.

'Two. Female mages reinstated and new ones accepted among the Ten.' Bastien ticked off the second demand while tension grew among the women sitting with Kermon.

'Three. Female mages are to have the same rights as male mages to marry and to have children.'

The drumming fingernails made the only sound in the room

until Puggy laughed, a melodic cascade that showed no interest whatsoever in proceedings.

'Can I go now?' she asked in a low, husky voice. 'I'm really bored.'

Hamel stopped drumming, regarded the husk of his old adversary and squeaked, 'We're all bored, Puggy, but we have to be polite about it. Keep quiet now, there's a good girl.'

Bastien flushed. Puggy re-crossed her legs and swished her skirts but said no more.

'So,' continued Bastien as if there had been no interruption, 'we should consider our appointments with the peace treaty in mind.'

He took a deep breath and announced, 'I nominate Mage-Smith Kermon for a seat on the Council, to employ his skills as both smith and soul-reader on our behalf. Of course, we can't replace Declan ... may the walls take his spirit. But we have his successor.'

'Declan was his own man and a genius at forging. This one's weak. You just want a successor as your yes-man, your Shenagra,' observed Hamel.

Bastien winced.

'Looks like that was a hit,' Hamel crowed. 'Let me aim again. He's not going to be part of the Maturity Test because you promised the Queen of the Warrior Bees that there'd be no more forging and no Maturity Test. So this little follower of yours will have nothing to do but mind-read, gossip and suppress freaks. A bit of smith-work in between of course. All very tidy. You might as well suppress me now, Mage-Smith Kermon.' The green mage flung open his arms, distorted his face like a gargoyle's and dropped his head on his small chest in an obscene parody of death throes.

Power flickered round the Council Chamber and for a second Kermon thought Bastien would accept the challenge beneath the taunting. Then he spoke.

'On the contrary. I would grieve your suppression deeply,

Mage Hamel, as my father's memorial requires skills only you possess now that he is dead. Mage-Smith Kermon will be yours to train for this new test, which will be far better than the old one and – how did you put it? He will be *your* yes-man if you make him such.'

Kermon's heart raced but he didn't dare speak. If he doubted his power in a duel, he knew for sure he was doomed against the mages' combined assault.

'I'm intrigued, dear Chief Mage,' crooned Hamel. 'And I accept your nomination.'

Three voices echoed each other. 'And I.'

Kermon moved away from the mind-wrecking perfume of Puggy and took his place at the Council table. *Stones*. What had they planned for him? He must ensure he had his say before they had theirs!

Two female mages were appointed to the Council without demur: the fussy little seamstress, Mage Fabrisse, and the demoted Maturity Mage, Yacinthe, now Library Mage. No doubt she missed her Assistant Librarian, thought Kermon, as he watched her tight black curls bobbing in excitement when the two women stood up. They were already discussing the making of robes for all the new mages as they took their seats at the table.

'I haven't had time to add gold embroidery to Verity's gown,' apologised Fabrisse. 'And ours will be black of course, traditional mage robes.'

'It's almost a pity to be a mage; the stripes look so flattering, especially with my body shape,' Mage Yacinthe sighed.

'I didn't know what to use for a Councillor who's not a mage. White robes were always for Maturity candidates so that was no good, even if things have changed … and then it just came to me like that – stripes! Never been done before.'

Yacinthe patted Fabrisse on the arm. 'Perfect,' she told her.

The third female appointment was Veebo's wife, Lady Zora, who seemed a Perfect example of successful forging as she humbly took her place beside her husband. Veebo had pointed out that women would find it difficult to understand Council matters and he could help her. Bastien could hardly argue against the woman for not being a mage, given Verity's status. And Veebo had supported all the other appointments, asking only this favour. Appointing his wife was a smart move as Veebo now had two votes on the Council.

If Mielitta could see the results of her attempt at 'equality', women twittering about dress fabrics, she'd nock an arrow and shoot herself, Kermon thought cynically.

Only one place was left at the table. One of the seven minor mages sitting on the edge of their seats would be asked to join the Council. Now that the Ten had opened up to so many artisans, outside the noble families, surely the mages would choose the Cobbler Mage, who shifted uneasily in such elevated company. His face was the texture and colour of his leatherette apron and to the advantage of his years could be added his responsible use of magecraft. Kermon had heard only praise for the mage's work. Solid, reliable. Yes, he would balance the youth of the Council nicely and he would soon get used to the pomp of procedure.

Not that he was automatically rejecting the other candidates because they were female, he defended himself to an imaginary Mielitta. It was just that they were all very minor mages, unknown quantities, except of course for–

'My turn to make a nomination,' Hamel beamed. 'You are wondering why I invited Mage Puggy here.'

Puggy clapped her hands, her blue eyes sparkling. She'd survived two Maturity Tests as a candidate; first to become an Adult Mage and then, under Rinduran's orders, she'd been given the pink potion and forging that sealed off her deep thinking, prevented her misglamour, left her to a future as the Chief Mage's beautiful, silly wife. Now his widow.

Kermon knew what the other Councillors did not: that she'd defied them all in one last act of supreme courage. She'd protected Drianne's mind with every particle of her own magecraft, poured power into the girl. If it hadn't been for Puggy, none of them would have escaped and the Forest would be dead.

Pity crowded out desire as Kermon remembered the mage Puggy had been. Powerful, intelligent, every bit a match for Hamel.

The green-skinned mage nodded his pointed head, said, 'If we must have females on the Council, who is better suited to join us at this table than Lady Puggy, who sat here by right for so many years? And now that female mages are allowed to marry, it is my honour to ask Lady Puggy if she would like to be my wife.'

He spoke as to a child. 'Would you like that, Puggy? Would you like to be a Councillor again and to marry me? To wear a pretty dress for a wedding.'

'Oh yes please!' Puggy clapped her hands again, smiled her dazzling smile. 'If I'm allowed?'

Her self-deprecation caught at Kermon's heart.

Even Bastien softened his speech when talking to this woman his father had wanted to be turned into a good citizen. This ex-mage his father had wanted for a tamed wife.

'We must vote on it, Lady Puggy,' he said gently.

'On me marrying Mage Hamel?' she asked, puzzled.

'No,' said Bastien. 'On whether you can join – rejoin – the Council.'

Her beautiful face smoothed. 'Oh that's all right then. I can still wear a nice dress and have a wedding.'

Kermon's stomach heaved as Hamel ignored his bride-to-be and addressed his peers. 'There is clear precedent. Mage Veebo's wife was elected. And my wife was born with magecraft. Perhaps she'll get it back.' His smug smile declared his certainty she wouldn't.

But procedure and expedience were on his side so it went to the vote. Bastien declared 'Against.' Verity with a moue of distaste, against; Veebo and Zora for, Fabrisse for and Yacinthe against, muttering 'She always thought she was better than me.

'Against,' said Garth. 'Distracting. Rinduran was right to remove women from Council!'

None of the distractions saw fit to reply.

Only Kermon's vote remained and he cursed himself for not speaking up earlier. What would be better for Puggy? He didn't know. What would be just?

'For,' he mumbled, looking down so he couldn't see who sent him black looks. That seemed to be the main survival technique in Council meetings.

'Come and sit here, sweetie-pie,' Hamel told Puggy. And she did, in an elegant perfumed swish that was spoilt only by her saying, 'Is it nearly finished now?'

Everyone ignored her.

'About my father's memorial,' Bastien began. Verity looked daggers at him, so he corrected himself, 'About *our* father's memorial, *we* know he would have wanted his work in the walls to be continued and for Perfection to benefit.

'The people have requested an award in his name so we are offering the Rinduran Award to our nominated mage, Kermon. He must prove himself worthy by returning to Council a week today with an account of his experience in the walls and a plan for the new Adulthood Test. Clearly, we need a new Maturity Test. And who better than our Forge-Master, Declan's successor, to add the Adulthood Test to his duties.'

Stones.

'It is an honour,' responded Kermon mechanically.

Garth nodded slowly. 'We do need a test.'

Zora looked to her husband, who smiled encouragement. She spoke in a tiny voice, barely audible. 'If the boys go into the walls, maybe the girls could be supporters.'

'Excellent idea,' Veebo beamed at her with affection and she blushed.

Puggy, the ex-Maturity Mage, asked, 'Will there be a Courtship Dance afterwards?'

'Of course,' Bastien confirmed.

Kermon could only imagine how he would report this new development in Perfection to Mielitta. But he could at least try to make capital out of it, while he was still alive.

He screwed up his face to indicate the brainwave hitting him. 'It would help me devise such a Test if I could spend time at the school, teach the children.'

'As Shenagra did,' pointed out Hamel. 'Yes, he must assess them.'

Kermon refrained from pointing out the difference between teaching and assessment.

'You will make the name Rinduran live again, Mage-Smith Kermon.' Bastien radiated pleasure at the response to his plan. 'Is there something we can grant you in return?' This time he ignored Verity's frown.

Stomach churning, Kermon had no time to weigh the wisdom of what he was about to do. Pity was indeed a powerful emotion and it wasn't as if Mielitta would ever love him in that way. He had nothing to lose.

'Yes,' said Kermon. 'I would like Mage Puggy to be my wife. If anybody can heal the damage done in forging her, then I can. Or at least I can try.'

'You're making a mistake, boy,' Hamel grated, his power flaring an angry green.

Bastien's colour rose in response, showing he was prepared to discipline his older colleague, who calmed, not ready yet to test the new Chief Mage with more than heckling.

Perhaps it was the thought of annoying Hamel that appealed to Bastien, for he decreed, 'If you survive the walls, make a discovery worthy of our father, then Mage Puggy shall be your wife.'

Puggy's face puckered. 'No wedding?'

'Oh yes,' Bastien assured her. 'Everything will be exactly the same, just with a different man.'

'That's all right then.' Puggy's face cleared.

Verity whispered something to Bastien and although his face

clouded in disapproval, he announced, 'Councillor Verity wishes to speak.'

Brittle as glass, the girl's voice cut across the mages' chatter. 'You will all support our Forge Master in his preparation for the ordeal. Hamel must pass on all that my father taught him, as best he can. If Mage-Smith Kermon comes back from the walls—' she paused long enough to remind the mages that coming back at all from the walls was never a certainty. 'If he comes back from the walls with the required contribution to Perfection, then he will deserve his reward and be worthy of his place at this table.' Her eyes made her expectations clear.

'Who's to judge if he's succeeded? *If* he survives,' asked Hamel.

Bastien laughed. 'Us.'

His gesture embraced all at the table, the Council of Ten, complete again and united as ever. 'We will,' he told them.

Then he closed the meeting and Kermon hurried to leave the chamber before he collapsed. He had to pass Bastien, who whispered, 'Nicely played, with Puggy. That gives you a second vote at table too. But watch your back. Hamel doesn't like being outwitted.'

So they thought he'd pulled a political coup! If only they knew. And if only he could figure out how to survive the walls after Hamel's 'training' His only experience in the walls had been the compulsory group visit as a student, under Rinduran's close supervision, but he'd never visited on his own. Only one person could help him. He rushed out of the meeting before anybody else could speak to him. He had to get back to the privacy of his chamber and contact Drianne. After he'd emptied his pockets.

CHAPTER TEN

'Seeds?' Mielitta stuttered again.

Kermon's face wavered as if seen through flames but he was not in the forge. Behind him in the greylight she could see the beige walls and regulation chair of a Citadel bedchamber. She could even see his black robe, flung hurriedly onto the chair, sleeves trailing like the arms of a corpse.

She didn't want to think about corpses. She wanted to think about Kermon going into the walls, about a new Maturity Test. Did Kermon even know what had happened in the old one? She wanted to explode, to shoot arrows into somebody.

And in the short time they'd had together, all Kermon could do was babble about seeds and magecraft lessons.

Anger misses the mark every time. Mielitta remembered one of the sayings her archery teacher Tannlei drilled into her and focused on her breathing, counting exhalations to calm herself down.

'Mielitta?' asked Kermon. 'I think the Forest put them in my pocket for a reason but how can I grow them here?' He gestured at his bare surroundings.

He wouldn't stop thinking about his precious seeds until she helped him. Or at least tried to. She was surrounded by seeds and their full-grown offspring, so already it was hard to remember how barren the Citadel was. And she'd condemned Kermon to that sterility. No wonder he sounded so hysterical at finding seeds in his pocket.

'Water,' she said. 'They need water.'

'Do you think the purified water here will do?' He sounded panicky. Over growing seeds? What the stones was the matter with him?

'I don't know,' she said. That too he had lost: the health-giving Forest streams. She saw his face fall. 'But it might. Especially if you grow them in...' She looked around her. She was already so used to walking on the natural ground that she rarely looked closely at it. Now she did, she saw shoots pushing up and roots pushing down. Up into the air and down into earth.

'Air,' she told him. 'they will grow up into the air.' But how would the roots feed and find stability? Grassette would kill anything Forest-born. All the Citadel flooring was mage-crafted, sterile.

She reached out to a tree-stump, felt its knobbly old wood. A small piece of bark, covered in lichen, broke off in her hand. She trailed her fingers through the little particles of green, linked to each other even when detached from the wood. Around the stump, at a respectful distance, tall offspring of the same species leaned towards each other, high leaves rustling in the breeze. Or in tree conversation.

'It's not enough.' Kermon's eyes were fixed on the lichen. She suddenly realised what torture this must be for him, to see all he had lost. If it was painful for her to see the prison from which she'd escaped, how must he feel!

'The walls,' she said. 'tell me about the walls. Maybe we'll think of something for the seeds while we talk.'

'Drianne went into the walls, after instruction from Rinduran on how she could survive there. If I show her – and Jannlou – my lessons with the children, I can help her control her magecraft and she could teach me what she learned.'

Did Mielitta's face show the yearning she had seen on Kermon's? 'I wish it was me,' she said quietly. 'Going into the walls.' She'd always believed that she'd find the answers in the walls. Why she'd come from the walls into the Citadel as a foundling. Who her parents were.

'Would you look, while you're there?' she asked. 'For anything that shows where I'm from.' Her heart thumped. She'd told herself she didn't care any more. That she was self-sufficient. But what if Kermon found some answers?

'If I can, but I don't know what to look for. All I know is the story Declan told everyone, that you just appeared from the walls in a basket, in front of him, with your name on a label.'

'Yes, that's all I know. A label pinned to my white baby clothes.' She'd regained her composure. It was only natural to be curious. She thought for a moment. 'And on my eighteenth birthday, a present appeared in my chamber: some kind of prophecy written on a scroll, along with a phial of perfume. The smell set the bees on me when I went to the Forest. I remember the writing too, spidery, in green ink. I always thought the gift came from the walls, from my parents even.'

Kermon wasn't encouraging. 'Finding answers in the walls is like searching streams for drops of water. But I'll keep my eyes open for anything that might be a lead. Do you remember the prophecy?'

She hesitated but surely there was no harm telling him.

'When the bottle is empty, you will be full.
No life ends while The One lives.
In the year of the prophecy, choose well.'

Kermon repeated the words, memorising them, as she had, then considering them, as she had. 'Obviously you're *The One*, with your bees, and you had to make choices. But so many lives *have* ended. What's that supposed to mean, if anything? Does it make *any* sense to you?'

'It might,' Mielitta admitted. 'Something the mage said, the one who died, Crimvert. He said that Citadel life was just existing, not living. And Jannlou's mother said the same sort of thing. "This is no life." Maybe we're going to change that, put an end to 'no life' in the Citadel, through the children and your work with them.'

Kermon made no reply.

Mielitta remembered the walls' trickery, sometimes helping her and sometimes staying blank, mere stone. She'd run down the dangerous path to the water gate, trying to escape Bastien and Jannlou, rubbing against the cold, wet lichen-covered stone on one side; the walls had stayed indifferent.

Lichen-covered. 'I've got it,' she told Kermon.

'Then you'll ask Drianne?' His expression barely brightened.

'No. I mean, yes. But that's not what I mean. The seeds,' her words tumbled over each other. 'They'll grow in the moss that's on the walls. It's natural, wall-born, nothing to do with the mages. Gather it and pack it into something. Then just keep it wet.' She had no idea whether that would work but Kermon needed her assurance: not 'might' and 'maybe'. *A half-loosed arrow falls short,* Tannlei had taught.

Her reward was the glow of determination in Kermon's eyes. 'I ordered new boots,' he said. 'I'll see the Cobbler Mage and get them tomorrow, plant the seeds in the old ones.'

'Perfect,' said Mielitta and they looked at each other. *How did you unsay a word?'*

'Forest,' said Kermon quietly.

'Perfect Forest,' she agreed. *Stones. Let's hope these mysterious seeds do grow in greylight, purified water and wall moss.* Could you trust the Forest any more than the walls? What were the seeds anyway and what would they do?

'I'll ask Drianne,' she told him. 'And Jannlou.'

Kermon's expression barely clouded at Jannlou's name. He must really be intent on growing seeds.

As the vision from the Citadel wavered and disappeared,

Mielitta felt the Forest alert behind her, knew that Jannlou and Drianne were back and she turned to greet them.

'One day, I'll catch you out,' Jannlou grinned. 'You won't hear me coming. I'll sneak up on you and give you a fright.'

'What'll you do? Growl at me?' she challenged him.

His grin disappeared and he shook his head at her. Why wouldn't he open up about something so important?

Drianne was preoccupied with the contents of a scarf tied at the corners to make a sack. She checked each brown object's cap and gills before sorting them into two groups.

Mushrooms, thought Mielitta, noting how small the 'inedible' pile was, thanks to Jannlou's capacity to distinguish between what could and couldn't be eaten by humans. And she knew why he had such an ability.

Drianne was out of earshot, busy, so Mielitta took the chance to speak *sotto voce* to Jannlou, who sat on the mossy trunk, easing tired limbs. 'We should talk about it,' she said.

He stilled but said nothing. Day's end sunshine gilded the brown curve of his warrior's muscles, picked out the sculpted line of his throat, the angles of his cheekbones. She could have traced each curve and line blindfold, without using her bees' direction dances, and yet the two of them were as far apart now as when they'd been knight and freak in the Citadel.

Had he really asked her to the Courtship Dance or had she imagined that?

Finally he spoke, his blue eyes on hers. Azure deepening to navy, then darkness against the sunshine. 'I have nightmares,' he told her. 'About Rinduran's death.'

'But–' she said, perplexed.

He nodded. 'But–' he agreed as if that was the end of the matter and all had been said.

She would not let it rest there. 'But Rinduran deserved his death! You had no choice.' She struggled to understand. The battle, the deaths, were her responsibility, not Jannlou's. What if she'd been the one who killed Rinduran? How would she feel?

She remembered arcing her back, injecting her bee's stinger into his eye as he used his power to expose her in the Citadel. Her fierce joy in his pain, then the realisation a bee had paid with her life.

Mielitta remembered him opening her mind up, ripping her private thoughts from her deep thinking, mocking her as she cried for the mother she'd never known, as she revealed her feelings for Jannlou. Mocking as he destroyed frame after frame from the beehive, destroyed her bees' will to live and hers with it. The bear had saved them all when Mielitta had nothing left to give.

'I don't have nightmares about it. I'm glad!' she told him.

His voice was soft and sad. 'I'm glad too but I do have nightmares.'

Totally frustrated, she said, 'We need to talk, properly. And include Drianne.'

He just shook his head. 'I'm not ready. Give me time.'

She put a hand out, touched his arm and he flinched as if scalded. 'I'm not ready,' he repeated.

Don't touch him! Don't touch him! warned her bees. *Dangerous!*

Oh shut up! she told them. Aloud, she said, 'Drianne, how did it go today?'

We will feast tonight! came her friend's proud reply. Then, confessing. *We gave up on the magecraft lesson and went gathering food instead.*

Knowing full well that Jannlou couldn't hear Drianne, Mielitta punished him by leaving that side of the exchange a mystery to him.

'Kermon will take over the magecraft lessons,' Mielitta told both her companions, who were equally downcast at the news. Well, she was no Tannlei to help them see that they were condemning themselves to failure by their attitude. She had enough problems of her own, just keeping them all alive.

Why couldn't you just sting everyone and everything when you were so angry the poison was filling your body?

Because part of you dies every time you use your stinger, replied her bees.

'It was a rhetorical question,' she told them. While she tried to explain in bee terms the use of a question to which you did not want an answer, she felt the poison evaporate.

'I have a lot on my mind,' she said to Drianne, Jannlou and the bees, by way of apology. 'News from the Citadel is … complicated. I'll tell you all the detail while we eat. You have both done so well, not just today.' She stared hard at Jannlou, willing him to accept his role in the battle, to move on. She sighed. 'I would be lost without you.'

Lost? panicked the bees, dancing frenzied maps in her mind.

She laughed and decided against explaining what a metaphor was.

CHAPTER ELEVEN

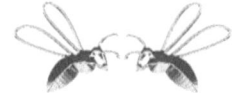

'It's not working,' Kermon told Mielitta. She could see the five youngsters who'd been sent to him for magecraft lessons looking around open-mouthed as he held a steel arrowhead and spoke to invisible beings. They sat cross-legged at his feet, fixated on his every move. Unlike Jannlou and Drianne.

Jannlou had faked magecraft throughout his schooldays, thanks to Bastien, so he knew what Drianne was supposed to do but he couldn't tell her what it felt like. And he couldn't hear a word she said.

It's not working, Drianne told Mielitta as she drew huge circles in the air with her index finger.

'That's supposed to represent the magecraft cycle in power and renewal so you can visualise your magecraft, send it around a circle and return it to your core, under control,' Jannlou explained, an edge of irritation hardening his voice. 'So you won't spend all your magecraft by the end of every morning!'

'We don't say 'spend', Jannlou,' Kermon corrected. 'We say 'endow'.

'I know,' Jannlou snapped. 'I did the training. Magecraft should only be used to benefit Perfection so we don't spend it, we endow it on the world. Whatever the words, when his magecraft is all spent, so is the mage!' He turned to Mielitta, opened his mouth.

She said it for him. 'It's not working,' she agreed with Kermon.

'I can't hear Drianne,' the Smith-Master told her. 'So I can't help her and–' Nobody there needed to be told that Jannlou wasn't helping.

'And,' continued Kermon tactfully, 'I can't find out what I need to know about the walls. I really need support. I'm sure Hamel is lying through his teeth every time he tells me something about the walls but there's not one of the mages I can trust. Every one of them has his or her own agenda and if I feature in it, then I'll be wall history.'

Mielitta clutched Steelwing even tighter. 'There has to be some way to make this work.'

She jumped as Jannlou's hand closed over hers, gently prised her fingers open, freed her hand again.

'Relax. You're making us all tense up,' he told her.

Oh, she thought. *Maybe it's not Jannlou who's blocking Drianne.*

Kermon's eyes widened. 'Do that again!' he told Jannlou.

Self-conscious, Jannlou put his hand over Mielitta's, spread her fingers. In doing so, he touched the glinting metal underneath.

'So stupid,' Kermon was muttering. Then he beamed. 'I don't need you.'

Mielitta could have sworn she saw Jannlou's hackles physically rise but he turned to go without a word.

'No, not just Jannlou. Both of you. Give Steelwing to Drianne. I could read Jannlou when he touched it so Drianne and I will be fine without either of you!'

'What did you read? asked Jannlou, his hand instinctively on his sword-hilt.

'Nothing important. I wouldn't – not without permission. I'm not that kind of mage!' Kermon was growing tetchy again.

Why wouldn't Jannlou let it go? Instead, he insisted, 'You're replacing Shenagra on the Council. I know what her role was. If my father ordered her, she'd suppress everyone in the Great Hall, permission or not. And what do you think Shenagra did to the children in the Maturity Test? That's what you'll end up doing for Bastien. All of it.'

'I won't!' Kermon's eyes blazed. 'I'm no Shenagra.'

'How do you think she began?' retorted Jannlou. 'You should leave, now, while you still want to.'

'Jannlou!' Mielitta intervened. 'You're – we're – not helping!' She laid a hand on his arm but he shook it off, roughly.

She tried to lighten the mood. 'Let's go, Jannlou. Leave the mages to it. We can spend our time in the Forest instead of all this...' She drew mocking circles in the air and screwed up her face as if in the effort of making magecraft, earning frowns from all three of her companions.

Better they're annoyed with me than that Jannlou and Kermon are at loggerheads again, she thought, as she unclasped her neck-chain and passed Steelwing to Drianne. Who sighed.

I'd rather spend the day in the Forest with you, she pleaded with Mielitta.

Work, said the bees.

'Work,' said Mielitta, shouldering her bow and quiver. She felt unprotected in the absence of her pendant, as if she'd passed her authority to Drianne along with Steelwing but she had no choice. She followed Jannlou into the Forest, leaving the mages to their lesson.

Kermon dismissed Jannlou's warning. The warrior always underestimated the mage's strength, mental and physical. He would not lose himself. He looked at the five eager young mages sitting cross-legged on the grassette outside the forge, their hands neatly clasped, as he had taught them.

'What do we call this position?' he asked them.

'The focus position,' they chorused.

'Yes,' said Kermon, 'the focus position. So whenever you want to practise focus, begin by sitting cross-legged on the ground, arms resting on your knees, hands clasped loosely, your body poised like your mind, relaxed but alert. Do you understand?'

Yes replied Drianne, slipping Steelwing around her neck on its chain, so she could follow instructions and still communicate with Kermon.

He continued with questions and repetition so that Drianne could follow the lesson, without his charges being ignored. He hoped there would be more sent to him, of different ages, but the teachers had insisted that the five 'best' among the oldest students with magecraft needed 'special attention'.

'Shut your eyes,' he told them. 'Imagine a ball rolling along a line…'

'A line is two-dimensional and a ball is three,' objected a boy called Nathan, his black hair erect in a spiky cone shape.

'Then imagine a ball rolling along woodette that never ends. The ball just keeps rolling. Watch that ball as it keeps rolling…'

Janette opened her eyes, her frizzy black hair bobbing in frustration. 'Mage Kermon, my ball's hit a wall and I don't know what to do.'

'The wall isn't there, Janette.' Kermon kept his voice gentle but he felt like he was smacking his head into that same wall. Janette found ways of failing he could never have imagined and yet her logic was impeccable. 'Look again and you can see your ball is still rolling, just like all the other balls. Your mind is very powerful. It can keep the ball rolling or it can make a wall. This time, I want you to keep the ball rolling and we can do this for longer each time.'

While the children obediently kept the ball rolling, Kermon turned his attention to Drianne.

'We can try *walls* another time,' he said.

Drianne took the hint, opening her eyes. *You want me to tell you all I know about the walls?* she guessed.

'Yes,' said Kermon, in the calm voice he used to keep the children focused. 'That's good work. Keep the ball rolling. Don't worry if it stops or bumps. Just make it roll again.'

You know Rinduran trained us before we went into the walls?

'Yes,' said Kermon. 'Good work, keep it up. You can hum

while you work if that helps keep the ball rolling.' Immediately the air filled with five hums, reverberating like working bees.

He told us it would be an assault on all our senses at once. Millions of people ghosting about us, with all their sounds and smells. Not just people but buildings and places we'd never seen before, beings we'd never seen before. He said it would be too much and we'd explode if we let ourselves be distracted, that we needed one search term in our minds and if we kept to that, we'd be all right. We could just find out what we needed to know, not get lost and stuck there. He gave us each a search term. I think somebody had Perfect Relationships and another one was Perfect Food. Mine was Perfect Parenting but I ignored it.

Drianne's voice held a note of triumph. *I searched for* Animals. *Not* Perfect anything. *And you know what I found.*

Kermon had used his powers to read her soul, present her testimony in the Great Hall when it came to her turn. He remembered her words.

She'd seen animals and fish being 'farmed'. They were nourished and their products harvested. Some were killed and eaten. This had shocked her audience but not as much as the revelation that people lived with animals as their friends and that some even preferred to live with animals, not people, as companions. They called such animals pets. And they liked to see wild creatures and plant life around them. Birds on trees, wolves, bears and squirrels in the Forest. Even though these animals ate each other. They thought this was natural.

Now, Kermon would have the chance to see this for himself, the way things used to be. He would need to think of his own search term and to devise some kind of Adulthood Test for children like those in front of him. If and when he judged them ready.

'How did you lose your voice?' he asked quietly under cover of the children's hum. They were concentrating too hard on their rolling balls to pay him any attention.

Rinduran followed me into the walls, said I wouldn't laugh at anybody again. His power squeezed my throat until my voice was trapped inside. He pulled me out of the wall, told the mages I'd used the safe word and he'd come to help me, just in time to save my life. That I'd lost my voice from the horrors I'd witnessed of life before Perfection. It's not true.

'I know,' murmured Kermon.

But I found my inner voice instead, with my mage powers, when Mielitta sent the bee to me. And I knew she loved me as I love her. And then Mage Puggy recognised me in the Maturity Test, knew I was like her.

Now I am going off the path. I've lost my rolling ball! You want to know about the walls not about me.

'It's all useful to me.' Kermon could hardly explain his special interest in Puggy with the children there. 'What do you mean 'Like me?''

That I was a mage and not interested in men. So she gave me all her power, enough to save me from the forging.

Poor Drianne. And Poor Puggy. No wonder they'd had enough of men after what they'd been through with Rinduran and Bastien. It would take patience to heal Puggy and Kermon did not intend to abuse his position as her husband. Surely kindness would bring her back to her womanhood, if not to her full mage's powers.

You need a safe word and a helper. In case you need to come out of the walls in a hurry because you're losing yourself.

'Who should I ask to be the helper?' Kermon's question was to himself as much as to Drianne.

Rinduran was mine.

There was a silence. Kermon imagined Hamel as his partner.

You're supposed to have somebody you trust, somebody you're connected to enough that the connection itself will draw you back from the walls to your living self. It's like being in a dream state when you're there.

'We can't always have the person we want.'

No. I know. Puggy shared this with me too.

Kermon turned his thoughts resolutely from yearning after

Mielitta to what was possible. He would not lose himself, not in the Citadel and not in the walls.

'Well done,' he said. 'You are now masters of infinity. If you can keep that ball rolling, you can control time. When there is no beginning and no ending, there is no time and your powers are infinite. The ball rolls of itself, without draining you. If you listen, the universe is humming too and will help you. In your own time, stop humming and let the ball gently slow down until it stops. Listen? Can you hear the universe humming?'

'That's just my heart thumping,' said Janette, round face screwed up in concentration, eyes closed.

'Yes,' said Kermon. 'That's your heart you can hear. Listen to it.'

CHAPTER TWELVE

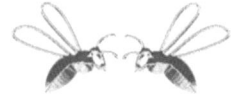

Mielitta floundered in Jannlou's wake as he strode faster and faster, as if he were trying to lose her. She saw his broad back appearing and vanishing between the trees, his pace even, as if he walked on grassette. She stumbled and cried out, sat down among the pine needles to check her ankle.

She took her boot off, then wondered whether she should have. If her ankle swelled, she'd never get the boot back on. And there was no Cobbler Mage here. Too late now. She removed the other boot and her hose. Cautiously she wiggled her foot. A small twinge but no more. *Thank the stones!* She really couldn't afford an injury when mere survival was a daily effort.

The leatherette jerkin had disappeared completely and Mielitta accepted defeat for now. Whatever was wrong with Jannlou, she couldn't chase him through the Forest, in the futile hope he'd open up to her when he stopped running away.

She checked her ankle again, just to be sure. Then she flexed her toes, tried moving them one at a time. Yes, no, yes. She laughed as her three middle toes insisted on moving together. How had she never discovered this. Could she train her feet as she had trained her archer's aim? She relaxed, concentrated and tried again, could visualise different movements, a separation where before she'd just been aware of a lump on the end of her leg, a 'foot' – whatever that was. How funny that she'd spent more time discovering her body as a bee than the one she lived in as a human and took for granted.

Was the other foot the same? No, she discovered. Like the leaves on the trees, each toe moved differently. Her toes were part of the infinite variety of the Forest. She belonged here.

She shared this life with her companions but they too were different leaves, attached to her, shaken by the same winds but fluttering in their own ways. A knot in her shoulders loosened and she felt ready to walk on. She strung her boots and hose around her neck. If she hardened her feet, she wouldn't need boots at all.

There was no chance of finding Jannlou so she'd follow her own path, discovering more of the Forest's riches. Maybe they all needed was some time apart.

Yes you can, said the bees. *But don't. Too dangerous.*

'I can what?' she asked.

Follow Brown Death.

That was a bit strong even for the bees! 'He's never hurt any of you. In fact he saved our hive,' she reprimanded them. Then she wondered. Was that how he saw himself?

'How?' she demanded. 'How can I find him?'

Bee minds squirmed away from telling her but they had no practice in evasion. They shared everything and Mielitta was one with the hive so she was soon in possession of all the bees knew about tracking. How could she have been so human as to rely on sight when she had her nose? She didn't have to sniff the last place she'd seen Jannlou to fix his scent: brown, earthy, male, unique as the imprint of her five toes on damp ground.

She shouldered her weapons and set off once more, this time at her own pace, following her nose.

The sun had moved a quarter-circle and still Mielitta was following the scent, sure she'd come across Jannlou. She was fit but she was no match for a warrior at the peak of his training. With who knew what strange boosts to his stamina.

Water, the bees told her but she already knew from the freshness in the air, cooler and scented sparkling turquoise, stone and minerals. Then she heard the rush and fall, water running fast, down a rocky drop. By the time she saw the waterfall, she had already pictured the scene in every detail bar one. She had not predicted the bear, splashing in the pool at the bottom of the fall, claws extended as it lunged into the bubbling water with its great paws, fishing.

She sniffed, wondering how she had missed the bear's smell, but she still caught only a faint whiff, even now she could see him. And she was sure the bear was male. His scent must be masked by the water but, even without that confirmation, she was sure she knew the bear. After all, she'd tracked him here. What better way to fish than as a bear? She'd had enough of secrets.

Mielitta left her bow, quiver and boots on the bank, and walked towards the stream. The bear was too absorbed in timing his move, watching the silver wriggles underwater, to notice her coming and the waterfall was loud, covering her splashes with its own.

Like a child playing tag in the playground, she reached out and patted the matted wet fur on the huge brown back.

'Got you!' she crowed and would have jumped on him to topple his balance if she hadn't heard a shout from the trees, distorted by the pounding waterfall but still clear enough to chill her to the bone.

'Mielitta!' yelled Jannlou at the top of his voice.

The bear was surprisingly fast as he turned to confront the stranger, rearing on his back legs, not one trace of humanity in the stony brown outrage of his tiny, round eyes. She'd interrupted his fishing. He swiped at her. One touch with those claws would have ripped her open but the second's warning from Jannlou had been enough. The great paw passed through thin air and a bee zigzagged in crazy flight back to her weapons and boots, where Jannlou waited, watching in open-mouthed incredulity.

She shifted back to human shape and punched him, hard.

He punched her back, not gently.

And then they were rolling on the ground, ignoring cuts and bruises to grapple for hair and hand-holds. Clothing grew as frayed as tempers but neither of them would surrender. Jannlou was the stronger but slow and clumsy. Mielitta's advantage in speed and agility was combined with a total lack of ethics.

Jannlou winced as she bit him, again. But she'd flipped to a distance beyond his arms' reach before he could punish her. Then she made her mistake, throwing herself at him, her legs wrapped round his waist, head-butting him in the chest, while he was still in the same position. His slowness to move had left him perfectly placed for defence against her assault. He only had to close his arms and crush her. Which he did.

A mouthful of Jannlou's curly black chest hair choked Mielitta as her back muscles screamed, then all pressure was released as her opponent dropped backwards onto the pine needles. She found herself astride a man who had stopped fighting and was looking at her oddly. She hit him again, just to make a point.

Then she leaned towards him, found his mouth with her own, allowed his arms to close once more round her back. She ran her hand down his thigh, under his ripped britches, found the bear sigil he bore. She shut her eyes, traced its shape with her fingers, knew him for what he was.

'You taste like honey,' he told her, his eyes hungry for more.

Fly high and fast, the bees reminded her, *so only the best catch you.*

She kissed him again and let the Forest take them wherever it willed. She had been right when she told the bees what a maiden flight should be like. For a human, this was personal. He was her first flower.

'We must have frightened off the bear,' Jannlou said, when

time started again. His fingers, so much bigger and broader than hers, were surprisingly gentle.

'The other bear,' she accused him. 'And I didn't need you–'

'–to rescue me,' he completed. 'You never do. I know.'

She touched his bear tattoo. 'When did you know?'

'I've always had it.' he shrugged. 'A birthmark that didn't mean anything. I thought it showed I had magecraft but – nothing. Just me being different. I tried, you know.' They lay on their backs, watching the clouds play tag across the sky, like they should have in the schoolyard, gently, for fun. 'My father told me the Forest was becoming more dangerous, but when he talked, I didn't feel the same as he did. I was more – curious – about the Forest. I even took a book out of the library, to find out more. About the enemy, I'd have said, if I'd been asked. But that's not what I felt.'

'*Predators of the Forest*,' Mielitta remembered smugly, earning a suspicious glare.

'You were stalking me!' he protested.

'Self-defence.'

'That's your usual excuse! Anyway, when the tiger came for us, I felt something. I could feel the mark, changing.'

'Like a hot glow,' she said.

'Yes. And then when the bear charged through the woods, this connection, like I'd called to him for help. And since then, I know why I'm different. I'm like you.'

She watched the clouds. 'I wonder why you were born with the mark and mine came later.'

'My father.' He was following his own train of thought and stumbled over the words. 'My father wanted so much for me. I tried not to disappoint him. And Bastien understood. His father was the same. I didn't want to hurt you.'

'But you enjoyed it, didn't you? It wasn't just because Bastien made you.'

'Yes,' he admitted. 'I was mean.'

Who was she to judge him? 'I guess we all have our mean side.'

'Like biting?'

She ignored his dig. 'I guess I disappointed my father too, my foster-father.'

'Are you still angry?' he asked. 'If I get up, will you hit me again?'

She looked at this man she didn't know, who was closer to her than her own heartbeat. 'Maybe,' she said. 'Try it and see.'

The sun made a fiery silhouette of his body, the bear symbol glowing on mahogany skin. 'Do you really have no magecraft?' she wondered aloud.

'None at all,' he grinned. 'Only natural charm.' Already his thoughts were elsewhere, the sigil fiery in summons. She could almost see him replaying the bear's fun in the stream, his urge to play. And now the waterfall was empty, inviting. The other bear must have run away from the sound of two predators fighting. She smiled.

'Go on,' she said. 'Catch some fish. I'll wait here and watch. I don't want to throw myself at the wrong bear twice in one day.'

As often as he'd seen *her* shift shape, Jannlou was shy and turned his naked back on her as he gained pelt and snout, paws and a lumbering gait when he dropped to all fours. She saw the ripple of muscles under his shoulder-blades, fur where her fingertips had traced silken skin. Once he was in the stream, he lost his self-consciousness and was soon lunging with expertise.

Danger her bees told Mielitta. *Brown Death. Bear and bees. Enemies.*

'No danger for me,' Mielitta repeated.

They held their peace while the bear's black claws darted underwater and rose up splashing with silver. Six times. Then the beast reared up on his hind legs, shaking rivulets of water down over a body that smoothed to human as Mielitta watched, tracing in her mind the path her fingers had taken earlier. The bear sigil was dimming, its mouth a roar that diminished to a smile as the toned thigh muscles rippled. Jannlou did not turn away when he caught her looking, just stooped in one powerful movement to gather his catch and come back to her.

He showed her the fish, so fresh their eyes had not dulled yet, then pulled out the snood-net and tied them in it.

The bees didn't like the snood any more than they'd liked the bear but they buried their concerns in silence.

She couldn't resist curling her fingers once more in the hair on his chest before he dressed fully.

'We should go,' he told her. 'Find out how Drianne got on.'

Oh stones. Would they know? Drianne and Kermon? She didn't want them to feel she ranked Jannlou above them in any way. She *didn't* put Jannlou above them but all these feelings for him were too new, too raw for her to explain even to herself. And she hadn't had the talk with Jannlou that she'd planned, about Rinduran's death, about Jannlou's second nature.

'Will you tell Drianne now?' she asked him.

'Will you?' was his response and he did not mean about his shifting shape. He must have read the answer in her eyes.

'Then I'm not ready yet either.'

Instead of uncovering one secret, she was returning with two, but it couldn't be helped. For now.

She reached up, kissed him lightly. 'Soon,' she said.

They shouldered their catches and walked together through the Forest.

CHAPTER THIRTEEN

Drianne must have been watching out for their return. She slid down from a tree, hopping from one foot to the other like the child she still was beneath her magecraft and forced maturity.

I met a beekeeper! Drianne's words tumbled headlong into Mielitta's mind, wiping out the warmth of Jannlou's kisses.

'Drianne says she met a beekeeper.' Mielitta automatically translated for Jannlou. Her bee sigil flamed gold and dangerous, no cuddly worker bee but a queen who scents a rival's birth and plans her death. How dare some other human interfere with *her* bees!

And where were they? What did they have to say about this? 'Well?' she demanded. 'What do you know about this beekeeper? Why haven't you told me?'

Her mind faked silence, the scuffling of small creatures who were pretending to be invisible. She'd used such tricks herself too often to be fooled by them.

'It's no good hiding,' she admonished them. 'You know about this beekeeper – of course, you do! And bees are supposed to share everything. I'm ashamed to call you my hive!'

Of course they knew about the beekeeper and so should she

have done. All the signs were there: the hive itself was a man-made box and the tiny sheds into which they'd chased the invading beetles must have been placed there by human hands.

Drianne was staring at her, one side of her scarred face twitching in bewilderment. *You didn't know there was a beekeeper?*

'No. The bees didn't tell me there was a beekeeper and I never saw her.' She knew from her twisting guts that the beekeeper was female. A rival queen. And she wasn't wrong.

You'll like her, continued Drianne. *She has a cottage and chickens and a cow and goats and–*

'If there's one person, there's more,' Jannlou cut in, interrogating Mielitta. 'How many people are there? Where do they live? How is it defended? This could be a Citadel trap. How does she know–'

A whisper of bees began, tentative, *You weren't there when the beekeeper was. She's not part of the hive and she doesn't hurt us so we never needed to tell you about her. She's not a queen, not hive, she's a beekeeper.*

'I can't listen to you all at the same time!' snapped Mielitta. Already the bee tattoo was calming down, controlling the instinctive rivalry, reserving judgment. 'Drianne, you were supposed to be taking magecraft lessons from Kermon. Tell me all about what happened, from the beginning. And wait while I translate for Jannlou.'

The lesson worked. Half of Drianne's face beamed. She removed Steelwing from her neck and handed the arrowhead back to Mielitta. *And the beekeeper will help me practise–*

Mielitta glared at her.

Sorry – all right, everything in order, a bit at a time.

With occasional tangents, and glares in response from Mielitta, Drianne told her tale. After her lesson, she'd gone foraging, on tracks she hadn't explored before, picking roots and berries. Once again, she'd found a clutch of eggs but this time she'd seen the hen who'd laid them. Russet-feathered and clucking, she had waddled off along the path, as if in invitation. Drianne had put the eggs in her cloth basket and followed.

She and the red hen had collected other followers and by the time they reached a cottage, a dozen chickens were squawking hunger and homecoming. They dived onto the corn offered them when they arrived and proceeded to eat and to scratch the ground around the doorway, which they had cleared of all greenery, making the entry as neat as a Citadel passageway.

When a person appeared, introduced herself as the beekeeper, everything made perfect sense.

Mielitta's face must have shown her thoughts as Drianne protested, 'It did! You'd have felt the same. There's just this atmosphere... you'll see. Anyway, the cottage is hers. It's a farmhouse really.'

The beekeeper had made Drianne welcome, saying she was expected. They'd had cheese sandwiches and Drianne had been allowed to thank the goat whose milk had made the cheese. She'd wondered whether she should thank the corn too, from which the flour had been ground to make her bread but the beekeeper said the spirit of appreciation was what counted.

At this point, Mielitta couldn't help asking, 'Drianne, are you sure this wasn't some glamour thrown on you by Citadel mages? It sounds a bit ... incredible.'

Jannlou said nothing but his sceptical expression added weight to her doubts.

Drianne was adamant. *Real* she insisted. *But you can judge for yourself. She invited us all to visit tomorrow.*

Mielitta translated for Jannlou and saw his raised eyebrows echo her own thoughts. A trap? If not a Citadel trap, then some new danger?

She's a mage, stated Drianne, with blithe indifference to their fears.

Mielitta snorted. The beekeeper was *expecting* Drianne and the homestead exuded magecraft. The beekeeper was *obviously* a mage.

When Mielitta made her go back through the details, Drianne said she had seen nothing but Forest ahead of her as, escorted by chickens, she felt 'wavery, like going through the rainbow gate from the Citadel to the Forest' and then, out of nowhere, there was a cottage and farmyard in the middle of pastureland. Animals everywhere: goats, cows, pigs, ducks, dogs, cats, chickens – Drianne's dream come true.

'Which is why it sounds like glamour, a magecraft trap,' cautioned Mielitta.

Again, Drianne shook her head. *I would know. Puggy's power inside me would know. That was one of her special skills, distinguishing glamour from reality. That's why she was so good at covering herself in glamour, at disguise – and why she was never fooled by it.*

'How did you know she was a beekeeper?' asked Jannlou.

Drianne's half-smile widened. *She introduced herself. She said, 'I'm the beekeeper and you're the flower.'*

The hairs rose on the back of Mielitta's neck.

Mielitta's true flower, commented the bees smugly. They'd always thought of Drianne as Mielitta's flower, from the time she'd pictured the girl for them and sent a scout after her.

Not the bear, added the bees, in case she'd missed the point. *He can't be your flower. He's a bear.*

'All right!' Mielitta said aloud, tetchy.

You came back together, observed Drianne, suddenly noticing, as if she'd sensed the bees' input.

'We bumped into each other in the woods.' Mielitta's studied nonchalance was prize-worthy.

'Do you want me to prepare these?' Jannlou indicated the fish strung on his line and suddenly food became the priority.

'We'll visit this beekeeper tomorrow, so Jannlou and I can make our own minds up about her,' stated Mielitta, closing any discussion.

The routine of fire, food and drinking water needed no words but Mielitta was aware of Jannlou's every movement, each time they brushed against each other, which was surprisingly frequently. He was imprinted on every pore of her skin. They avoided secretive glances, which merely added to the charge of suppressed electricity in the atmosphere between them.

How could Drianne not notice? Where would this lead, this *thing* between her and Jannlou? There were no Courtship Dances in the Forest, no weddings – no society. Just the three of them – and a beekeeper.

Later, in replete human silence, Mielitta opened her mind to the bees.

'Now,' she commanded, 'tell me everything you know about the beekeeper.'

'Everything' turned out to be of little use, from a human perspective. Hands dominated. Hands that pulled out frames from the hive and replaced them. Hands that changed the scent in the hive, added bees who reeked of the new scent. Hands that were slow and gentle, strong, didn't react when a bee panicked and used her stinger.

There was a voice too, incomprehensible but soothing. The murmur of human words, a rhythm that was almost bee-like sometimes, humming, singing.

'How do you feel about the beekeeper?'

The question caused confusion. *The beekeeper is the beekeeper. We don't feel anything about her. If we are frightened by the winds or a storm coming then we show her our fear. If we are happy making honey, we show her our happiness. We know her smell and we share our feelings with her. She shares her feelings with us too and she is serene so we let her hands do what they want.*

'Well, I don't trust her and I don't like her.'

That's because you feel dislike and distrust. Not because of her.

What would they know? They were only bees.

What does 'only' mean?

Mielitta started to explain and then flushed. 'It means I was thinking like a human. Not good thinking.'

You can't help it. We must teach better bee understanding.

What am I? wondered Mielitta. *Not only a human, not only a bee. And Jannlou. What is he?*

Her thoughts were interrupted by fifty thousand cries for help. *No, no! Trapped!*

Mielitta felt the panic spread through the home hive but her bee sigil stayed dull. She was not being called back to support them. Twilight was deepening around her but that did not explain the blackness she sensed through her bees' eyes, nor the jolting sickness as they clung to their frames.

'What's happening?' she asked her own cadre of spirit bees. They seemed uneasy but nothing more.

Moving, they told her. *The beehive is moving, being moved, with all the bees inside. We will find it again tomorrow.*

'Why can't I go to help?'

You aren't needed. The beekeeper is the one moving the hive.

Mielitta's stomach lurched in sympathy with the colony, travelling in the dark, losing all their mind maps. She didn't dislike the beekeeper. She hated her.

CHAPTER FOURTEEN

Kermon sought the heart of flame in his forge, in the white-hot centre, beyond the distraction of flickering red and yellow. Even though no face formed, no fiery mouth spat accusations, he could not concentrate and the steel knew it. He swore as the metal broke into pieces.

'Master?'

Kermon almost looked around the forge to see whether his master had returned. Declan's spirit didn't need to appear in flames to haunt this place. But of course Kermon was the master now and one of his new apprentices was observing him botch his work.

However, Janette was watching him rather than the fires. He should have turned her down as an assistant but how could he face Mielitta if he'd rejected the only girl who'd shown an interest? Even if it wasn't her gender that worried him but her magecraft. He could feel her gentle questing, attempts to understand him that went beyond empathy. What if she too was a soul-reader? Must he defend his thoughts even in the forge, usually his haven?

He sighed. He'd promised to nurture these children and failure was a good lesson for them too.

He put the glowing tongs down on the anvil. While the red dulled to black and the broken metal flaked onto the stone, he gathered the young assistants, spoke with the control his smith-work had lacked.

'I have much on my mind,' he told them. Their eyes glowed in grubby young faces. 'I let that distract me from my work and I didn't notice the furnace overheating. The steel could not bear the stress I put on it.'

Like me, he thought. *Learning wall-craft from Hamel, who wants nothing more than to leave me lost in the walls. With Verity watching my every move. If I don't come out of the walls with some idea for a Maturity Test, she'll cry 'Traitor'. I'm about to marry someone who can't speak one word of sense. Teaching a few children who might have been changed by a taste of honey – or who might not. Giving Mielitta false hopes, based on what?* His little group learning magecraft and his forge assistants, deliberately chosen from those without magecraft – these were the only ways he could reach such children. But what sort of example was he?

And then there was the gift of the Forest, seeds planted in moss-filled boots, watered every day and no doubt dying in the greylight. Now *that* summed up his life!

'Master?' asked Janette again. 'Do you want to try again?'

No, he didn't. He really didn't. But there was something in those young faces that he could not destroy. Call it hope. Even if he had none, he could not lash out at these innocents when his sole purpose in life was to nurture them.

He picked up a nugget of metal left on the cold stone.

'I should not have tried something complicated when I knew I was distracted,' he told them. 'You have to learn what is easy for you and what is hard, so you can judge what you can do now, at this moment. Sometimes, you can test yourself and build on your skills. Sometimes, you need easy work that is both practice and reassurance.

'Today has started badly for me so I want to save something from my failure and tackle an easy job so I feel better. What do you suggest? The easiest job you can think of as I can't cope with doing something else badly today.'

Kermon paused, let them think.

Ioan, a stolid and reliable lad, who achieved through stubbornness what he couldn't through talent, risked the first suggestion. 'Clean and tidy the forge?'

Although he could think of little that would increase his depression as much as cleaning and tidying, Kermon expressed warm approval. After all, that might work for others, perhaps for Ioan himself.

Encouraged, the young apprentices showed their own characters in suggesting easy tasks – or rather, tasks they found easy: sharpening a knife, stacking wood, oiling blades and handles, repairing a joint.

'I read the list of commissions this morning,' began Janette, a born organiser, 'and there's one for a belt trophy. That would only take a little metal and it would be fun to engrave it.'

Kermon nodded, careful not to show more enthusiasm for this idea than for the others, but she'd read him perfectly. Simple but fun. Exactly what was needed.

'Who's the trophy for and what is it?' Kermon should have known but he'd been so preoccupied, he hadn't checked through the orders for days. He really did need good assistants! The men who'd helped Declan carried out their usual duties and no more, as if they too felt the master was absent from the forge.

Janette closed her eyes as if that helped her recite from memory. 'Chief Mage Bastien requires a belt trophy of a tree with a cross through it to show the victory of the Battle of the Forest.' She opened her eyes. 'A belt trophy is a small metal badge commem – commemorating–' She was young enough to stumble over the word and determined enough to go for it again.

Kermon remembered Drianne stammering before her voice had been stolen from her, if not by Bastien then by Rinduran on his son's behalf. '–an event or achievement in the life of the knight who wears the belt.'

Not fun at all, then, thought Kermon. Just another of the daily lies filling his life. He wiped the wetness from his eyes. Sweat probably.

'Perfect suggestions,' he told them. Let Janette note what a good citizen he was in his choice of language. 'Each of you should now carry out the task you suggested and afterwards we can talk about how that felt, whether my bad start to the day has been rescued and turned into good work.

'Janette, you can help me make the belt trophy. I want you to draw the symbol required, the tree and the cross, then make a template. I'll make the badge and then help you transfer your design to the metal for engraving.'

And if the stones are with me, I won't be the one who engraves that lie on metal. The glorious victory of the Battle of the Forest! But Kermon knew that evading one lie could not clean his soul of the many he must tell each day. His mettle was indeed stressed beyond bearing.

Despite himself, at some point between hammering and chiselling, he slipped into the focus that had eluded him earlier and his spirit calmed. Surrounded by the sounds of his young apprentices at work, he gave praise where it was deserved and encouragement where it was needed.

While he was not thinking at all about his predicament, a plan of action formed in his mind. Mielitta would have said his deep thinking was at work. He even smiled at the thought. Next time he spoke to her, he would be able to tell her more positive news.

He would tell her how well the children were responding to his lessons, both in the school and in the forge. How Drianne too was learning from him and was finally working to control her magecraft.

He would tell her how he could defend himself against Hamel's treachery by triangulation, using two other experts on wallcraft. He could compare anything Hamel told him about wallcraft with what Drianne knew, and with what Bastien knew from his father. It would be easy to state some tenet of wallcraft in front of Bastien, when Hamel wasn't there, and read his reaction.

He would confess that he'd promised to marry Puggy, because he could see no other way to save her from Hamel; that he intended to use his soul-reading to reach her and try to heal the damage done in the Maturity Test.

He would ask Mielitta for her suggestions about a new Maturity Test. Why hadn't he thought of that before? He would be going into the walls very soon and he would find out who her parents were. Everything was going to work out.

Except that when he held Perfection Unfinished, in the gathering gloom of day's end, nobody responded. The arrowhead glinted as he reached out for Mielitta and met only a wall of cloud, insubstantial but barring everything beyond to his senses. As if magecraft had blocked him from reaching Mielitta. His optimism snapped like overheated steel.

He trudged back to his room, sat on the solitary chair in his greylit, locked chamber and stared for a long time at a pair of old boots, filled with moss. The seeds were probably dead. He'd throw them away in the morning. Face the reality of the rest of his life imprisoned in the Citadel, find some way to make the best of it.

Bastien thought he'd exiled Mielitta, Drianne and Jannlou but it was he, Kermon, who was the exile. And he was alone.

CHAPTER FIFTEEN

'Am I interrupting?' Verity seemed taller in her striped robe, more confident, and the question was polite rather than genuine as she entered the Council Chamber.

'Not at all,' grated Hamel, his pointed head nodding welcome. 'We were just finishing. The Mage-Smith is now fully prepared to visit the walls and earn the Rinduran Award. I see no benefit in him delaying further.'

Nice touch, making me sound like a coward, Kermon thought as he bowed.

He shook off his gloomy thoughts to greet his fiancée as, shy and dreamy-eyed, she followed Verity into the chamber. He wondered whether she would remember who he was. Hamel scowled at the new arrivals and left the room.

'Lady Puggy wanted to wish her fiancé luck for his ordeal in the walls.' Verity motioned Puggy to sit and followed suit. 'I'm sure Mage Kermon would love to tell us all he's learned about visiting. Ask him, Lady Puggy.'

'Mage Kermon, do tell us all.' Puggy graced him with a dark-lashed blue gaze but he felt a diminished response to her beauty. His fear of visiting the walls took priority over any softer emotions. Hamel's jibe had hurt because it was true. He couldn't delay any longer and he wasn't just scared. He wanted to scream.

However, he was a trained mage and his lessons to the children meant nothing if he couldn't discipline his own base emotions.

Verity prompted him. 'You've been in the walls. What's it like? Why would anyone be scared? My father was never scared. He told me he could see millions of lives, walk amongst them and navigate to wherever he chose, in whatever time period he chose, but that his existence there had no reality.' Her eyes shone with loving memories and something more: curiosity.

How could Verity's reality be so different from his, Kermon wondered. How could Rinduran be murderer, tyrant and Perfect fundamentalist – as Kermon knew him to be – and yet also the brave father idolised by his daughter?

'Students with magecraft all visited the walls,' he told Verity, 'as part of our History lessons, to learn the origins of Perfection and see for ourselves the horrors of the social systems it replaced. We stayed together as a group and Mage Rinduran was always with us, directing what we saw, making sure nobody got lost.'

'Chief Mage Rinduran,' Verity corrected.

Puggy toyed with long strands of blonde hair, plaiting them, running her fingers through them to loosen them before weaving them together again.

What was it like in the walls? Kermon searched for a word. 'It's overwhelming,' he said at last. 'The weight of all those lives. You could drown in somebody else's pain or spend all your own years watching another person's life. On your own, you can get lost in so many ways: by losing track of time or losing the route back. Immersed in so many other lives, you can forget your identity. Splinter into a million trillion shards of living matter with a million trillion names.' Kermon stopped suddenly. This was the first time he'd voiced his fear and to Verity of all people. He might as well have handed her his head on a plate.

However, there was no sign of triumph in her face and, when she spoke, she was merely solving puzzles.

'When somebody dies, we say, 'May the walls take them.' Can you see people again, people you know?'

'No.' Kermon was sure about that. 'We were taught that it takes centuries for the imprint of people's lives to have any form in the walls. So what you see took place hundreds of years ago or more.'

She hid her disappointment but Kermon knew what she'd hoped. What orphans always hoped.

Verity returned to the practicalities. 'Is it because you're a soul-reader? That you enter too deeply into others' lives? And that would be dangerous in the walls?'

'Of course not. I'm used to being a soul-reader, to controlling my magecraft,' Kermon replied without thinking. She wasn't even a mage. She knew nothing about the hours of practice, the discipline he'd mastered.

Verity just gazed back at him.

'Maybe,' he admitted quietly. 'Maybe that makes it more dangerous for me than for other mages.'

She nodded. 'So you will need to be careful. Not use your soul-reading. Can you do that?'

He hesitated. 'I think so. We don't read minds without permission.' *Unless ordered to do so by the Chief Mage.* He was not going to remind her that her brother held *that* power. 'So I have trained to use soul-reading consciously, not by accident. But to hold back in the walls will be like visiting blindfold.'

'If it risks your life otherwise, that's what you must do. Hold back.' Verity was imperious. 'And the other kind of getting lost. How do you go into the walls and how do you get back? I know it happens at the bottom of the spiral staircase here in the tower. My father told me. But he wouldn't tell me how.'

Puggy was still twiddling plaited locks, looping them into knots and undoing them again.

'It's hard to explain. I only know what it was like for me. I stood facing the wall, shut my eyes, told myself that the walls were not barriers but entry points and I walked forward. Into a different world, where I had no corporeal existence but I could see the other students and Mage Rinduran.'

Frowning in concentration, Verity didn't even correct her father's title.

And he had *been a mere mage at that time,* Kermon thought defiantly, *not even a member of the Council.* His support for Mielitta was reduced to acts of rebellion so tiny they weren't even noticed.

'So how do you find your way back?' asked Verity.

'From what Hamel says, I need an anchor, somebody I am connected to, who I can find, who will draw me back.' What Hamel had actually said was that Kermon should take a cup with him from the kitchen. Fat lot of use that would have been! Thank the stones Drianne had given him such good advice.

'The tradition of entering the walls in the same place might help in fixing the return in space. I think the walls can be entered anywhere but that just adds to the confusion,' he explained. The story of Mielitta's appearance from the walls as a baby supported his theory but it was hardly politic to mention that to Verity.

'Nobody has the wallcraft your father had,' he admitted. 'Mage Rinduran was the anchor, for students, even for the volunteers who went into the wall.' *Drianne,* he thought, *one of those so-called volunteers.* The world inside the walls allowed Rinduran to take a girl's voice. 'He had great powers.' *That* was true. 'Hamel wants to take over, be my anchor.'

Verity glanced at Puggy. 'And Hamel is not motivated to keep you safe.' She nodded. 'That's the other reason for your fears.'

There was no point denying it. Kermon shrugged, helpless.

'Does the anchor have to be a mage?' she asked. 'From what you say it could be somebody important to you, so that the connection draws you back. My father never had a mage as an anchor. I don't think he had anybody as an anchor. But he found his way back without ever worrying so he must have had the connection in his head.'

Like Mielitta and her bees, their mind maps. The thought lifted Kermon's spirits. 'Maybe,' he conceded.

'Then that's the answer,' Verity declared with evident satisfaction. 'Puggy will be your anchor.'

Puggy looked up at the mention of her name. 'Are we going now?'

'Soon,' replied Verity. 'But first there's something very important for you and Kermon to do. He is going to be your husband soon and he needs your help.'

Puggy smiled vacantly. 'I can't do a lot. He'd better ask somebody else.'

'No, dear. It should be you,' Verity persevered, with more patience than Kermon would have believed possible. He felt only growing horror. Have his life depend on the bond between him and Puggy? He'd intended to save her life, try to find her lost soul. Would she now cost him his own?

His mouth was too dry to speak and while he licked his lips, hesitating, Verity took Puggy's hand and explained, 'You can do this. All you have to do is to stand by the wall when I tell you to and think very hard about Kermon. Shut your eyes.'

Puggy obeyed.

'Now picture Kermon in your mind's eye. How strong he is. The smudges he usually has on his skin from working in the forge. His manner of looking away to think before he speaks; then when he meets your eyes it's like magecraft, a force. Can you see him?

Puggy opened her eyes and smiled. 'I can see him now. He's just there!'

'Make her understand! Take her hand!' Verity pleaded with Kermon but she didn't wait for him to act. She grabbed Kermon's hand in her own small, elegant fingers and joined it to Puggy's as if in marital binding.

Kermon did indeed feel a jolt, a force like magecraft. Puggy jerked her hand away, her eyes wide with physical repulsion.

He laughed. He had hoped to find a trace of Puggy's character, the woman she had been before the Maturity Test that turned her into this childish siren and his hopes had been realised. There was indeed more to Puggy – she hated him. *This* was where his chivalry had led him. He was doomed to a marriage from hell. He didn't even feel physical attraction to her any more.

One moment's rejection had ended any thoughts that he'd find comfort in this woman's touch.

Kermon suddenly realised that Verity was still holding his hand. Gently, he prised her fingers free. 'It's not your fault,' he told her.

'I will do it,' she said, ashen-faced. 'I will be your anchor. I'm my father's daughter even if I have no magecraft. I don't need to be a mage to do this. I'm sure I don't.'

'I don't understand. Why would you help me? You accused me of treachery. This is supposed to be a test, an ordeal.'

Grim as death in the walls, Verity said, 'I've changed my mind. I want you to be my knight. You carried me in that evil place and you *were* gentle, whatever orders *she* gave you. I don't want to kill you. I want you to help me kill *her*.'

CHAPTER SIXTEEN

In the dark alcove at the bottom of the spiral staircase, Kermon studied the ancient stone wall in front of him, gleaming from the touch of mages who'd passed this way before him. Thousands of years ago, men had carted the building materials here, fitted one rock to another. They'd selected each one for the best fit, turned them to minimise the gaps, grunted with approval as the wall grew, solid, one stone at a time and the mages' tower had been born. Not, of course, that it was for mages in those days but for knights, their ladies, and children, horses and hounds.

Kermon reached out to touch the past, to find the state of mind he needed to walk through the barrier.

'We should do a practice run,' said Verity, jolting him back to the present with her matter-of-fact tone. 'If you just pop into the walls for a minute and come back, while I'm here, we'll know the anchor works and you can get on with it then. I won't have to stand here all day but I'll come back this evening and call you, in case you need help finding your way.'

Her prosaic certainty was reassuring even if Kermon's racing imagination presented as many possible dooms for him as there were past lives in the wall.

'I think touching hands helped make the anchor,' she said, 'so let's do it again. This is home for you.' She held out her right hand, the one for oath-making, and Kermon remembered the raised redness of her palm where she'd been stung but he could see only a pale gleam in the shadows.

He placed his hand on hers, palm to palm, felt again that jolt. *Verity's sting* he thought, with that bitter humour which surged up so often nowadays. He noted the hollow between their hands, the pressure between thumb pad and fingertips, hers so much smaller than his that he could have hidden her fist in his own just by curling his fingers. He held his hand steady, half of the prayer they made together.

'The stones be with you,' she intoned solemnly, her voice still a girl's but the weight of her responsibilities lending gravitas to her words.

He bowed, disengaged, turned to the wall and focused on what was beyond this illusion of stone. One step at a time, without hesitation and looking always beyond the surface, Kermon entered the wall.

Even though he'd expected it, the teeming current of lives caught him up in a riptide of others' emotions.

He took a few steps after an angry teenager who was muttering and fingering the knife in his pocket. *No*, Kermon reminded himself. *This is the past. Whether the knife is used is not the story I need to follow. Focus!*

He touched Perfection Unfinished, hanging round his neck, cold against his skin, hidden under his shirt. He reached out to Mielitta, to Drianne, so he could share all this with them. They could learn from these techniques, pose questions of their own about all the societies he sensed around him. A million trillion opportunities to learn. And Mielitta had asked him something, hadn't she? What was it?

Ah, yes. *Find her parents.* She could search with him, thanks to the arrowhead.

He reached out again. *Mielitta. Drianne.* Nothing. Just cold steel in his hand.

And in front of him a man in a workshop, soldering joints on wrought iron gates, judging the small, steady movement to melt the alloy evenly in place. Not directly touching the wrought iron but heating the solder to leave a tiny amount. Wiping the oxide off the tip of the soldering iron with a wet sponge.

He stopped to watch the techniques, wondered idly where the metal came from and immediately found himself in some kind of mine. He could do this! He was navigating like an expert!

The mine walls were grey rock speckled with orange, green and pale glints shining in miners' headlamps. Hewn chunks were loaded into a truck and Kermon wondered why the men would bother. He listened to their thoughts as they worked and looked again at the rock face. He still couldn't see the gemstones – diamonds even! – that were in the rock but these men knew where to look – kimberlite rock – and what they were looking for. He looked closely at one section of rock. *Now that's interesting. I didn't know...*

'Kermon,' a voice called, as unmistakeable as a fingerprint and very irritated.

How long had he been in the walls? He was supposed to go back, let Verity know their anchor worked. Verity's hand. He couldn't visualise it, panicked, shut his eyes.

There. He felt it, palm to palm. All he had to do was step through the wall, back to the Citadel.

'What on earth were you doing all that time?' Verity stamped her foot. 'I thought you'd never come back. I waited hours!'

'It didn't feel long to me. I'm sorry,' he stammered. *She waited hours.* Mielitta, Drianne – and, of course Jannlou – were too busy enjoying their new lives in the Forest to even contact him but there was one person in this hostile community who cared whether he lived or died.

'It worked,' he told her and was rewarded with a smile. 'You're my anchor.'

'I told you it would.' But she hadn't completely forgiven him.

'Now you can go back and work without me having to stand here all day and catch my death.'

There was an awkward silence, which she broke with a forced laugh., 'I haven't talked about my death for weeks and now I'm joking about it.'

Carefully, Kermon said, 'You're looking so much better. We've all been hoping that a miracle has happened, that you've been cured of allergy.'

'I might be feeling a bit better.' Her eyes narrowed. 'But don't think it's anything to do with some bee sting. My mother had good days and bad days. Before she died.' She coughed. 'There. We shouldn't talk about it.'

Kermon said nothing but he knew the difference between the racking coughs of her invalid days and one forced for effect.

She waved a hand in the air. 'Go on then. Go back into the walls. You need to produce quality research and come up with a test for adulthood that won't make Bastien ill as an oath-breaker but that will meet the Citadel's needs. Go and earn the Rinduran Award.'

That was clear enough. 'Yes, Chief Councillor.' Kermon's bow hid a smile and when he stepped into the walls, he was better prepared this time for the whirling infinity of past lives. He had to hold himself apart but to do so, he needed to know who he was.

Verity had described him to Puggy as a man who looked away from eye contact. Was he such a furtive creature now? He had not been so as Declan's apprentice, open-hearted when creating Steelwing for Mielitta, a gift of love, forged with his own tears. Had he been so changed by the Battle of the Forest, by Declan's betrayal, by his double life in the Citadel? He knew the answer and was ashamed. It was his own forging and tempering that he must face in the walls before he devised any maturity test for others.

He was under orders and that would be his starting point. Quality research required focus and navigation, not whims and tangents. His nose twitched as tempting smells came from a bakery. Mielitta would have words for such smells but he could only describe reactions: hunger, salivation. What was different about bread here from the sustenance in the Citadel? He wouldn't need to spend long in the bakery to find out...

He caught himself short. That's exactly what had happened before, skipping from one attraction to another like a child in the schoolyard. *Focus, self-discipline.*

Somewhere in the maelstrom of a million trillion lives and his own confusion, Kermon found his path. What if he could be loyal to the Forest and to the Citadel? So he could look everybody in the eyes again, even himself? Newly-baked bread wasn't a distraction. It was the answer. Daily bread, the common element in human lives, in whatever form the sustenance took.

His research would focus on food, the variety in the walls, how it smelled, tasted and looked, how different it was from citadel purified water and sustenance. And why. There must be some way of linking that to a new Maturity Test. Something that connected with a taste of honey, with the children he'd been teaching and the reason he was teaching them. He wasn't sure how it would all come together but he knew that it would. And he had a starting point.

He followed a lady with a basket on her arm into the bakery, where a man was kneading and stretching a lump of dough, kneading and stretching it thinner and thinner into a long sausage shape. Hands dipped in flour and lightly twisted the dough. Hands scored the circle of dough with a knife, brushed it with oil, placed it on a tray and started the whole process again. The power of human hands.

Maybe Kermon should research hands instead?

Food. Focus, insisted his new inner taskmaster, as a blast of heat filled the bakery and trays of oiled dough circles went into the oven.

Oil, Kermon demanded and found himself watching as the golden liquid was extracted from sunflower seeds. Sternly he forbade himself to trace the seeds back to their origin, fields golden with flowers that tracked the sun. But he noted the idea: food origin. And he moved on to his next quest. *Fruit.*

He saw apples growing on trees, picked and eaten fresh, cooked for pies, mashed to make cider, sold in the greengrocer's. He indulged himself by following the shopkeeper home, sampling his thoughts gently. After working all day with fresh fruit and vegetables, the man was joyful at day's end, at the prospect of a home-cooked meal. *Food again!*

After sitting invisible at the table with the greengrocer's family, savouring creamy sauces and crispy fries through their mouths, scenting strawberries so bursting-sweet they needed no accompaniment, Kermon was replete with the taste of home. He wanted to be that man and to sit quietly beside his wife as she talked about her day but a voice in his head said, 'Kermon!' and he knew he must go back to the Citadel and write down all that he'd learned.

He needed a moment to distance himself from this scene of domestic happiness, so he walked out of the greengrocer's house onto a street thronged with people, crazy and colourful. He was too wrapped up in his own thoughts to notice that one of these people stopped dead and stared at him, then slipped back into the anonymous crowd.

The impossible variety of minds and feelings let Kermon reconstruct his mental barriers. It hurt to cut off the warm sense of belonging he'd felt in that little house, among only four people. Could one family be a community? He thought of his friends – were they still his friends? – in the Forest. His lack of friends in Citadel.

He started writing up his research in his mind. He knew now what was important. *The children should know where food comes from, what it is.* Perhaps he should change that to past tense? So the presentation would read as a plan for a trip into the walls, into the past, not jump too quickly into a comparison with the present. Or not jump at all, perhaps let the Maturity Candidates make their own comparisons, come to their own conclusions.

He controlled his growing excitement, readied himself to reach out for his anchor. He shut his eyes, saw clearly the hand that would draw him to the place he called home. He felt no joyful anticipation but there was relief that he could do this. He took a step, then another, steady, confident, although there was a strange sense that something was holding him back.

He opened his eyes but it was not the dark alcove at the base of the Mages' Tower that met his horrified gaze. Nor was it Verity. Instead, her father's ghost gave a mocking grin, dropping his hold on Kermon's cloak. Magecraft. Kermon's return was blocked by magecraft.

'Apprentice Smith Kermon. I knew somebody would come but who would have thought you'd be the one. Snivelling snot-faced friend of the Freak that you are, you'll have to do.'

For a ghost, Rinduran sounded horribly real and his blinded eye still had Mielitta's bee-sting protruding in its milky soup, exactly as Kermon remembered it.

Behind Rinduran, hordes of past people went about their business, impervious to the drama being enacted on their street.

As if he could read Kermon's thoughts, Rinduran said, 'Don't worry – I'm still dead in your world. But not in this one. So you and I need to do a little deal. I need a go-between, willing or not.'

Kermon touched his arrowhead. *Mielitta!* his mind screamed. *Verity! Help me!* But there was no response from either the Queen of the Warrior Bees nor from his anchor. Why would there be? One was busy in her beloved Forest and the other? If it came to a choice between Kermon and her beloved father, Kermon's life was worth as little to Verity as he'd believed a few days earlier. He was on his own. As always.

CHAPTER SEVENTEEN

Drianne led the way. Barely snapping a twig as they passed, Mielitta and Jannlou followed, the connection between them like the tilt of treetops towards each other in the canopy overhead, a force of nature. In contrast to the hunters' woodcraft, Drianne's noisy insouciance set off a rainbow of wings and trill of alarm.

Each belonged to the Forest differently. The young mage was fearless, convinced that her powers rendered her invincible, whatever warnings about exhaustion Jannlou and Kermon gave her. Mielitta had heard the warnings but she knew nothing of magecraft. She could feel the bees' affection for her 'flower' and the presents Drianne brought back each day from foraging showed her bond with the creatures in the Forest. Squirrels shared nuts, birds offered berries and deer showed her edible leaves. An eagle had even dropped a dead rabbit at her feet and a fox shared its plunder, a pigeon apiece. Snakes wound around her naked feet, hissed and passed on. She was never bitten by mosquitoes or ants, nor troubled by the plants that brought Mielitta out in a rash.

Following in Drianne's footsteps, Mielitta felt inferior, an impostor. Truly, the mage was the Queen of the Forest and she merely the mother of bees.

Queen Mother of bees, reproved the voices in her head. *And not merely. We are going to the beekeeper's. And she is proud of her title. She doesn't say* merely *about her bees.*

Doubly inferior then. Doubly an impostor. Mielitta felt an arm snake gently round her waist, Jannlou stepping too close deliberately, holding her just long enough to kiss the back of her neck. Released so quickly she wondered if she'd imagined the contact, she felt the swish of her plait swinging back over her tingling flesh. *Small hairs that have collected pollen. Cuddle Bee.*

Her bees were not impressed. *Not Cuddle Bear,* they pointed out.

Drianne paused, listened. Sure enough, chickens were clucking and soon emerged from between the trees, ducking their heads to peck at the path Drianne was following. Little bantams darted about with puffed-out chests and large red matrons rolled from one leg to the other. The hens voiced their impatience with the humans. They added pecks of encouragement to their squawks at Mielitta and Jannlou.

'Ouch!' *Chivvied by chickens* thought Mielitta as a tiny white nipped the back of her ankle. She was sorely tempted to bag one for soup but she didn't think that would endear her to the beekeeper. *Not without asking first,* she silently warned the nearest feathered herder.

Here! Drianne declared triumphantly and Mielitta automatically voiced the thought for Jannlou. Not that anything could be seen. Just a continuation of the path through more trees. And then Drianne vanished, as did several chickens.

Mielitta had no option but to keep walking along the path until visibility wavered and, suddenly, she wasn't walking along the path any longer. Or rather the path was now part of a farmyard, where chickens fought over corn feed. All around the homestead, as far as the eye could see, were miles of pasture, with occasional copses but no Forest. Distant four-legged specks could be cows, horses or both.

Drianne was hanging on the arm of someone who could only be the beekeeper, bringing her towards Mielitta.

'Like the rainbow gate!' exclaimed Jannlou as he suddenly appeared at Mielitta's side.

'Must be the same kind of magecraft barrier,' she agreed absent-mindedly. All her attention was on the beekeeper, who was old and small, birdlike with her beady black eyes and fragile body. Her face was as tawny-skinned as Mielitta's but wrinkled like a dried golden plum. Her neck lay in loose folds and more wrinkles ran down her neck and throat, deep as storm channels in mud. The hand she held out to Mielitta in welcome was bent into an arthritic claw and the only possible reaction was to hold it gently, then let go. It was difficult to harbour resentment against somebody more ancient than Mielitta had ever imagined it was possible to be.

The beekeeper's voice was quiet but stronger than Mielitta expected, with a hint of power underlying the words. 'All boundaries look different from the other side, don't you think?'

'It is a boundary then,' Mielitta replied, wary.

'Oh yes, my dear. I can't be doing with tigers, wolves, foxes and bears among the livestock. They'd scare the horses and eat the chickens. And you already know what the bees think, don't you. They are safe here. We live in the Forest but we are not of it. The Forest creatures have their habitat and we have ours. I think Drianne told you? All who live here on the farm are safe.'

'Like in the Citadel.' Mielitta kept her voice expressionless but her anger must have shown.

The beekeeper's serene smile reminded Mielitta of somebody but she couldn't quite place the resemblance. 'Now I understand why you don't trust me. No, indeed, not like the Citadel at all. My daughter and I created the boundary and this haven.' Her face wrinkled more. 'Her magecraft was more powerful than mine. And she loved the Forest as I do. Come inside and we can talk at length. But first you want to check on your bees. I must speak to your companion.' She held out her hand to Jannlou, who raised it respectfully to his lips, showing no signs of a growl or other ursine surliness.

Mages who loved the Forest? wondered Mielitta. *Mother and daughter?* How was this possible when female mages had been banned from marriage and of course banned from motherhood? This was one of the very changes that Mielitta had insisted upon in the aftermath of the Battle of the Forest. And the beekeeper had used the past tense. What had happened to her daughter?

Bees reminded the voices. Mielitta's mind saw the dance of directions leading her home to the beehive, which she had last seen hanging from a tree in the clearing. She rushed across the yard and into a meadow, at the far side of which were twenty beehives.

Home hive identified the bees but Mielitta didn't need to be told. The familiar scent of queen, home hive and happiness calmed her instantly. They didn't need her but she asked anyway.

'Cuddle Bee? Young Queen? Is everything all right?' Predictably the response was in chorus.

We moved. Did you stay out in the dark and get lost? Here are our new directions so you can come home if you go foraging.

Mielitta saw the new mind map danced into her mind, replacing the route to the tree in the Forest clearing. Although she could see all the other hives, they were irrelevant and smelled wrong. The mind map took her straight to home hive, where the smell was right.

Relieved, she returned to the yard, where the beekeeper was telling Jannlou about bees. He was either very polite or genuinely interested.

'Why did you move them to the Forest in the first place?'

'To produce honey with a different flavour than that of the meadow flowers where they are now. You can taste them both.' Her smile included Drianne and Mielitta, whose defences were weakening. To be safe, if only for one night, would ease her burden, just for a little while.

'Come into the house and meet Arven,' the beekeeper invited. 'He's been waiting to meet you for years.'

Drianne skipped after the beekeeper, scooping up a long-haired ginger cat on the way and settling the purring mass around her neck, where it seemed quite contented. She disappeared through the doorway and Mielitta hesitated on the threshold. Another boundary? Was this as perfect as it seemed? Hadn't she warned Drianne that all her dreams coming true here meant there was something wrong, some glamour?

If that were the case, she would call on her bees, all of them.

We're here they told her, in a long buzz like yawning. *But you don't need us.*

For all his politeness, a bear *had* come onto the farm. Her bear. Conscious of that hidden weapon, Mielitta didn't hesitate any longer. She walked through the door straight into a family room where a teenager sat in an armchair, knitting. He looked up without breaking his rhythm, the clickety-clack of needles sounding like the rain, which had just started pattering on the window.

'My grandson Arven,' declared the beekeeper with pride.

Grandson? Two generations of illegitimate relationships and offspring? How could this be?

'I'm Mielitta,' she said.

The knitting needles stopped and Arven stared at her. His grandmother's black eyes and tawny skin, a trace of a face she should know, but younger this time instead of older.

Arven started knitting again, faster. 'I know,' he said. 'I told Granny you would come. The flower, the bear and the bee.'

The rain fell harder, pelting loud against the glass. Drianne sat down on a marigold-patterned sofa and the cat shifted position slightly, settled back against the soft padding, its paws dangling either side of her neck.

The bear? she queried.

CHAPTER EIGHTEEN

'My story has been waiting for you,' began the beekeeper. 'Won't you sit down?'

Mielitta and Jannlou did not look at each other as they dropped onto a huge sofa, also upholstered in bright flowers. The whole room looked as if designed by a giant bee.

Drianne stared at Jannlou, her question unanswered, while the rain settled to a steady drumming in the background, punctuated by Arven's needles. He sat in a straight-backed armless chair, his hands repeating an effortless routine, pulling blue yarn from the wicker basket at his feet, working a row, turning the needles and knitting again. Clickety-click clickety-clack and elbows flapping like a hen's wings. In between his strange pronouncements, he seemed relaxed, only half-listening to his grandmother but watching them all closely, without any interruption to his knitting.

Mielitta didn't like being observed in this way and stared back at Arven.

Like two cats she thought as his gaze moved on to Jannlou. But she didn't feel as if she'd won. She felt as if she'd been caught out in some petty misdemeanour by somebody older, wiser, superior.

Stop feeling so inferior, she told herself and concentrated on the beekeeper's words.

'You're wondering how old I am? And how anybody can be so old? That's because you've never seen an old person. Because they're all suppressed in the Citadel.'

Mielitta's guts twisted. She'd seen how traitors were 'suppressed', reduced to ashes by magecraft.

The beekeeper showed no such revulsion as she explained, 'Old people have no place in Perfect society. We are a drain on resources and make little or no contribution. We have been replaced by the next generation.' She smiled fondly at Arven but that didn't take the sting out of her words. 'Like misfits in the Maturity Test, we are suppressed.'

'That's murder!' Jannlou's face showed the same incredulity as Drianne's. Mielitta envied their innocence. The moment the beekeeper spoke the words, she knew they were true. She'd seen the ashes in the Maturity Barn, remains of those candidates who failed the test and were suppressed by magecraft. Misfits like her. And like Jannlou; he'd been protected by his father and by Bastien, without either of them realising what kind of man they were protecting.

'And that surprises you? I told you this place is not like the Citadel and we have reason to hate Perfection.'

How could people be suppressed without the citizens noticing? Mielitta thought of the ashes in the Maturity Barn, the vagueness of successful candidates regarding how many had entered the Barn and how many had come out. 'But surely the grandparents would be missed? By their children, by their neighbours? There would be outrage.' She thought of her table companions at dinner in the Great Hall, rendered good citizens by their forging. 'Or at least complaints,' she amended sadly.

The beekeeper nodded. 'It is Perfect that old people die, so nobody minds too much. Maybe a little grief sometimes. And each year, the suppression age is reduced. When I was a girl, we saw people suppressed in their sixties. Now the death age is fifty.

Apart from the Council members, and even they go into the walls at sixty.'

Gone into the walls. Mielitta thought of Kermon with a pang of guilt. She should have contacted him, checked he was all right. She knew he was afraid of this mission into the walls. At least she had the chance now to find out information that might help him. She would contact him tonight.

'What does it mean 'going into the walls'? I know we say that about somebody who's died. 'May the walls take them.' But what does it mean?'

The answer was disappointing. 'Only those who've gone can tell you that, my dear. I hope that they will live on in the walls in some fashion. That the lives they lived will be recorded among all those that have gone before. But I don't know. And I've never visited the walls nor heard of any mage seeing the recently departed.' For the first time there was bitterness in her voice. 'Not that anybody would have told an ordinary citizen like me.'

Ask her. Drianne shifted to the edge of her seat and leant forward, causing much annoyance to her living scarf, which tumbled forward onto the carpet. The red cat recovered its balance and stalked off, pretending that the indignity had never happened. *Ask her how she could be a mage and have a child. Why she says she was an ordinary citizen. And I want you to tell me about the bear.* Drianne's cheeks were pink and her magecraft was leaking, a fine rainbow-coloured ribbon dancing in the long blonde hair.

Oh, Stones. She'd have to explain about the bear, afterwards, whatever Jannlou's reservations. For now, she just nodded. How to put this tactfully? 'Can I ask…' she began.

'That is the purpose of this meeting,' Arven said in his strange manner. The rain paused. He'd come to the end of a ball of wool so he reached down, pulled another one out of the basket and married the two ends together. Then needles clacked and rain pattered once more, drawing together those sheltering in the cosy room. 'You will find no secrets here except those you brought in with you. And it is time now to unburden yourself of those.'

Mielitta didn't want to think about the secrets she'd brought into the room with her so she rushed ahead with Drianne's question for the beekeeper. 'But you were a mage, not an ordinary citizen? And powerful, judging by your work here. How was it possible that you had a baby? And how are you here, not...' She couldn't bring herself to use the term 'suppressed' while facing a survivor.

A table lamp glowed golden in the gathering gloom, smoothing out the beekeeper's face, already softened and slack with age. In contrast, as he watched his grandmother, Arven was all edges, sharp-cut cheekbones and jaw, his Adam's apple prominent in the profile of his throat. The family face, changed across gender and generations. Again, Mielitta was reminded of somebody.

'I was in love with a boy at school so I hid my magecraft,' the beekeeper said and her face glowed with the memory. 'So I could marry him and have children. It wasn't such a sacrifice, you know. Many women hide their powers.'

Mielitta remembered her own Maturity Test, the moment she'd almost succumbed to forging, the joy of dancing with an imagined Jannlou and of more than dancing. The loss of her bees.

Never she told them. *I would never give you up. Not for any man.* She felt the warmth of the hive mind, the contented buzz of their combined lives, like a cat's purr.

'I only had one child but she was a joy to me. She had magecraft and she made a different choice. She came into her powers and she trained daily. She was the most disciplined mage in the Citadel, in mind and body – except for one failing. She too fell in love and he with her. You know it is forbidden but it happens sometimes, in secret.'

'*Was* forbidden,' said Mielitta, hoping that Bastien's blood oath would hold him to the terms she'd dictated.

The beekeeper nodded approval. 'For them, in secret meant in the Forest. They used the water gate to be together in the Forest and they created this place, the farm. My husband died of allergy and I was nearing sixty, the age of suppression then, so my daughter brought me here and her lover lied for me, said he'd fulfilled the law. Nobody was interested enough to investigate further.

'Then the miracle happened. Or the disaster, depending on your point of view. My daughter became pregnant and that would never have been tolerated in Perfection. She and the baby would have been suppressed.'

Arven's knitting filled his lap and he gave no sign that this was his story as the needles parted and joined in their implacable rhythm. He must have heard it as many times as Mielitta had heard of her own birth from the walls.

'So she came here to give birth to Arven and I have raised him since then, I don't know how many Citadel years ago. Time is not the same in the Forest as in the Citadel although I'm not sure how it ebbs and flows. My daughter and Arven's father came here when they could but they had to be careful, for Arven's sake, so they didn't come together. One day, she went missing, and then the news in the Citadel was that she'd died. So we guessed she'd been caught leaving the Citadel and killed. All we knew for sure was that she was dead or she'd have come here.'

'And Arven's father?' asked Mielitta.

'I'm an orphan,' stated Arven.

'We're all orphans,' snapped Mielitta, then felt ashamed again. He hadn't been seeking sympathy. That was *her* weakness.

No I'm not, Drianne objected. *My parents still live in the Citadel.*

Oh. Mielitta flushed. 'Drianne's parents are alive.' She translated for the others' benefit. 'But how did you...' she tailed off. She could hardly ask how Drianne could be callous enough to leave her parents behind but her friend responded to the unspoken question.

They were models of Perfection, Drianne said. *They were embarrassed by my stammer, by me being different. They were ecstatic at the thought of me marrying Bastien and being a good citizen and I should think they've forgotten I ever existed now I'm not there.*

'Arven's father was a good man.' The beekeeper's voice cut across Mielitta's confusion, continuing the story. 'He came here when he could until one day he too came no more and we cried for both of them.'

The beekeeper smiled tenderly at her grandson. 'Your parents would have been very proud of you,' she told him.

'I was little when they stopped coming,' said Arven. 'I knew the moment each of them died because they gave me their power, just before it.'

Like Puggy did for me!

'Drianne experienced something like that,' Mielitta said.

'Can you knit?' asked Arven, looking down at the fabric he'd created.

'Yes,' said Mielitta, realising the rain had stopped.

'I was asking the bear.' Arven fixed Jannlou with a level stare, possible only because he was sitting in a high-backed chair and Jannlou was slumped on a low sofa.

'Warriors are not taught knitting,' Jannlou replied with the hauteur of one high-born.

'That's what I told Granny when I was a child,' answered Arven. 'And she proved they should be. Do you want to learn?' He dipped into the basket and produced two knitting needles and a ball of wool. 'It seems to me your close-knit ties are unravelling and you could use the skill to re-make them. Besides, it's good discipline for a mage.'

'Then I'll pass,' said Jannlou in his deep voice that now held a hint of growl. 'I'm no mage.'

Arven poked the needles through the ball of wool and returned them to the basket. 'No, you're not, are you.' He spoke calmly but the unspoken challenge turned into a spoken one. 'I think it's time you told Drianne about your second nature. And although Granny loves the Forest, she loves her bees more. I saw you looking. A hundred beehives. Mouth-watering, irresistible.'

Jannlou stood, towering over the youth in the chair. 'If I

couldn't control myself, you would be the first to know, not a beehive.'

Unimpressed, Arven said, 'You'd be surprised what can be done with knitting needles, if you take my point.' He resumed his work, his jutting elbows moving fast as pistons. The rain started again, hammering down.

Drianne too was on her feet, eyes blazing. *When is somebody going to tell Drianne what this is all about? What about a bear? What does it mean, Jannlou's second nature?*

'I wanted to tell you but Jannlou finds it difficult to talk about,' Mielitta began, earning glares from both friends. 'The same way I... with the bees... a bear is his second nature.'

A bear. That bear. The one that... And you didn't tell me! Neither of you told me! Drianne's cheeks flared with colour as hectic as the rainbow-coloured ribbon of magecraft seeping out around her hair.

'Yes, that bear,' said Mielitta and felt a growl building in the room, unstoppable.

'It's not your story to tell,' roared Jannlou. 'Why don't you tell Drianne about us being together? Why do you find *that* so difficult to talk about?'

Incandescent with rage, Drianne screamed in Mielitta's mind, just one word, *'Noooooooooo!'*

And that's when it happened. What Kermon and Jannlou had warned her would happen, again and again. Drianne lost control of her magecraft and the cat fled as furniture smashed walls and windows in blinding shafts of random power.

CHAPTER NINETEEN

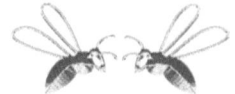

The rain on the window turned to hailstones, battering the window, barely heard against the storm unleashed inside. Drianne whirled in a silent scream, loosing rainbow flashes of power that sent books tumbling, a carpet flying, tables banging into each other. Two bone china teacups smashed against the wall, in a jagged hail of floral fragments.

Instinctively, Mielitta froze and, for the moment, remained unhurt, despite the chaos all around her, as if Drianne's magecraft recognised her friends, even in blind rage. Instead of releasing the tension, the wild magic fed on itself, grew ever more destructive. Only in the Battle of the Forest had Mielitta faced such raw power.

Should she call her bees? She felt them cowering inside her, not just because of Drianne's storm but because the growl filling the room was now shaking the very foundations of the farmhouse.

Bear, whispered the bees.

Jannlou's face contorted with his struggle. As burning as his touch in passion, she could feel his hurt, an unspoken accusation that seared her.

Unfair! she thought. *I'm not ashamed of you. I don't wish we hadn't ... aren't ... but I have to consider all three of us. Kermon too. I was right not to say.*

The bees' silence was heavy. They didn't need to point out the consequences raging round the room. Nobody else heard her thoughts. Drianne was lost, her own magecraft consuming her.

Jannlou was losing his own fight for control, storm-blue eyes hardening into round brown stones. He grew taller, bulkier, a hint of teeth and claw visible, then sheathed again.

'You must leave,' Arven told him. Half the size of the creature Jannlou was becoming, the youth was standing now, holding his knitting calmly as if the scene was exactly what he'd expected. 'Go quickly. Stay on the path until you are in the Forest and you will be safe. Keep your mind and your body away from the beehives.'

Did Mielitta imagine a flash of bloody hunger in those brutal eyes? Was it just the reflection of a shaft of power from Drianne, who was now so red-faced she would surely burst into flames any minute?

The bees shivered, shrank, wanted to fly home. *Warn home hive the bear is coming.*

'No,' said Mielitta aloud. 'He would never do that!'

The bear gave her an anguished look and then the door swung open, blown by magecraft indoors and out, ripped off its hinges. Jannlou rushed out into the hail, roaring, and disappeared.

Torn between friends, Mielitta moved to follow him but Arven was quicker. He jabbed her in the earlobe with a knitting needle, sharp and piercing as an arrowhead but not barbed, the stones be thanked. She rubbed her ear instinctively then reached for Steelwing to retaliate, drawing her hand across her jerkin, smearing it with fresh blood. The bastard must have struck deep!

Before Mielitta could stab him with the arrowhead, all Drianne's power focused on Arven in an outraged howl. He still stood calm as ever. Just before the rainbow shafts hit his chest, he held up the needles, horizontal, with the knitted yarn dangling below like a curtain – or like a shield. The power blasted into the wool, changed all the colours to rainbow and stilled. In the silence that followed, Drianne fainted.

'I'm sorry,' Arven said. 'It was the only way I could think of to stop her.'

The beekeeper tutted as she stooped over Drianne, gently put a cushion under her head, stroked the girl's hair.

'Never mind all that now. You can talk later. I need Arven's help to bring this girl back from the stones know where she's gone after losing all that spirit.'

Arven had already lost interest, was working a cast-off row to complete whatever it was he was knitting.

Realising that her wound was more bloody than painful, Mielitta rushed to Drianne's side, touched her forehead and flinched from the heat.

As suddenly as the storm of magecraft had begun, Drianne's skin turned from red to snow-white then to ice-blue and the delicate pulse in her fragile throat stopped.

Arven jumped up, pushed Mielitta out of the way and draped the rainbow knit over the girl's upper body. First the red, then yellow, then each rainbow colour in turn drained from the fabric till it was beige as a field mushroom. Drianne's skin responded to each colour, gradually regaining its usual creamy porcelain tone.

Please, please, prayed Mielitta. *Give me a chance to make it up to her, to both of them.* She held her breath, watching for some sign of life in that still body. Nothing.

Arven too had been holding his breath and the sound of his sigh made Mielitta jump.

'It's all right,' he said. 'Look.' He held a downy white feather, no doubt a chicken's, under Drianne's nose.

The tiny movement in the white fluff was the miracle on which Mielitta had hung her heart. Sure enough, the barely perceptible pulse was beating again. The boundary between life and death, so easy to cross, no doubt quite different viewed from opposite sides. Mielitta shivered and took Drianne's hand in hers.

'I'll make some peppermint tea,' said the beekeeper, tutting. 'We could all do with a cup of something calming, if I have anything left we can drink from.' Debris littered the room: pieces of china and fragments of broken furniture.

Drianne's eyes opened, blinked, clouded, blinked again.

'I'm sorry,' said Mielitta. 'I thought I was doing the right thing but I was a coward.'

Go after him, Drianne said. *I'll be all right now. He needs you more than I do.* But her words were at odds with the bitterness in her eyes and Mielitta hesitated. She did not want to choose between them.

When Drianne sat up, the knitted fabric fell off and she picked it up, looked at it, puzzled.

Arven said, 'You may keep it.' He wrapped it around her shoulders and the material moulded itself to her body, joined back to front at the sides and formed a simple woolly slip-over. Or perhaps not so simple. The knitted garment was changing colour, taking on the pale pink of Drianne's lips, of a spring flower.

Fascinated, Drianne watched her new clothing express itself.

'To help you control your magecraft,' explained Arven. 'So you can tell when you are in harmony with your powers and when you are in danger – or causing danger. The colours will tell you.'

The beekeeper came back into the room with a tray. 'Peppermint tea and honey biscuits,' she said. 'And you, my girl, need proper magecraft lessons, not just a pretty knitted top!'

Go, Drianne repeated to Mielitta.

'If he learns to control himself, he can visit, but not overnight,' declared Arven. 'I would not put him or us through that ordeal. By night the bear is king of the Forest, which is where he needs to be. If he doesn't learn control, we can do nothing for him. Drianne is like us. We can teach her what she needs.' He waved his knitting needles, already showing a new work in progress as he nodded at Drianne. 'Without Granny's teaching, I would have been the same.'

Mielitta didn't need to be told to go a third time. She mouthed an apology about not staying for peppermint tea, about everything, then grabbed a honey biscuit to eat on the way and made her escape. She had to track a bear, survive his wounded rage and talk to the man within the bear about controlling himself.

CHAPTER TWENTY

Kermon's first instinct was to find Verity. She glowed in his mind, a beacon to draw him home and he felt an almost fatherly tenderness towards her as he stood on the Citadel-side of the wall, recovering his breath. He felt a little unsteady but he had done it. He'd visited the walls, watched artisans at work, the ironmonger, the baker, the farmers. Most important of all, he had an idea for the new Adult Test and he had all his notes to write up and present to the Council.

No, he wouldn't go to Verity yet. He would write up his notes, develop his idea for the Test until it was Perfect before he made it public. Something troubled him about that word 'Perfect', as if its flavour had changed on his tongue.

Perfection has no flavours, just purity.

Yes, of course. How strange that he might have thought otherwise.

You should see Verity.

There was something irritating about this need to see Verity so he resisted. He would see her but not yet. And he would make sure that girls were properly considered within the Test, in appropriate roles as supporters and helpmeets. Very much the role that Verity was playing for him. He felt a stab of pain, maybe an adjustment after coming back from the walls. And of course Verity was far above him. He should not presume to think of her in such a way.

When he'd regained his composure fully, Kermon realised he felt hungry. He had no idea how long he'd been in the walls, without sustenance, and now he'd thought of food, he was starving. The greylight suggested it was daytime but whether a meal was due or not, he couldn't tell and didn't want to wait to find out. There would no doubt be something to eat in the kitchens and even though the Cook and Stewards preferred to keep their domain out of bounds to mages and citizens, he was sure they'd make an exception for him, especially when they knew what he planned for them.

You could call on Verity as you pass the mages' quarters.

Where had this sudden obsession with seeing Verity come from? He remembered their pact to help him travel the walls, the connection of her hand on his – pain ripped through his guts again.

Don't think of her like that.

With the discipline of his mage training, Kermon focused on his task in the kitchens, which should also solve the misbehaviour of his empty stomach. How long *had* he been in the walls? And did time behave the same way there? Mielitta had said time was different in the Forest.

Mielitta. Another name that tasted different since he had been into the walls. Colder.

He should contact her. *Yes, contact her.* He'd tried, he remembered and she hadn't replied.

No doubt she's too busy with that traitor, Magaram's son, just like his father.

Kermon stopped short in the passageway, touched the stone wall to steady himself, traced grit and crevice. Why had he thought of Jannlou as a traitor, or as Magaram's son? Whatever he felt about Jannlou's connection with Mielitta, there was no question of Jannlou's loyalty to her, to their cause, to the Forest. And

Kermon had never known Magaram except as a distant figure at High Table in the Great Hall. Why should he suddenly feel such hatred towards both of them?

How strange. As if he didn't know his own mind. He groped for an explanation: stress, illness or– no, it wasn't possible.

Another spasm of pain struck him and his mind went blank. What had he been thinking about? Oh yes. Mielitta.

He must contact Mielitta. But then he would have to tell her he'd found nothing in the walls about her origins. She would guess that he hadn't tried. And he should tell her about his forthcoming marriage. It was all so complicated. The Forest seemed like a place he'd imagined and his friends there ever so distant. It wasn't as if he had anything to tell them, really. There was no change in the Citadel. And they could contact him if they wanted to…

He reached the door to the kitchen and pushed it open, expecting a scurry of servants and perhaps the noises of cooking, if not smells and steam. This was Perfection after all, where sustenance and drink were pure and healthy. But the room was deserted. He'd obviously missed mealtime preparation and clearing up. He had no idea how much of kitchen work was magecraft and how much was human toil. As with other labour in the Citadel, the balance had been decided in the past, using the wisdom of the walls, and each specialist Mage or Craftsperson maintained Perfection on his domain.

There was nothing to stop Kermon exploring and, he hoped, finding something to eat in the process. Drink was easy. There were bottles with contents in different shades of brown, white and red, lined up on shelves. He read the labels: tea, red wine, coffee, ginger beer. Most were clear and without labels. Citadel purified water, no doubt.

Trays of mugs, cups, glasses and goblets stood on more shelves. Kermon picked up a cup and chose a bottle labelled 'tea'. He unscrewed the cap and poured the brown contents into the cup, where they immediately frothed into a steaming liquid. He took a sip, swirled it around his mouth to cool it enough to drink and he swallowed.

He imagined the taste and scent of tea. Thanks to his visit into the walls, he'd experienced tea through the minds of those drinking it and he could revisit a crunch of broken leaves, dark bitterness with citric zing, hazelnuts. Mielitta said there was no taste to any food or drink in the Citadel and that only in the Forest did water have flavour but she was wrong.

He knew now why the mages in the Council swirled their 'red wine' with pleasure. They brought to the Citadel drink all the flavours they'd experienced when they visited the walls. Or perhaps even those flavours they'd been told about. What if imagination could create experience? After all, Mielitta said that all the books she'd read stayed in her mind and the words came to her to fit the experiences, which came afterwards.

Did it work for sustenance? Kermon opened cupboards until he found a store of sustenance, in concentrated cubes, dense as stone. The majority were yellowish and without labels but there were racks of 'meat and fish' (brown or white), 'vegetables' (green, orange, red or brown) and 'puddings' (all hues except blue or black).

How did it become edible? The 'tea' had transformed when poured so perhaps he needed to put a cube of sustenance on a plate? These were easily located, on more shelves, so he pulled one down and placed a cube of sustenance on it. Sure enough, on contact, it expanded and changed to the yellow sustenance that served as daily bread. He shut his eyes and sure enough, his imagination brought back the smell of the bakery in the walls and of freshly baked bread. He tasted buttery crumbs, a hint of cinnamon and the warmth of home.

He opened his eyes. The remaining sustenance was as unappetising as ever.

He closed his eyes and tasted. There it was again. The whole wonderful experience of fresh bread. What did this mean? And could every citizen use his imagination in this way? Or only mages? Or just soul-readers? How did this relate to deep thinking and the new Maturity Test?

Now that his stomach was no longer rumbling, he suddenly felt exhaustion sweep over him. He had to get back to his chamber and sleep before any further consideration was possible. Stumbling, he forced one foot in front of the other in the longest walk of his life, to regain his bedroom. Once there, he fell onto the bed fully dressed.

Boots, he told himself. *Mustn't get the bed dirty.* He hauled himself to a sitting position and as he bent down to untie his laces, he noticed his old boots, standing like prisoners against the opposite wall. Filthy with moss and damp, the cracked leather smelled of failure. His failure. As if Forest seeds could grow here in this room! Tomorrow was a new day, a Perfect day and he would start a fresh life by throwing away those old boots. Then nobody would know he'd failed.

He was asleep as soon as his head hit the pillow. His dreams were troubled by a one-eyed ghost and bee stings but such flights of the imagination were only natural after an intense visit to the walls. Or so he told himself the next day, puzzling over what was real and what was not, as he crossed the boundary from sleep to wakefulness.

Mielitta could have told him that boundaries look different from both sides but he had no intention of contacting her any time soon. And he'd figure out how to get rid of those damned boots without drawing unwanted attention on himself.

CHAPTER TWENTY-ONE

Kermon rushed down the slippery cobblestones – real cobbles not cobblette – to the water gate underneath the Citadel, clutching his filthy old boots to his chest. He just had time to get rid of them before the Council Meeting and he wanted to make his presentation to the mages without this pointless act of treachery on his mind. The mossy mould inside the boots was turning to slime and he did not want to be questioned by Perfect citizens about a pair of old boots full of mud. Why he'd thought the seeds in his pocket were a gift from the Forest, a sign, he had no idea. He wasn't that naive person any more.

No, indeed.

He slowed down, careful with his footing as there was a sheer drop beside him on the left and he could hear the stream rushing below. His head swam at the thought of tripping, falling over the edge into the race of water, drowning. Maybe that would be for the best. Maybe...

No. You have work to do, my work. Why do I have to suffer such a weakling?

A surge of inner strength jolted him upright and he steadied himself with a hand against the stone wall on his right-hand side.

If it gets too much, you can always go into the walls and stay there rather than make a mess in the Citadel's purified water. Think of Perfection for the stones' sake and not just of yourself!

Kermon found it strange that his thoughts grew harder and more self-critical as he felt himself weaken. Perhaps he'd spent too long in the walls these last few days. Or perhaps it was the lack of contact with Mielitta. He felt himself drifting, even if not yet drowning.

He walked down to the end of the pathway, where the only options were to turn around or jump across to the stone ledge below the water gate. Had he really carried Verity down here, helped her across to the ledge and out through the gate into the meadow beyond? That was when the password still worked, when the gate wavered to rainbow and the Citadel children were able to leave and discover the Forest.

The water still streamed in through the gate, purified at the boundary, but from this side nobody could know the wild beauty beyond. He felt the tug of homesickness and was then flooded with disgust. Treachery indeed, far bigger than a concealing a pair of boots. He took aim, threw one carefully to land on the sill of the water gate. Then the other.

The pair of boots, containing the dead seeds, collapsed a little more in the spray through the gate but they clung to their place on the stone, no doubt thanks to the mud seeping through them. Ordinary boots, falling apart. Nothing special.

Just on the other side of that gate, Kermon had said his final goodbye to Mielitta, promised her he would nurture the Forest in the children, in the Citadel. Easy to make promises when he was on the Forest side. From where he stood now, he could see only the silvery outline of water over muddy boots and a gate that was closed forever. Better to turn around and head back through the darkness to the known corridors of the Citadel and the Council Chamber, where he was awaited.

'Sit here,' Verity told him, indicating a chair beside her at the table.

Kermon felt a warm glow as he took in how much she'd changed. She was growing up into a slender maiden, pale but alive, thanks to him. Isolating her throughout her childhood had paid off. If she was careful, she might be able to take her proper place as a woman in the Citadel but she should drop this foolish attendance at Council. It was bad for her fragile health and she was a mere hindrance to business.

As were the other women seated at the table. It was so wrong. After all he'd done to restore Perfect standards. He was tempted to mute them during proceedings but men could do that effectively without resorting to magecraft. Powerful men had always known how to mute women in a meeting; they had honed their techniques in the schoolroom each time a girl tried to answer a question. If only females would accept how much better their lives would be if they accepted their limitations.

He'd made his point with dear Lady Puggy and there she was, back at the table again but as beautiful and brainless as he'd left her. So much more attractive that way. Kermon smiled across the table at his bride-to-be, whose expression froze an instant. Her fear of him was increasing.

Good. That will make our second wedding night more entertaining. He always felt more desire when a woman put up a fight. He felt a leap of anticipation at the prospect of rediscovering Puggy's body, a pleasure indeed.

So good to be back amongst the Ten, where he belonged. He nodded to the other male mages. His friend Hamel must be so pleased to see him after all that time he'd spent in the wall – barely recognisable! And of course sharing the body of this pathetic excuse for a Mage-Smith. How Declan would mock.

A rush of anger at how Declan had died was interrupted by the entry of the last and most important mage, bar himself of course. Bastien, grown into his inheritance, his father's son. Look at how all deferred to him, bowing and waiting until he sat before dropping onto their own chairs.

Except Verity, who had the effrontery to behave as if she were Bastien's equal. She remained seated and greeted her brother casually. What an unfortunate consequence of her isolation! She'd been raised in Perfect ways and should know better but she was no longer his little girl. He'd over-indulged her and now a lesson in humility was needed. She didn't even show the hero-worship for her brother that had been so touching. And so well-deserved.

Better to dwell on Bastien's qualities than his sister's failings. Resplendent in his Chief Mage's robe and crackling with barely suppressed power, Bastien could be relied upon to do what was needed. He just had to wriggle his way around the constraints placed on them by that freak after the Battle of the Forest. Not an occasion to dwell upon. Now was the moment for Kermon to expound on his tedious plan for a new Maturity Test, so let him get on with it.

Verity nodded to Bastien, almost as if she was giving him permission to speak first. How ridiculous.

'We welcome back Mage-Smith Kermon from his mission into the walls and my sister assures me that she is satisfied of his loyalty and his fitness for the Rinduran Award so we hope he can satisfy the Council with his report.'

What nonsense. Before you bore everyone to tears, at least pay tribute to the Chief Mage whose award you hope to win.

Kermon didn't remember planning this part of his introduction but he felt inspired to return Verity's support with a glowing eulogy for her father.

'Chief Mage Rinduran was a legend in his own time,' he began.

This was more like it.

'Peerless, honourable, dauntless, indefatigable. He upheld the values of our Perfect society against all attempts to erode our standards.' Kermon looked with distaste at the females around the table.

Distraction and so wrong.

'He defended the Citadel from attack by our greatest enemy, in this very room! Thanks to his courage and exceptional magecraft, he defeated the vile creature, single-handed against the forces of darkness. But he bore the scar, a reminder to all Perfect citizens of the sacrifice he made for the society he loved beyond himself.'

Verity and Bastien were glowing in the reflection of their father's reputation, eyes glistening. Around the table heads nodded. Even Hamel had stopped tapping the table with those irritating fingernails.

'In this very room,' Kermon built up to an emotional crescendo, 'This giant among mages also faced the treachery within, the betrayal of Perfection by a faction in the Council itself.'

He paused, look around the table for signs of guilt, continued, 'He faced up to Perfection's terrible need and drew deep on his powers to do what nobody else could. He executed the tyrant who masqueraded in the robes of a Chief Mage.'

Ah, the killing of Magaram was a sweet moment. And of his whore, the epitome of degradation, neither pure in womanhood nor pure in female magecraft. Under Perfection there should be no Shenagras. Nor Puggys.

Kermon glanced at his fiancée, whose beautiful mouth tilted in what could have been approval or could equally have been an air kiss, aimed randomly. The flash of fear had disappeared like dust on the woodette floor, leaving only Perfection.

'The enemy saw Chief Mage Rinduran and massed all its vile forces against him.'

'Vile' twice was clumsy. Practice in speech-making is needed to achieve the ends of Perfection. More adjectives would help. 'Consummate', 'proficient', 'masterful' and, of course, 'great' could have been included to improve the eulogy's impact.

Kermon dropped his voice, dripped sadness. 'Through trickery and dark arts, the enemy took Chief Mage Rinduran from the people who love him.' Verity and Bastien were crying openly now. 'But he lives on!'

Yes, he does indeed.

'He lives on in hearts and minds, in his son and daughter.'

Bastien took his little sister's hand in his own. Two sweet orphans.

Kermon completed his introduction on a triumphant note. 'He lives on in the Rinduran Award and it has been my privilege to be the first to follow humbly in the footsteps of the greatest wall-mage who ever lived—'

Now that had a nice ring to it.

'In the name of Rinduran the Great, I present to you my research and conclusions from my visits to the walls, along with a proposal for a future Maturity Test that should meet the terms of the generous pact given by the Chief Mage to those who live in exile—' A nod from Bastien. 'And also the needs of Perfection, our society, which was created from the wisdom of the walls. May we never repeat the mistakes of history!' A nod from Verity.

Kermon gripped the table as he suffered one of those stabbing pains to which he seemed prone these days. Thankfully they were always brief and his mind was clear again.

He described his experience in the walls, his deductions and his proposal. 'As in the previous system, the designated mage will visit the schoolroom, test students and indicate which of them are ready for the Adulthood Test. The males among these students will visit the walls in a guided group and the females will be their anchors, to provide security for the return journey and also to listen to the accounts from the returning Candidates.' He smiled at Verity, his anchor, who was certainly listening.

'The focus of the test will be wall research into the origins and flavours of food and drink. Each New Adult will present his findings to the Council in a brief description of one item of food or drink. This will enhance our lives through feeding our imaginations and we can choose the best students to repeat their speech in the Great Hall so that all citizens will enjoy their food more.'

Verity was frowning and Kermon hastily added, 'Each New Woman will also make a speech, from what she has been told by the Candidate whom she serves as anchor. And I am sure some of them will repeat the words of the New Men in a very accomplished way because their imaginations too will be at work.'

There was complete silence around the table and Kermon wondered whether he could sneak out without anybody noticing. Maybe he hadn't explained well enough how important imagination was in their lives. Maybe it was just a stupid idea.

Bastien was the first to speak, as was proper, and unlike Verity he hadn't heard the proposal before. 'But there's no distinction between candidates who are mages and those without power,' he said, frowning.

Verity withdrew her hand from underneath her brother's.

Then the objections rained in from around the table.

'Everyone will pass.'

'Unsuitable candidates need to be suppressed – how will we find them?'

'I suppose *you* will be the tester and the guide!' Hamel was greener than usual and scraping his nails again.

'Why would anybody want to know where food comes from? What an appalling thought! Children would stop eating!'

'Imagination is dangerous and you want us to encourage it?'

After the first flurry of objections was over and there was a pause, Puggy said, 'I like chocolate torte topped with cream and black cherries that have been marinated in Kirsch.'

All eyes turned to her and she twiddled a lock of hair, looked down bashfully.

Hamel exploded. 'That is the kind of trivial nonsense we'll have to listen to all the time if your Adulthood Test is accepted. I thought even you had more sense!'

Kermon could feel the contempt poisoning all his plans, reminding him he was an outsider. Worse than an outsider, if only they knew. *Much worse.*

Before he could reply to any of the questions, Verity stood up, her face as white as in the old days, when she was imprisoned in one room.

'I like chocolate torte too,' she said, as if flinging a gauntlet onto the table 'And if men were discussing the statistics of chocolate composition, would that be considered appropriate? Instead of discussing flavour. Which men have decided is trivial. I am tired of women's activities being considered trivial – unless they are legitimised by men and their numbers. Is knitting trivial? I can assure you that the intricate skill involved is every bit as hard to learn as the use of magecraft.'

The mages looked at her when she said 'legitimise' as if their sustenance had jumped up onto the table and begun to dance a jig.

'And another thing,' blazed Verity. '*Why* should non-mages be second-class citizens? I was declared equal to my brother as leader of this Council and I take that responsibility very seriously. As I take my nature as a woman. *My* Perfect nature.' She moved her hand away from Bastien's soothing attempt to capture it.

'How can we avoid the mistakes of history if we don't know what they were? Or why Perfection is the way it is now? And seeing where food came from seems to me to be the Perfect way for all Maturity candidates to become Adults. I don't see why any children have to be suppressed at all if they are educated in Perfection's ways. And I don't see why non-mages should be considered inferior.'

She was warming to her theme and two hectic spots of colour appeared in her cheeks. 'In fact, I think magecraft should be banned in the Council Chamber so that non-mages *are* equal, not treated as disabled.'

The ripple of shock ran around the room and Verity spoke over it. 'I support the proposal from Mage-Smith Kermon and I suggest we put it to the vote, with amendments to be considered after there is broad acceptance.'

She ignored her brother, reached out and took Kermon's hand in her own. He felt the electricity shoot down to his core. Did she really have no magecraft? Suddenly his head cleared of the muggy confusion he'd been suffering.

It was as if some demon had been perverting his thoughts. Maybe his spirit was still sullied from cleaning Declan's blood off Steelwing. Had he really felt such violent desire for Puggy? He flushed, seeing the damaged woman opposite with only pity. Hamel's contempt for him mattered little as there was only loathing between them. How could he have taken the mage for an old friend? Paternal pride in Verity and Bastien gave way to something very different, almost loyalty.

Verity removed her hand but the clarity remained. Kermon knew who he was.

'Let's vote,' said Bastien.

CHAPTER TWENTY-TWO

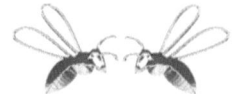

Kermon gazed into the heart of fire, taking longer than usual to focus on his work. He'd had enough of Citadel politics. Let the other mages bicker over their amendments to his proposals. They'd voted for his Adulthood Test in principle and now they could argue themselves to death over the detail, for all he cared. He'd excused himself – work to do – and left the Council Meeting after the vote.

If he'd had to put up with the tinny silliness of the female councillors any longer, he'd have hurled magecraft round the table. At all the females bar Verity of course. He felt a rush of paternal pride at her intelligence, sharp as a dagger-point. She just needed a reminder of her proper place. To see Bastien ruling with his sister's support almost made him feel he could leave them to it. Almost.

What a wonderful society the Citadel would be if all but the most intelligent and talented were suppressed, keeping only a few women of good bloodlines as helpmeets and bedfellows. Perfection indeed.

In a flicker of yellow, the steel vanished into the hungry black mouth. Kermon struggled to concentrate, wary of the forge itself, struggling against the pains and fog that affected his mind. Would

Declan suddenly appear again? If he did, what would Kermon ask?

He was worth a hundred weaklings like you. If the future depends on your Maturity Test, we've only more weaklings to look forward to until the Citadel pisses itself to death, too scared to breathe. His own thoughts had become his worst enemy, dragging him ever further down.

No face appeared in the flames and he didn't know whether he was glad or sorry that the forge belonged to him alone now. Forge Master had a hollow ring, however much his young assistants might be impressed.

'Am I disturbing you?' a light voice disturbed his thoughts and, with a sigh, he retrieved the burning rod from the flames, placed it on the anvil.

Show some respect, that insistent, critical inner voice told him. He wiped his hands on his apron, bowed in greeting. 'Lady Verity. What brings you here?'

'I thought you would want to know that the Courtship Dance will go ahead this Saturday as planned. The citizens would be disappointed at any postponement. There will have to be another one after the Test but nobody will mind a second opportunity for dancing and courtship.'

Kermon hadn't even thought about the tradition of a Courtship Dance coming after a Test, so the New Adults could pair up, then marry.

Ah, marry. Kermon's wedding was planned for the day after the Courtship Dance, so he should show pleasure that all would proceed as planned.

'That's Perfect,' he said.

Verity gave him a sharp look but merely added, 'I'm to present you with the Rinduran Award at the Courtship Dance.'

'That's Perfect,' he repeated mechanically, caught himself. Verity deserved better. 'No, I'm sorry, I do appreciate all you're doing for me and for Puggy.'

'You don't love her, do you,' observed Verity in that detached way she had, like a little girl talking grown-up. Yet she was no longer a little girl and her blunt manner remained, her habit of stating what others preferred to leave unsaid.

'I didn't know you liked torte,' he hedged.

Her gaze was straight as his welding rod. 'I had never heard of a torte before Puggy mentioned it,' she told him.

There was silence as he took in the implications.

Little meddling minx, he thought with a mix of pride and disapproval.

She put her hand on his and, as before, his head cleared of all its confusion and that inner critic was silenced.

'You mean to be kind in marrying Lady Puggy and I mean to be kind to her too. I think we women need to help each other, as the traditions of the Council can be… difficult for us.'

Kermon just nodded.

'I know you can't tell me what used to happen in the Maturity Test. Bastien explained to me that it was only for those initiated to know.' Her voice dropped sadly. 'So I never will. And as Chief of the Council, I can hardly take part in the new Test, like some child, so I feel at a disadvantage.'

What did she want from him? Kermon tried to reassure her. 'You've been my anchor so you've done everything a New Woman will do during the test.'

She looked at him as if he were some schoolroom infant himself. 'I don't need status. I need knowledge. Whether it's torte or forging, I need to know everything about the Citadel, especially what *they* don't realise I know. Knowledge is power.'

Her father's daughter indeed. Kermon was not going to ask who *they* were. He had enough problems of loyalty and betrayal, without being dragged into the Citadel's internal politics.

'No,' she said impatiently, 'what I want from you is your help.'

Her glare was so fierce that he had no option. 'Of course,' he said, even as his stomach sank, wondering what impossible feat she would demand. He did not have to wonder for long.

'I know that Lady Puggy is the wreck of the woman – the

mage – she used to be. No, you don't have to come out with any 'Perfect' nonsense about women's roles and all that.'

Kermon could not have been more shocked if the cobblette had reflected trees and birds. Verity was *not* completely her father's daughter after all!

Luckily, being speechless was a safe response and Verity rushed on, 'I wonder whether we could bring her back? Whether Mage Puggy is still there, inside that feather-brained shell? If we could restore her to her senses, she would be my ally and I could find out so much that I don't know! Fabrisse and Yacinthe are not... helpful.'

'I've wondered whether I could heal her,' admitted Kermon. 'But it might be dangerous, for her. And maybe for us too.' It was his turn to speak directly. 'I'm not sure Chief Mage Bastien would approve. Nor Hamel or even the other mages. They agreed with–' he didn't want to say *your father's plan* 'the change to the composition of the Council.'

Instead of rebuking him for lack of respect, she seemed to be thinking it through. She nodded. 'That's why we'll leave it until you're married. Then, as her husband, you can decide what is right for Puggy.' She flushed. 'It's a pity but that's what must happen.'

What is a pity? he wondered. Surely not his wedding to Puggy?

'After you are married, when nobody is watching, we will go to the Maturity Barn, just the three of us, and you will use your soul-reading or whatever magecraft is needed, to take her back in her mind to what happened. I think we can restore her and anyway,' she shrugged, 'even if we don't, I will know more about what used to go on here.'

'We could try,' Kermon agreed cautiously. 'But don't get your hopes up. I suspect nothing will happen.'

'And you must go back into the walls. Find out more about tortes.'

How quickly Verity changed from subtle politician to imperious child. Kermon could not explain to her how he dreaded going back into the walls. His previous objections had proved to be figments of his imagination. And yet, some worse fear had taken their place, none the less terrifying for being nameless. He just *knew* something terrible waited for him in the walls and he felt its shadow growing with each visit he made.

'Yes, my Lady,' he said.

CHAPTER TWENTY-THREE

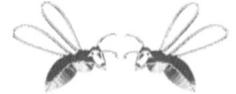

Mielitta blinked, adjusting to the shafts of sunlight lancing through the canopy, after the storm gloom in the farmyard. Her bees sulked in silent disapproval. They'd been rash enough to ask why she didn't stay safely in the house with the nice beekeeper. Let them stay silent! She only cared about Jannlou, who was on the run, hurt and alone.

First, she must find him, so she stilled her mind in the way Tannlei had taught her.

What is the target, Mielitta? To find Jannlou, or the bear, or whatever he is.

That's merely the flight the arrow takes to reach the target.

Mielitta had learnt that time spent on such thoughts was never wasted. She observed the bear prints in the damp earth, so human with their five toes and heel. Her tracking instincts guided her in pursuit while she still posed the question. *What is the real target?*

To put things right with Jannlou. But what did that mean? Why was he so secretive about his second nature when she was open about hers? She didn't understand him at all. And she'd been right to keep their relationship secret from Drianne – look what had happened when Drianne found out! She had no idea why her friend had been so extreme in her reaction but it was exactly what Mielitta had been trying to avoid. Why couldn't Jannlou see that, instead of taking that reaction as a personal insult?

Grumbling to herself about the two of them and how difficult they made her life, she paused, inspected the ground, sniffed that dark brown scent she'd know anywhere. She had to find him, reason with him, bring him home.

Her bees were not sleeping. *Not home!* they panicked. *Not the bear!*

'Not home hive,' she reassured them. 'Our human home.' Which was where exactly? Some high branches in the Forest?

How could she call herself a leader when they had nowhere to live and she couldn't even keep the three of them from arguing! She'd helped save the Forest but that was now in the past. Her grand idea of changing the Citadel and its Perfect society was never going to happen. Even her bees were looked after by the beekeeper. Nobody needed her.

She'd failed as a leader, she'd erred, abused Drianne's loyalty by keeping her in the dark, then hurt Jannlou when she had revealed his secret. But that was his fault for–

Just as her thoughts were circling again, the scent of Jannlou-bear hit her full-strength. He was close. She trod more carefully, knowing that he was as skilled in woodcraft as she. She quietly nocked an arrow, just in case the bear needed stopping so the man could think. Just in case.

Crushed and trampled undergrowth filled with his scent showed he'd lain here but the pit wasn't as deep or as hidden as a bear's usual day bed. He'd merely paused, lain down briefly. He must be close. The breeze was fickle, playing scents past her nose in different directions, so when she realised the new trace of Jannlou-bear came from behind her, it was already too late.

She whirled around as the great paw wrenched her bow from her hand, scratching her with claws she'd seen kill. Close enough to see the heart beating under the brown fur, to look up into pebble-hard brown eyes, Mielitta realised that this was what

Rinduran had seen in the last moments of his life. She could shift into a bee, fly. And increase her chance of being killed if caught. Bears and bees: enemies. She shut her eyes.

After an eternity of seconds, she opened them again, watched the bear's eyes soften, change to stormy blue. He sat down on a tree trunk, tried to scratch his back, contorting his body in a way Mielitta could only envy. Somehow, the tension lessened. Grooming did that. She remembered Cuddle Bee and the pollen, combing fur.

Very slowly, Mielitta moved towards the bear, ignoring her bow on the ground, keeping her hands out in front of her. He put his leg back on the ground but remained sitting, some humanity in his eyes now but none in his body. When he was seated, his shoulders were at a height she could reach with her hands. She moved so close she could smell his breath: berries and mushrooms, no honey biscuits.

Don't think of honey warned her outraged bees. *We don't give bears honey!*

He sat statue-still, staring at her. She stretched her arms out towards him, hands open and sank her fingertips into the deep brown fur covering the muscle of his shoulders. Then she began grooming him, raking the fur with her nails. He gave a low growl but made no move to stop her, so she took that growl as signifying pleasure.

Carefully, watching for any sign that he objected, she moved to one side and around behind him so she could continue her work on his back. She combed, scratched and kneaded, in the ancient animal language of appeasement, known to both man and beast. There was pleasure for her too, both in what she gave and in touch itself. His fur was dense and darker at the root, finer and almost silvery at the tips.

Finally, he sighed. She adapted her touch as the fur thinned to skin, so she was stroking and smoothing, gentle. He put a hand on hers, stopped her, pulled her round in front of him and they just looked at each other, for as long as was needed. She looked into his eyes: blue with depths of fluttering leaves. Reflections of the trees above and the soul beneath.

'I'm not ashamed of you,' she said. 'or who you are. I just didn't want Drianne to feel left out.'

His words seemed to come from a distance, as if shaped by a bear's jaw. 'Maybe *I* am. Ashamed. I have nightmares about what I have done. Rinduran; other prey.'

'You know he would have killed us.' If only he'd accept what he'd done, what they'd all done, and stop chewing it over like bad meat.

'It makes no difference to the feel of flesh tearing between my claws.'

Chewing it over like bad meat. Yes, just like that, she thought. But she must walk in his pelt, reach for his thoughts, not impose her own.

'Tell me,' she invited.

'You said we are the same but we're not. You are connected to creatures which are feared only by stupid Citadel dwellers.'

The bees buzzed in irritation at this lack of respect.

'Wherever I walk in the Forest as a bear, creatures hide, fear me even more than they fear men. Only other predators are my equals and they're competitors, not friends. My own kind want no contact with each other, let alone with a half-brother. Unless I want to beget cubs, I walk alone.'

Mielitta flinched at the thought of Jannlou mating in bear form but there were many aspects of her own shape-shifting that she had not told him – and saw no reason to now. There was one part of her past that might help though.

She spoke quietly. 'I know it's not the same but I had to do things, when I was in the hive as their queen, that are difficult to think about, when I'm human.' She paused, wondering whether this was a good idea or not, then forged ahead. 'I had to kill rival queens.'

He snorted.

Before he could speak, she rushed on, 'Not just in a fight, as you did, where it was my life or hers. But,' she swallowed, her mouth dry. No attendant bees dripped nectar down her throat or protected her from outside evil. She was just as alone as Jannlou.

No, you're not, her bees buzzed, indignant. *Home hive and flower.*

They were right. 'And bear,' insisted Mielitta. They were a team: he, she and Drianne. She would do whatever it took to keep them together. Just as she had done whatever it took in the beehive, to keep it safe. 'I murdered the other queens in their cells,' she confessed. 'Before they were born. They heard me coming and sang out. I can still hear it, the last song of the unborn queens.

'Our nature as beasts and as humans can be brutal.' She looked him straight in the eyes. 'But I can live with that and I would do it again. To protect the bees, to protect you and Drianne, or Kermon, or the children in the Citadel. I would not hesitate. Nor would you. Whatever it takes to protect each other and the Forest, *that* is what we will do. Even if it hurts afterwards to know what we are capable of.'

He nodded but didn't reply. Instead, he asked, 'Do you miss it? The Citadel?'

'Do you?' she countered.

'Sometimes,' he confessed. 'I miss Bastien. No,' he added hastily, 'not harassing you. I don't miss that at all! But you didn't see the training for warriors, the friendship.'

'No,' she said tightly. 'I didn't.'

'Instead, there's a challenge with knitting needles!' A flash of brown darkened Jannlou's eyes. 'I don't like him.'

'He saved Drianne.' Mielitta recounted all that had happened after Jannlou had rushed out the farmhouse and, despite the bees' rebukes, shared a honey biscuit with him.

'I don't know that I like him either but the fact is that he and his grandmother can give Drianne something we can't – training in magecraft. Without it, she's a danger to herself and everybody around her. You saw that.'

'But Kermon was working on it, with me helping,' Jannlou

objected.

'Working on it isn't good enough. And we can't ask Kermon to do everything.' Mielitta felt a pang of guilt. When had she last spoken to the friend who'd gone back to the Citadel, who was so isolated?

'You heard them. I can visit but that's all. Are you and Drianne going to live with the beekeeper?'

'Of course not! At least I'm not. We need to talk to Drianne when she's not hurling furniture at us.' He wasn't getting off the hook so easily. 'She's not the only one who lost control.'

His voice had a hint of growl when he snapped back, 'And you? When the bees call you back into the hive? What control do you have?'

'None,' she admitted, 'but that doesn't kill my friends or their acquaintances.'

'So you agree. We're different.' He shrugged.

'If you say so. The point is that all three of us need to know more about our gifts and learn to use them better. Maybe Arven and his stupid knitting needles can help Drianne, maybe the beekeeper can help me – I don't know. Maybe we can all help each other. Let's just find out, can we?'

'You want me to dig a day-den and stay in it. And at night I'm not allowed to visit you.'

How could a man be so deaf? 'I told you. I'm not going to live in the farmhouse. Like you, I can visit. What we need is a place of our own, where all three of us can be ourselves. We need to find somewhere we can make a more permanent shelter in the Forest.'

'Gifts, you say,' repeated Jannlou bitterly. 'We could have lived ordinary lives.'

She put both hands on his shoulders. 'No, we couldn't,' she said and kissed him, bee, human, bear and man, nothing held back. *And I need to contact Kermon,* she thought, *before I lose another friend.* Then all thoughts of Kermon vanished in kisses.

CHAPTER TWENTY-FOUR

'Kermon's marrying Puggy.' Mielitta blurted words out as raw as her own reaction when she'd finally made a connection through Steelwing and seen *that*.

Jannlou sat bolt upright, his eyes wide, shocking blue, indubitably human. 'But I thought...'

'That's not the point! This isn't about me, or whether he still has... feelings for me. Although I hope he does but not *those* feelings.' She held the steel arrowhead firmly but the Citadel scene still shimmered like a mirage, without any sound. Perhaps it *was* a mirage? Some trick of glamour? What if Kermon had been discovered and now the mages were trying to reach her, to mess with her mind? And she still didn't trust the beekeeper.

Mielitta rubbed the arrowhead as if to clear the picture it presented in her mind but there was no change. The Great Hall was decked out in wedding trappings: golden lightspheres on the tables, beige garlands of sustenance strung above the tables like canopies above four-poster beds. When the last couple had made their vows, the knight promising to protect and his lady promising to obey, the garlands would break and the gathered assembly would tuck into the wedding feast raining like manna from heaven onto the best silvery platters.

Seven couples stood before the mages' High Table, hands clasped and in wedding purple. How strange to see Kermon in anything other than his smith's workwear and leatherette apron or mage's robe. More than strange to see him clasping hands with the willowy blonde husk who had once been Mage Puggy.

She felt a twinge of something that she refused to name. She'd dreamed that she and Jannlou... a dance and a wedding. Kermon looked so handsome, his smith's muscles showing to advantage in metal arm rings and his sleek black hair a contrast to the fair beauty beside him.

She wanted to see his face but that too shimmered in and out of focus so she couldn't read his expression. A smile – but was it genuine? Had he been forced? She couldn't believe he was in love with Puggy, who could barely speak. Especially when so recently he'd shown strong feelings... Was that what men were like? Strong feelings one minute and with somebody else the next? She glanced at Jannlou, who reached out, squeezed her hand. He showed no sign of having tired of her but how could you tell?

She studied Kermon again, trying to make sense of this impossible scenario. How strange to see Kermon clean, without smuts on his face. His hands must be clean too, especially the one clutching his bride's.

There, she'd said the word. And Kermon would be wearing his new trophies on his belt. He'd barely had time to forge his engagement emblem before making his married one, she thought. And he hadn't even bothered to tell them.

'He can't hear me,' she said. 'Or doesn't want to. This must be why he hasn't been in touch.' She let the anger carry poison through her veins, numbing the pain. 'He didn't tell us. He's gone over to them.'

'You don't know that,' objected Jannlou. 'He has to maintain a veneer of normal citizen behaviour.'

'But – married to Puggy, of all people! What are we going to tell Drianne? She'll go off on another magestorm!'

'I don't think Kermon marrying means as much to her as you

being with me.' Jannlou looked at her strangely then shook his head, as if she were the stupid one who'd been forged to brainless. He rubbed his back against a tree-trunk, a habit he'd slipped into even when in human form.

'Can I see?' he asked.

She shrugged, placed his hand around hers, curled like a walnut shell around its kernel, with Steelwing in her palm. She concentrated on the link, the Great Hall, Kermon and Puggy, the garlands breaking and all the mouths opening, to cheer, to eat, to share in the happiness of the couples' Perfect day.

And here she was, Jannlou's hand clasping her own under garlands of leaves, which rustled in the wind, a parakeet chattering approval before flashing red through the branches and away. The moment lasted an eternity during which she could hear the very ants soldiering on under their burdens of seed, heading back to the nest. Her bees politely held their collective breath, which was the closest to understanding that they would ever show.

She opened her eyes. Had she closed them? She no longer knew where the boundaries were between worlds, between her and this man. Protection and obedience were words meant for different sides of the boundary and they did not need such words for the promise that lay between them.

'Yes,' she told him or he told her. Afterwards they were never sure who had begun it but they knew where it led and what it meant. There was an eighth wedding that day, witnessed by the fur and wing of Forest, danced by the sunlight through the canopy.

He still held her hand as she brushed leaves from her hair and clothes and she clasped the moment to her tightly. If only time could stop here, now.

'You deserve more,' he said, eyes sapphire, too dazzling for her. 'The wedding of Magaram's son and heir would have transformed the Great Hall with a week of feasting, golden goblets and platters, fire-eaters and jesters.'

'I don't want more,' she told him. 'I want this.'

The fire in his voice calmed, became almost dreamy, melancholy. 'You are stronger than I am. Steelwing showed me a reminder of the world that was. My friend Bastien, Chief Mage. A world in which I was not a bear.'

She shivered, not knowing what to say. They'd been so close and now she felt as if he'd pushed her away, become a solitary creature again. Maybe his hand holding hers was just pollen-gathering together, not soul deep.

You have us whispered her bees. *One hive, always.*

'Your beekeeper is right,' Jannlou said gravely. 'I must learn to live with my second nature and to control it. Perhaps I can use all those lessons in magecraft I endured for years. Or perhaps I need to find new ways.'

Mielitta listened with a growing sense of foreboding. She could feel the goodbye in his words, so cruel in its timing.

'I can help you,' she pleaded but she could see his decision in his eyes.

'A bear lives alone,' he told her bleakly. 'I need to be on my own.' He tried to soften the blow. 'Just for a while.'

But she knew he meant, 'Until I can control myself.' What if that day never came?

She sought Tannlei's wisdom but all that came to mind was being told *Arrows tipped with honey cause the deepest hurt.* Knowing that did not help.

Jannlou raised her hand to his lips, said, 'Keep believing in me.' He turned to go, paused and hesitated.

'I did see Kermon and Puggy,' he said. 'I saw their eyes, how they stood, how they touched. He doesn't love her. He pities her.'

'And Puggy?'

'She is so scared of him she couldn't stop shaking.' He turned to walk into the Forest so she barely heard his last words, spoken as if to himself. 'I know what love looks like.' Already he'd let his humanity slip and was covered in thick brown pelt as he rushed off between the trees. Mielitta heard the startled yelp of a fox as the bigger predator lumbered past him.

She sat down with a thump on a tussock of grass. So much for proving her leaderships skills! She'd driven Jannlou away by forcing him into too much, too quickly. And as for Kermon? What in the stones was going on and why hadn't he told her? The only one left was Drianne and, despite Jannlou's strange pronouncement, Mielitta was sure the young mage would set loose her crazy power and destroy the farm when she heard about Kermon.

And Jannlou, thought Mielitta gloomily. *We've lost both of them.*

Her stomach gave another lurch but she'd suffered so much emotional upheaval that she didn't recognise the symptoms until she heard the voices.

Help! Help! Queen Mother.

With a sickening wrench she found her eyesight and body changing as she was transported into the beehive, in the middle of a full-scale war.

CHAPTER TWENTY-FIVE

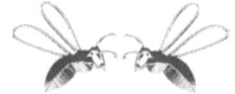

The roar of enraged bees filled Mielitta's core and she instinctively batted her wings faster, increasing her contribution to the general hullabaloo as bees zoomed past her in all directions. The banana-scent of stinger poison filled the air, rousing all the workers to keep their own weapons in readiness.

Am I a queen or worker? Mielitta asked herself as she quickly assessed her body's equipment. In the past, she'd duelled against her rival in the larger, clumsy body of a queen but in a battle like this, only workers could act as warriors. The queen would be hidden by an increased bodyguard, her person and the hive's potential descendants protected from the invaders.

The buzz told her clearly that there were invaders but all she could see around her in the blue and ultra-violet dark of bee-sight, were other bees.

Move! A bee knocked her out the way as another one, smelling wrong, zoomed in with loaded stinger. Mielitta sniffed the wrongness, an alien queen's scent, from a different beehive. The bee attacking did not belong here. Her scent was hive-wrong. A drip of poison fell from the tip as the invader succumbed to frenzied bites and a sting from Mielitta's hive-right rescuer.

'Are you all right?' Mielitta asked anxiously, hating the

thought that the bee must surely die, its stinger gone. Even here in the beehive, she was making wrong choices, destroying others' lives. She felt the bee's confusion at such a stupid question. What did one bee's death matter in a hive of fifty thousand?

My stinger is intact but no poison left now. I can still bite.

Oh. Of course. Mielitta had forgotten that bees sometimes retained their stingers if used on skin less tough than that of a human. She shivered, realising that she was in worker form and to use her stinger could mean her death. And that she had no option. She was called upon to be a warrior bee.

Robber bees after our honey, the bee told her quickly. *All foragers are recalled to defend the entrance. Intruders like that one will head for the honey and the hive-cleaning bees can pick them off one by one as long as we prevent reinforcements breaking through. Unless you're on nursery duty or in the royal bodyguard? Those are protected occupations.*

Mielitta touched antennae with the other bee, communicated her availability at the front.

Follow me. The other bee zoomed off, ducking the occasional wrong-hive bee going in the other direction, upwards to the honey stores. Mielitta could barely see daylight coming through the entrance for the black bodies of fighting, dying bees.

Right-smell workers were trying to move the dead bodies back through the entrance, off the landing ledge, but they risked attack from the mass of wrong-smell bees, filling the air with their triumphant raiding song.

As Mielitta flew down closer to the mêlée at the entrance she could see why the defence was so difficult. The metal portcullis, which usually occupied the long opening that ran right across the bottom of the beehive, had been removed. There was an open entrance instead of a dozen or so bee-sized openings in the metal, each of which could be defended by one bee, overseeing and approving incomers.

Damn that meddling beekeeper! thought Mielitta as she reinforced the line of warrior bees holding the entrance against the oncoming hordes. A surge pushed her backwards and she retaliated, heaving with all her might then clamping all six feet to the floor to hold her in place. She dug her tarsi claws into the wood for good measure but there was no time to consider the practicality of a bee's feet as another shove claimed her attention.

Cleaning, cleaning! announced a stressed whine beside her. *Let me through!*

Mielitta automatically made room for the right-smell bee to pass her and carry a dead body out through the entrance and off the platform. Usually the procedure would have been a normal part of keeping the hive sanitary. But today was not normal and Mielitta rushed to block the hole created by the removal of corpses, before the invaders perceived the weakness.

'No,' she buzzed frantically but the right-smell bees were fighting for their lives, not listening for reports from scouts and odd-bees like her. How could she reach them?

In the front row now, she could see the air black with robber bees, hear their intimidating war-cries, even see her own reflection in the giant hexagons of their eyes as they landed and charged at her. She bit, kicked and lunged with her stinger, heedless of risk. One bee's life was worth nothing.

Dance it! her inner queen told her. *Do it calmly, repeat and repeat again. Believe in it enough and they will hear you.*

So she did. In the midst of battle, whirling as if she were trying trick shots in the archery yard, Mielitta drew on the strength of her inner queen to dance a mind map in the manner of bees. She showed the entrance blocked – not by a metal portcullis but by corpses – and the right-smell bees defending this restricted entrance. She danced the compass points required, the hive's need and most of all, she danced her certainty, like a scout who knew she'd found the best new home for the hive.

Jabbing and hacking, ignoring the bites and rips her own body was suffering, Mielitta repeated the dance, over and over, until she could feel her co-workers repeating the dance, until she was blind from the bodies piling up in front of her.

And then she realised why there were bodies piling up. Her message had got through. No more cleaning. The right-smell bees had closed up their entrance with corpses, nudging then together like a wall to keep the invaders out – or trapped inside.

Mielitta dropped to her six knees, exhausted.

Let me take over. A right-smell warrior edged past her gingerly but already the fight at the front was ending as the last corpses were moved to block any trace of light or invasion.

The remaining fight was inside the hive now and Mielitta could hear the high-pitched screams of wrong-smell bees as they were mobbed. She hoped they were being hotballed to death. How could they turn against their own kind!

We smelled wrong to them, her bees told her, always keen to answer a rhetorical question. *And our honey smelled good. Their scouts told them they were strong enough to take it. Maybe they needed it or maybe they just wanted it.*

'Humans are the same,' acknowledged Mielitta, stretching her feelers, her legs, blinking.

Propolis, explained a cleaner bee, patting orange sticky goo on Mielitta's worst bite wound. *Keeps it clean for you. Heals.*

Mielitta wished she were visiting as a queen so she'd be pampered more, groomed and given nectar and honey, rather than merely patched up and sent back to work. Especially after she'd saved the hive. She should have an award, really.

What's an award.

'Special respect for one worker,' Mielitta explained, showing a happy worker bee and the other bees dancing respect as they did to the queen.

Her bees tinkled with laughter. *Feel,* they told her. *Your award.*

Mielitta let the atmosphere in the beehive fill her, as rage had done before. The queen's joy and the hive's security thrummed in her abdomen, making her want to work and to dance, for those two things were one and the same. She had fulfilled her purpose and the hive was safe.

'Yes,' she agreed, humming with the hive's joy. 'My award.'

Thank you, Queen Mother, came a voice she knew well, honeyed and maternal, sending out its signal that all was well. The Young Queen knew what Mielitta had done. Of course she did – all the bees knew. And she knew what they had done. All would be well.

Mielitta looked towards the blocked entrance. What would they do now? They could stay inside the hive for a day or two, more if they used up their honey reserves, but they would need to forage again, while they could. If they unblocked the hive, would the invaders come back? And if they left the bodies there, what about putrefaction and disease? She began to worry again. What should she do?

She nudged a body, tentatively, but the right-smell workers had done their work too well and the wall was immovable, with corpses for bricks. Her pride crumbled to dust as she realised that her brilliant solution would kill them all, immured in the hive. Bees had no muscular strength and even working together, they would never clear a way out.

Even as she began this gloomy train of thought, the corpse wall moved, making her jump.

Ghosts! she thought.

But ghosts did not move in an organised fashion backwards from the entrance and disappear over the edge. As daylight appeared through a cleared hole, Mielitta could see the huge human hand methodically clearing the entrance.

The beekeeper! Thank the stones! Mielitta chose to forget her earlier imprecations against the beekeeper and couldn't wait to get into the fresh air. She was never enamoured of the bees' enthusiasm for clustering in a mass and just the thought of suffocating in the hive made her feel claustrophobic. She scuttled through the gap in the entrance, flew behind the beekeeper and shifted back into human form.

'You can help me,' the beekeeper said, not even turning round. 'Once we've cleared the entrance, we need to put the portcullis back in place. Then we'll suspend a wet sheet across the front of the hive, tuck it under the roof.' She pointed to a bucket, in which a pink sheet was soaking in water.

Mielitta joined in the work at the entrance, marvelling at how different it was to be on this side of the boundary. What was it the beekeeper had said about boundaries and seeing differently? She reminded Mielitta of her archery teacher, Tannlei, finding hidden meanings in the simplest activities.

What is the target, Mielitta? she asked herself. *Clear the entrance. And?*

Stop the robbers coming back, she realised, just as the beekeeper spoke.

'The sheet will deter the robber bees because the wet sheet will mask the honey smell and they don't have the same motivation to get inside the hive as the bees whose home it is. You know how strongly bees feel about their home.'

She did indeed. *Home hive.*

'Why didn't you stop it, the robbing?' asked Mielitta.

'All I can do is keep all the beehives strong,' said the beekeeper. 'But if one is stronger than another, which happens if a hive has a difficult year, or even if one queen is aggressive, then robbing happens. I just have to watch for it and stop it when it happens. So sad.' She indicated the grass around the beehive, black with bee corpses. 'So violent.'

Mielitta flushed. What she had wished in the heat of battle was not the sort of person she was. And certainly not the person she wanted to be seen as by others.

They tucked the sheet under the roof so it hung by its own weight, covering the entrance but with a small gap, either side, for bees who looked hard enough.

Already, one right-smell scout bee had popped its head out from behind the sheet, then disappeared back into the hive, where she was no doubt dancing the message for all the other foragers.

Mielitta smiled. 'They will find their way out and back, for sure. What will happen when the sheet dries?'

'I'll keep it wet for a couple of days. That's usually enough to deter the robbers – they're opportunists. I'll visit all the hives to see they have honey stores enough for themselves and then I'll ask Arven to knit us some more rain for a day or two. That will put an end to all interest in other hives' honey.' The beekeeper picked up her bucket and looked at Mielitta. 'I often wish I could go into the hive and help them, find out all that's going on. But I have to guess and do my best.'

For the first time, Mielitta warmed to the beekeeper, felt they were different sides of the boundary but working together.

'What is your name?' asked Mielitta. 'I can't call you the beekeeper.'

'Why not? It is a good name and I have earned it.' The beekeeper laughed. 'But my given name is Qingzhao.'

Mielitta had more questions but in the aftermath, the adrenaline rush of battle had left her now it was no longer needed. Her knees began to shake. She relived the terrors she'd faced in the hive entrance, the attack and murder. What if her stinger had remained in a wrong-smell bee, ripping her body apart? Would her human self live on if her bee self died? And if she survived, who would she be, shorn of her wings?

'Let's get the kettle on for tea. You've had quite a shock.' She offered an arm to Mielitta, who went into the farmhouse leaning on the beekeeper – Qingzhao, as she must learn to think of her. This time, the peppermint tea was for Mielitta, with a spoonful of honey.

CHAPTER TWENTY-SIX

Drianne and Arven were in the family room, with their eyes shut, presumably deep in a training session.

Or asleep, thought Mielitta cynically, stepping carefully around the two mages, who sat cross-legged on a cleared space of carpet. They were facing one another, or would be if they opened their eyes.

'Visualising,' whispered Qingzhao, leading Mielitta through the door into the kitchen. 'Sit yourself down there while I make the tea.'

Mielitta dropped into a battered old chair and wrapped the patchwork knitted blanket around herself to combat a sudden chill. Immediately the ginger cat dropped from his position as a bookend on a shelf, stretched and stalked towards Mielitta.

'Hui likes you,' Qingzhao observed, as she filled the kettle.

Fixing her with a green-eyed stare, the cat twitched his nose; presumably he felt he'd informed Mielitta of his intentions and he leapt onto her lap. She could feel his claws through the blanket as he landed. He retracted them enough to do no damage but still retain some grip, like a bee climbing a frame in the hive, and he climbed her chest up to her shoulder where he settled, flexing and kneading his claws in her hair while purring.

Despite herself, Mielitta began to relax under the warm fur and imperious attentions of the cat. He purred and her bees hummed, with the gentle noise of happy wings.

Qingzhao warmed the china teapot with hot water from the kettle, which now added its bubbling song to the purring, humming music of the kitchen. How strange that the teapot and cups, set out on a tray, should seem so familiar and homely, when this was only the second time Mielitta had been in the house.

As always, book-words from her days in the Citadel library came to her, fitting the experience. 'Hearth', 'inglenook', 'kitchen range', 'kettle' and 'tea-service' – so different from the functionality of 'sustenance' and 'drink' in the Great Hall of the Citadel. Somewhere to curl up in a chair with a cat.

'Here you are, dear. You can move Hui if you like.' Qingzhao had completed the ritual of tea-making and begun that of tea-drinking. She offered the cup on its saucer as if it were a jewelled goblet.

Mielitta received it in the same spirit. She couldn't bow her head properly without disturbing the cat, which Hui did not favour, but she murmured her thanks and looked into the dark green swirl of liquid before taking one sip and savouring it. Peppermint, of course. Not spearmint, apple mint, ginger mint, pennyroyal, pineapple mint, lavender mint.

Mielitta let her imagination dwell on each mint that she was not tasting, the more fully to appreciate all the qualities of the peppermint. Was it peppery? She thought so.

And in her second sip she appreciated the honey, its provenance in the Forest, from a bee colony she knew well.

Qingzhao watched her with approval, confirmed what Mielitta already knew. 'That jar of honey is from Forest forage, from your beehive. You can see why I place a hive in the clearing each year to get such a taste.'

Mielitta understood that she was being treated as someone special, that this honey was rare and quantities limited. This knowledge warmed her as much as the tea and the purring cat. She had not been treated this way since... maybe Declan? No, Declan's parenting had been harsh, even before... Her mind shied away from the thought. No, she had never known such attention to her comfort.

This must be what it was like to be spoiled. Why did 'spoiled' always sound like rotting food? She liked being spoiled. Didn't everybody deserve to be spoiled a little?

She sipped her tea, concentrating less this time and idly observing the scene through the door, where Arven and Drianne seemed to have finished their cross-legged closed-eyes heavy-breathing session and were standing now. Their position was the one Tannlei had always called 'readiness', poise before action.

'What is your anger?' asked Arven, his quiet voice carrying as clearly as if by speechcraft.

I want to smash everybody and everything around me. Drianne's knitted waistcoat flared in a scarlet stripe then returned to its neutral pink as she awaited the next question.

Mielitta moved some papers on the scrubbed table beside her, recipes in spidery green writing, so she could put down her empty cup and concentrate on the lesson in the other room.

She could not tell whether Arven heard Drianne or merely left pauses for her to answer his questions, think her own thoughts. He seemed comfortable with silences. Then he asked another question. As if he already knew which question to ask. As if all humans were subject to the same compulsions.

'What causes this feeling?'

They do. The way they treat me. Half of Drianne's face puckered into a scowl, almost matching the other half.

Mielitta had a good idea who *they* were and she flushed. Hadn't she had much the same thought regarding Jannlou and Drianne, when she'd stomped off into the Forest?

'Where is this feeling?'

In me.

'If it is in you then you have power over it. You cannot control what others do but you can control your reaction.'

It is too strong for me. It's a blaze that consumes me.

'By the time you have lost your temper, it is too late. So we must recognise the signs earlier, of disappointment in others or ourselves, of the pain behind the anger. The more I am aware of what is happening in myself, the more I will see anger coming and not be ambushed.'

Drianne was switching weight from one foot to the other, the colours of her waistcoat reddening and blanching in turn, with occasional zigzags of rainbow power sizzling above her head, then dying out as she controlled herself. Arven showed no concern but maintained the same calm tone. He left Drianne time to think, then questioned her again.

'Does anger make you happy?'

No! They cut me out, they don't care about me, only about each other. She *doesn't care about me!*

Mielitta's brief respite of calm was vanishing as she watched the rainbow flashes multiply around Drianne. She was losing it again! But Arven could read Drianne's degree of self-control in her colours.

'You display beautiful emotions but they pain you. If you would rather be happy, make your anger dance and play in the pattern you create. You are in control, not your anger.' He took rainbow-coloured knitting needles out of the basket by his side and handed them to her. Dull beige stitches were already cast on and the yarn trailed from a needle into the basket.

'Make your pattern in the fabric of this world. You have already begun the work. Express your anger.'

This is the most stupid thing ever! Drianne's silent shout rocked Mielitta to the core and she huddled up in the chair, making herself as small as possible to avoid the hurling of objects around the room that would surely follow.

However, Drianne took the needles and stood still to knit a row. Rhythmic clicking was the only sound. Only when the purring and bee hum started again did Mielitta realise that they'd stopped.

'Another cup of tea, dear?' asked Qingzhao quietly. 'He's so good at that now because he found it so hard to do when he started. You'd never believe he shouted at me that he wanted a warrior's training and not to shame his father with this namby-pamby needle-work. He was full of big plans for avenging his mother and father, when he was barely big enough to carry knitting needles and too proud of his masculinity to learn to use them.'

'What changed his mind?' Mielitta saw Drianne's needles turn to silver and the rainbow colours wriggle onto the fabric as she knitted, turning her needle different ways to make some kind of shape that pleased her.

'His own deep thinking.'

Mielitta would have bet her quiver on there being some silences and hard questions involved in the process but she was too engrossed in the spectacle of Drianne trying to dance while knitting, to interrogate Qingzhao further. The ball of yarn was tucked under her arms, the needles were clacking and the rainbow fabric was growing, waving like a flag.

'They have a connection,' Mielitta observed quietly to Qingzhao. 'Drianne and Arven. It would be wonderful if Drianne found somebody to love, a partner...'

Qingzhao looked at her as if she were stupid but said nothing.

The bees were less polite. *Silly human, thinking only of the bear and cuddles. Drianne-flower can think bigger than just being in a pair. How limiting!*

Maybe Mielitta was obsessing about romance but she couldn't help it. She was in love, with someone who loved her too, even if he was disturbed at the moment. She wanted everybody she cared about to know the whoosh and zing of love's glamour. No, not glamour. That suggested magecraft and deceit. What *was* being in love then, if not glamour?

Ow! Drianne had bumped into a table and stubbed her bare

toes. She held her knitting in one hand and rubbed her foot with the other but, even though she stood still, all the rainbow power stayed in the knitted pattern she'd created.

'You're in control again,' pointed out Arven, 'and you've made something beautiful from your anger. Because you've shaped it with discipline.'

Drianne spread the knitted fabric out, inspected her pattern and glowed.

'No reason why you can't dance and knit,' Arven challenged her. 'Look around you first. Dance in your imagination. Let your feet know where you can dance and where there are obstacles. Then, make the ground your friend, your partner,' he instructed, smiling.

Before he'd finished speaking, Drianne's feet and needles were flying across the carpet, crossing and making a pattern of dance and wool. As she whirled, the room filled with joy, a brightness following in her footsteps and lingering, a scent of crocus and violets. She danced to her own tune but everyone felt a new spring in their step.

Despite his protests, Mielitta unwound Hui from her shoulders and rushed to her friend, heedless that she was interrupting the lesson, heedless of any damage she would suffer if Drianne's colours flared rainbow, beyond control. She threw her arms around the young mage, who did not resist or start hurling furniture.

'It's beautiful! You're beautiful.' Mielitta spoke from her heart without stopping to think. Stopping to think had done her little good recently. 'Jannlou and you are the most important things in my life and I can't bear this, this–' she shrugged, lost for a word to describe the pain of them all being at odds.

And Kermon, pointed out Drianne. *And the bees. And the Forest.*

Mielitta couldn't deny it.

It's all right. Drianne laughed. *You don't have to choose. Honestly.* There was an irony beyond her age, a shadow Mielitta didn't understand that flitted across half of her face. And then she changed the subject.

I know who Arven is, she told Mielitta, *and so do you.*

CHAPTER TWENTY-SEVEN

Mielitta looked again at the slim youth, the sharp planes of his face, his black eyes and hair, reminding her of somebody else, softer, womanly. Who was he?

Drianne resumed her position of readiness, all her attention on Arven.

He spoke in that same calm, authoritative manner, which also reminded Mielitta of somebody else. His grandmother of course, but not just the beekeeper. Someone Mielitta had known longer.

'Before the anger takes you over, when you feel hurt or disappointment, the feelings before anger, you can channel them, express them in a work of beauty. Like that.'

Drianne held up the rainbow fabric, its centre marked by a relief pattern that held out a bent leg, blew its throat out in a bubble underneath wide nostrils, as the light caught on the knitting. The frog's face disappeared under a lotus flower and then reappeared again as the fabric rippled.

'A frog.' Mielitta spoke the word aloud and added, 'He's beautiful.'

She, corrected Drianne. *A frog and a flower. I think it's a scarf.* She caught up the hanging edge of fabric and placed it by the needle holding the stitches. Her face glowed along the web of silvery lines as she began to join the edges with magecraft. Then she remembered.

Oh. She sighed and worked the join manually instead. *I'm not supposed to use magecraft without need and purpose.*

Arven bowed, pleased with his student. 'Ask yourself *What is the target?* and you will find the answer changes. If you think about your target, you will regain control. At first, you wanted to hurt them, I think, because they hurt you. And then you wanted to stop the hurt because you were hurting yourself. Then you wanted to enjoy your power, to be happy. And now? You have made something beautiful from your hurt and confusion. You don't need to use knitting and needles to be creative. That's just my way. You will find your own.

'So, what is the target now?' he asked

The silver tracery still glowed on Drianne's face, which no longer struck Mielitta as damaged but as unique; as much an act of self-expression as the rainbow frog. The scars had healed, their puckering like rosebuds on the cream skin beneath and the asymmetry of expression merely a reminder that happiness and sadness co-exist. Some of the anger Mielitta carried in herself dissipated in contemplation of Drianne's face, the harmony of two halves.

To choose happiness. If Drianne thought aloud, it was for Mielitta to hear and share in the lesson and in forgiveness.

What's the target, Mielitta? she asked herself.

And then she knew who Arven was. Who his grandmother must be. But what this had to do with the spidery green writing that she also recognised, she had no idea.

'Tannlei,' Mielitta exclaimed. 'Tannlei, our archery teacher, was your mother. But she was so old. And she died.' Then she remembered the beekeeper's tale and held her tongue, didn't say how angry she'd been at her beloved teacher dying, leaving her friendless.

Qingzhao's eyes were wet, ancient as the black rocks under the waterfall. 'Not so old, compared with me,' she said softly. 'But you were young. You must tell me about her, what she was to you.'

'But who was Arven's father? asked Mielitta, too curious for diplomacy.

'One of the Council of Ten,' Qingzhao replied.

'The warrior, Crimvert,' replied Arven with pride.

Whose execution Mielitta had watched. After she'd received the prophesy in spidery green writing, on her eighteenth birthday – or what counted as such.

'This conversation must wait,' Arven stated, in his strange manner. 'Drianne can build on the understanding she has now, with help from the mage in the Citadel. But there is one lost in the Forest. I served him an ill turn and must go to him.'

Qingzhao's expression softened as she watched her grandson passing judgement on himself, in the same calm tones he had used throughout. No anger, no bitterness, no breast-beating: just truth and consequence. She stayed his departure with a gesture.

'Before Arven leaves, please tell us what happened to his father,' she said. 'I saw your expression and it is time we knew.'

Hesitant at first, Mielitta began the story she'd seen from her side of the boundary, of a much-loved teacher, a mage executed by Chief Mage Magaram for his love of the Forest.

'I will never forget the words Mage Crimvert used to describe the Forest. Until then I'd never heard adults speak of the place,' she turned to Arven but he kept his head down, hiding all reaction, 'and then your father gave his life to speak the truth. He said we must live, not just exist; nurse the spark in the children, not extinguish it. He told the Council of birdsong that hushes as you come near. He said the Forest never repeats itself. It dazzles, varies, enchants. When I heard his words, something awoke in me, a need to go there, even though it was forbidden. And everything he said was true! It's his vision that inspired me, that Kermon has taken up as his mission.'

Mielitta stumbled in telling of the Council's reaction, the

conviction of treason. She omitted the horrors of Shenagra's testing, her attempt to force Crimvert's mind.

'Magaram used his power,' she said, 'reduced Crimvert to ashes. It was instantaneous.'

But in her memory, she saw Magaram's hand glow red, felt the threat become action, a fistful of fire hurled across the council table and a man turned into a pile of ashes. She heard again Magaram's sarcastic comment that it was a fitting end to one who'd valued wood so highly. And she recalled the reign of fear in that room. Had Rinduran really been any worse? Or just different in his politics but not in his actions. *Watch their hands,* Tannlei had always said.

'With the password I overheard, I opened the water gate and discovered the Forest. Where the bees changed me and here I am,' finished Mielitta. 'Thanks to your father and your mother too, in a way. She taught me more than archery. She taught me to use my deep thinking.' *Watch their hands.*

Arven had withdrawn into himself, knitting with yarn turned black, frowning at the pattern he'd made.

Here we are, corrected Drianne.

Yes, us too, chimed in the bees.

Arven placed his knitting back in his basket, spoke as if he'd heard nothing of Mielitta's account.

'All lessons teach the tutor as much as the student, if not more. I provoked the bear from my own need to prove myself. This is for me to reflect upon, after I have made amends.'

'I tried!' Mielitta exclaimed. 'He won't listen.'

'He can't fight you,' was the strange response. 'He can fight me. And he needs to fight somebody other than himself. Anger comes out in different ways.' He picked up his basket of knitting and was out of the door before Mielitta could think of a way to stop him.

These mages were a law unto themselves! Arven would be wolf-dinner in the Forest before he had the chance to be bear-kill! She should chase after him, summon her bees.

No! Not near an angry bear! they panicked.

'Don't worry about him,' Qingzhao told her. 'He became far keener on my training methods when I showed him how to use a needle as a sword and to capitalise on being underestimated. He understood quickly the advantages of women's weapons and his gifts stay his hand when others would kill. You can trust him with Jannlou.'

'Even though Jannlou is Magaram's son?' asked Mielitta, sick with worry.

'Even so,' replied Qingzhao. 'Trust him.'

'I have no choice.' The responsibility for what might happen weighed on Mielitta like a tombstone.

The beekeeper was resolute. 'And we can talk, the three of us, without you worrying what a son should hear of his father's death. Staying his hand then could be more difficult for Arven.'

Mielitta's questions about a prophesy in spidery green writing would have to wait. To be considered later, when she could indulge in purely personal reflections.

She nodded. 'Yes, that makes sense.'

She told Qingzhao and Drianne what she'd seen in the Citadel. 'I don't know why Kermon is marrying Puggy. Jannlou says he doesn't love her, that it's pity or something. I don't understand why he didn't tell us, why he hasn't been in touch.'

She looked at her unlikely allies, a young mage barely in control of her powers and an old mage still grieving for the couple murdered in the Citadel.

'What should we do?' she asked baldly.

CHAPTER TWENTY-EIGHT

Kermon spent his wedding night lying on a bench in the forge, wide awake in the darkness. What had come over him?

All had been going to plan. He'd overcome his reluctance to visit the walls and taken the male magecraft students from his little group to pilot the new Adulthood Test. They had behaved with impeccable self-control, searching for the simple topics he'd given them without letting the myriad tangents distract them. Kermon couldn't protect them from the knowledge that the full range of sex and violence in human and animal history could be witnessed in the walls. Anybody entering the walls would be aware of a billion sordid byways in a zillion experiences. But he *could* inspire a sense of mission and integrity that would keep them on the right path – and he was there to stop them from straying, if need be. He could lead by example.

What an example. He thrashed around on the narrow bench, wishing it were harder, the punishment he deserved.

He was the one who'd been distracted by all the sordid byways, wondering whether … wondering how … as if he'd been taken over by some evil spirit. He didn't recognise himself. If he hadn't been accompanied by children, he might have followed his worst instincts. Instead, his responsibilities protected him and he pictured the sweet faces of the girls, their anchors, relying on the research from the visit for their own Maturity.

The children had plenty to report that was positive and were full of youthful enthusiasm as they met up with their female study partners and shared all they'd learned with their first listeners. The next task was for them to report to their classmates and for all the candidates to be paired up and choose their own food topics. Kermon would visit the classroom and liaise with the teacher.

He should be proud of himself but there had been something sleazy in his inclinations among all the temptations offered by the walls.

'Well done.' Verity's clear gaze and hand on his arm had made him feel whole again. 'You're quite an old hand at visiting the walls now.'

He couldn't tell her that he felt he was losing more of himself each visit. He'd sound so feeble, such a poor substitute for the father she worshipped, so he accepted the compliment – the lie. With her hand on his arm, he almost felt he could make it true. Almost.

He should tell Mielitta that her plan was progressing. But his urge to contact her was tinged with revulsion, like bile spoiling the taste of honey. Something in him was as reluctant to speak to Mielitta as another part of himself was afraid to visit the walls. He was torn in two and exhausted.

Then there had been the wedding, a surreal procession of meaningless pomp followed by hollow promises to a woman empty of character or feeling. Or so part of him had felt.

He'd also felt growing triumph. Here he was, where he belonged, the focus of attention in the Great Hall, with a desirable woman he'd mastered before and would dominate again. He remembered what she'd been like as a mage, ugly in the misglamour she'd projected but underneath, so desirable. He'd merely revealed what she should be like and muted or mutated what was undesirable. He couldn't wait to be her husband again.

Reality seemed more dreamlike to Kermon than did the world of the walls but he'd spoken, danced, eaten when he should have. The silver goblets contained tasteless Citadel water and the glittering platters held tasteless sustenance. His imagination offered no flavours to relieve the tedium.

His bride had fiddled with her hair and her dress, demanded his admiration for the lace trim, and had seemed as happy as a toddler with birthday toys. Until they were alone in their new, shared chamber.

Kermon had intended to escort Lady Puggy to the room, then return to his own, so he had no idea why he'd followed her, closed the door and grabbed her. Or rather, he wished he had no idea why he'd followed her into the room but his body still knew. Unforgivable, unthinking lust. He'd grabbed her and kissed her, ignoring the fear and repulsion in her eyes. She hadn't fought him. Why would she when he could overpower her in every way the Citadel allowed – and that was indeed in every way. He was her husband.

When he stopped to remove his shirt, his arrowhead banged against his chest – thank the stones! – and he remembered how he'd felt about Mielitta. Such a long time ago. Such a different man he'd been then. He'd liked her, not just wanted her. He looked at Puggy, the loathing in her eyes, and he turned on his heel, throwing his shirt back on as he went.

'Change the lock,' he told her curtly, as he left. He assumed she had. As long as he thought that, he could fight this evil desire to go back through the dark corridor and slide into a warm marital bed. Into a warm marital embrace.

Kermon shifted again on the bench and the arrowhead poked him. *Good.* He hoped it would make a mark, hurt him again. He deserved it.

Despite himself, he must have slept, because he was woken by banging on the door. He gave no explanation to the assistants, who'd turned up to work as usual, but hastened to the Great Hall for breakfast, hoping that his new wife wasn't there.

Ribald comments from male citizens were as welcome as post-wedding wishes for his future babies from the ladies he brushed past to reach the High Table. He dropped into the seat Verity indicated beside her, with relief. At least she knew the truth of why he'd married Puggy. He felt like he himself was forgetting.

'I can get away this morning,' she told him in a low voice. 'Let's try... that thing we said we'd do.'

For a moment, he had no idea what she meant and was annoyed at her presumption. Quite above her station. She put her hand on his arm and at once he remembered. They would take Puggy to the Maturity Barn and see whether she could recall what had happened there, regain any of what she'd lost.

'All right,' he agreed. Then he remembered what had happened the night before and flushed. 'Could you escort... my wife... to join me? I promised I'd complete some trophy work in the forge this morning but I would so love to see her. And you may tell her she needn't be afraid.'

Verity gave him a quizzical look.

'Of the forge,' he explained. 'There's so much noise and the sparks in the darkness can be quite startling for someone so delicate.'

There came one of those quiet moments that occur when people are eating, broken by remarks made louder than was intended. Vulgar comments regarding a bride's delicacy could be heard from the far end of the table, along with some coarse wedding-night jokes.

Verity flushed crimson. 'You may rely on me, Mage-Smith Kermon, to protect Lady Puggy's dignity.' She wiped her mouth, stood, glowered at the male mages around her and picked up her skirts to leave the dais.

'We will come to the forge later this morning,' she told Kermon and, her colour still high, she left him to suffer further ribbing, which increased once there were no ladies present. He wondered how long he could continue living like this.

CHAPTER TWENTY-NINE

Kermon had dismissed all the apprentices and assistants and let the forge grow as cold and dark as his thoughts. He almost missed the soft tapping when it finally came but roused himself to unlatch the door and blinked at the visitors.

Verity marched into the forge but Puggy hesitated on the threshold. Kermon stepped back to allow her to enter without coming near him.

'Don't be such a fusspot, Puggy,' Verity told her, while Kermon brought some lightspheres to life. Their diffuse radiance brightened what was within their reach but made the shadows seem even more ominous. 'This is just a workshop, the same as Mage Fabrisse's and you always love going there. She makes dresses and Kermon makes metal, so it's darker here, that's all. You'll get used to it.'

She seemed to have taken Kermon's words at face value. So much the better if she thought Puggy's fears were some kind of forge phobia. What if Puggy told Verity how he'd behaved? No man would take her seriously, nor most women, but there was a straightness about Verity. Kermon couldn't bear to imagine how she would look at him if she knew. Not only was he a lesser man in her eyes than her beloved father, he was *that* sort of man.

'We shall have go to Mage Fabrisse's afterwards, as long as you are very good and try your hardest to do what we tell you,' Verity told Puggy, who gave a sidelong glance at Kermon before heading straight for the back of the forge.

Without a word, Puggy found the small door, invisible in the shadows except to those who knew it was there. How many times, when she was a Maturity Mage, had she led candidates in the procession through the forge and out that door, across the greensward and into the Barn?

Kermon and Verity exchanged a glance. The hairs on the back of his neck rose as they followed in Puggy's wake, to stand in front of the Barn door, which used to be sealed by magecraft.

From long-ingrained habit, Puggy stopped in front of the door, placed her hand on it and her lips moved in what must be her old password. Luckily, the magecraft seals had been broken and never replaced. Now that Bastien was Chief Mage, and the old Test ended, there was no Maturity Mage – unless Kermon himself could be considered such.

The door opened to her touch and Puggy entered the Barn, showing none of the timidity she'd exhibited coming into the forge. Once, this was her domain, where she was all-powerful. She stood in the centre of the Barn, swirled her skirt a little, giggled, then performed some kind of sinuous wriggle.

Verity screwed up her face in embarrassment and Kermon realised that he felt much the same. Since entering the barn, he'd felt none of the internal conflict that had troubled him since his first visit into the walls. He realised that Puggy's intention was to be seductive in her movements but stones knew why. She'd made it clear she wasn't attracted to him so why behave in such a way? She looked like a large snake had dropped into her dress and was vomiting its prey.

He laughed, then covered that up with a cough. He felt the tingle of his own powers and as he watched the female husk who had once been Mage Puggy, he felt a rush of the pity which had led him to marry her. He would use all his skills as soul-reader to heal her if he could, as Verity wished.

'I can't enter her mind,' he told Verity gently. 'To do so without permission is–' he flinched from the term *mind rape*, too conscious of what he'd almost done. 'Is a kind of forging. And even if she gave consent, she isn't in her right mind, so it would be meaningless.'

'I don't know what forging really means,' confessed Verity. 'What are you going to do to get her to think?'

Puggy seemed unaware that they were talking about her or of anything but entertaining some invisible audience.

What would make her remember? Kermon walked around the Barn, saw the pile of ashes in a corner, the door they'd come through. Nothing else. He remembered what Declan had told him of the Ceremony. The procession of candidates entering the Barn, girls lining up on one side, boys on the other...

He went to the door, opened it and spun the story of the Maturity Test, to bring memories to life for the woman who used to be in charge.

'Do you see them,' he began, in a voice that held his soul-reader's power to reach another person. 'The girls and boys coming in, so happy to be chosen, to become adults. The girls come to this side and the boys go to the other. I don't know how you'll know which are the mages. Blue cups for the boys, pink for the girls and green for the mages. Perhaps you can see their flashes of power in the darkness. The green cups are drawn to power, aren't they?' He let his imagination add details, spinning the story while he walked about as if he were one of the candidates, stood waiting for his cup.

Like a nail scraping on a door, no trace of velvet in her voice now, Puggy said, 'It takes skill to identify the children with magecraft. And the boys should be this side. Who are you? Some new apprentice they've fobbed off on me? Hamel's always trying to undermine my authority. I warned Yacinthe but she doesn't see how they are.'

Verity gasped and Kermon warned her to say nothing, to keep still while he continued to recreate the test.

'...their drinks have worked and all are dreaming. The mages are come to their full powers, the boys are winning battles, the girls are–' Kermon took his cue from Puggy's movements as she acted out the story before he told it. 'dancing with the love of their life. So you tell Declan it's time...'

'Not all,' came the harsh interruption. 'I can see the freaks, the misfits, by their colours. Not pink, not blue, not green. Not Perfect and never will be.' She stood tall and fierce, threw out her arms, shuddered.

'What's she doing?' whispered Verity.

'Sending them to the corner,' replied Kermon, quietly, 'as ashes. She suppressed those who didn't fit in. Murdered them.'

'Executed,' corrected Verity automatically but she was stammering.

Puggy continued, 'I told the Council a hundred times it's better to suppress them now, even the mages, than wait till they're proven traitors, but Magaram was soft. Look at what happened with Tannlei, just because she had a gift for archery. If I'd been Maturity Mage when she came to the Barn, she would never have left it. It was only ten times worse and so messy leaving it till she was known in the Citadel. It's not nice suppressing somebody you know, that you've had dinner with. Shenagra wouldn't do it so I had to. As always, leave it to Puggy if there's something difficult. But I'd have done anything for Shenagra.' Her voice softened.

'So I do what's needed. Usually three or four of them. *Then* I call Declan to sort out the New Adults,' Puggy continued, 'and he enters their minds with hot steel and magecraft. The best Mage-Smith the Citadel has ever had.'

Was it Kermon's imagination or did Puggy glare at him? No, her eyes were still shut, focused on the past.

'He seals up their minds, stops their deep thinking and their imaginations making them unhappy, spoiling Perfection. Only happy Citizens left and we can celebrate!' Puggy threw her arms in the air, ready to leave the Barn and celebrate another successful Maturity Test, but Kermon stood between her and the door.

'Not yet, Maturity Mage Puggy.' He let his voice weave the story into her memory so that her mind opened of its own accord. Maybe it was a kind of seduction, he thought with a pang, and hesitated.

'Do it,' Verity ordered between gritted teeth. 'She deserves it.'

He was no longer sure whether their intentions towards Puggy were for her good or not but the truth laid its own claims, insistent.

'This time it's a strange Test, Maturity Mage Puggy, different. You've had that young upstart Bastien foisted on you and here he is, acting as if he's in charge. Something is wrong...' Kermon felt Verity stiffen and he didn't dare mention Rinduran, though he remembered well how Verity's father had announced his plans to end women mages before Puggy had entered the Maturity Barn. He remembered Puggy standing by Rinduran, losing the power struggle, muted and assuming this goddess-body she'd lived with since then. How could he lead Puggy back to that moment without bringing Rinduran into the story?

Puggy held her head, shook it as if in pain. 'No,' she whimpered. 'He's waiting for me outside. His powers are too strong for me. He took my voice, took my chosen form. But I can wait too. I'll hide inside this body like I hid in the other one, until I get my chance to escape.' She gave a harsh laugh.

'It's all as usual, green for the mage candidates, blue for the boys and pink for the girls. Let Bastien think himself so clever, doing the work. I'm watching him. But that's not right. He's giving a pink cup to that mage girl he wants to marry, the one they muted. That's not right. Can't he see she's a mage?

'What's he doing? Why's he turning his power on me?' Puggy's writhing was no longer an attempt to be sensuous but a genuine memory of torture.

Kermon looked at Verity, whose face glowed greenish white in the darkness.

'No,' she whispered. 'Don't stop her. We must hear it all now.'

Puggy was on her knees, head back drinking, spitting out the invisible pink liquid. 'Can't fight,' she sobbed. 'Going to be forged. But *she* won't be. Not if I can help it.'

Kermon could see Drianne in his mind's eye, mute, her nascent magecraft about to die thanks to drugs and Declan's Perfect smithcraft. Bastien's Perfect bride was to have been created here.

With a huge effort, Puggy gave a silent scream, sent all her magecraft as a last gift to protect the girl before the ex-Maturity Mage crumpled into a ball on the Barn woodette floor.

When she raised her face, smeared with tears and dirt, she said conversationally, 'I couldn't let her suffer like that. Not just the loss of her magecraft but having to bed a man. Her magecraft should have protected her, so nobody needed to know. But they couldn't be trusted, the men. That's why I wore the misglamour, to make sure. And even that didn't protect me. He saw through it, so clever. But not clever enough to see the truth.'

'Needed to know what?' asked Kermon, picturing Drianne, that disfigurement she'd chosen, her facial network of silver threads and scars.

Mage Puggy stood up, looked him right in the eye, her tone mocking. 'That we can only love women. But I think you know that, Mage-Smith Kermon, don't you. Husband.'

In case her words left any doubt that Lady Puggy no longer existed, the mage's face had resumed her preferred appearance. Long, lank hair, blotchy skin, eyes like raisins and a body dumpy as dough.

Kermon swallowed hard but he knew his duty as a soul-reader and healer. Whether he was skilled enough as a Mage-Smith was a different question. 'Mage Puggy, you were forged. I think you are returning to us but I don't know what damage remains. As Master Mage-Smith and as a soul-reader, I can investigate and carry out what healing is possible, if it's needed.'

The pause was long as the raisin eyes stared him out, accusatory. Finally, she said flatly, 'I am open.'

In an ironic parody of their wedding night, Kermon entered Puggy's mind. For a moment he was bombarded by Puggy's memories. Brutality from Rinduran; her private indulgence in beautifying before a mirror, in the scent of roses; and a woman's face, misty with love. Hastily, Kermon blocked all that was irrelevant, as in a visit to the walls. He sought the metal sealing off her deep thinking, Declan's work.

And master work it was, working Puggy's deeper thoughts into the very fabric of the metal that sealed off whatever magecraft was left, along with part of her mind. Wisps of power and thought wriggled their way through a hole in the metal, no doubt caused by Kermon's suggestions and Puggy's responses. The welding included the very fibres of Puggy's being so he couldn't remove the metal seal. Could he make the hole bigger?

If he were in the forge, he would heat it again, pierce the molten steel. So, that's what he did, focusing his magecraft to a fine blade of fire, a welding-torch that he applied to the edge of the hole, widening it particle by particle, careful not to affect the edges. His mind ached as he worked. If he lost concentration, he risked damage to the filaments of thought enmeshed with the metal. With infinitesimal progress, the hole grew, until finally he could do no more but cool the edges, let them harden so Puggy had free access to as much of her mind and power as was left.

Puggy shuddered as he withdrew from her mind.

'Thank you.' Her accent was now rough, flat and ugly, her tone mocking. 'I should be getting back to work, if you'll excuse me, Lady Verity. I *will* call on Mage Fabrisse but there's no need to accompany me. I won't be choosing gowns. I'd like to catch up on Council matters. It seems we female mages need to confer.' She glared at Kermon and left the Barn.

CHAPTER THIRTY

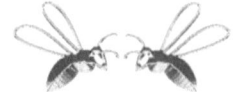

Jannlou lumbered along one of his favourite trails, seeing little in the gathering mist but following his nose without hesitation. Unlike Mielitta in bee form, he didn't need to adapt to a bear's eyesight, which was much like a human's. But having a snout brought an explosion of scents to him, finely distinguished and from miles away. Strongest and nearest was fresh meat but he could also smell the oily sunflower seeds in the prairie in front of the citadel.

His nose even detected the unnatural boundary where smell ended, the Citadel wall. That was his destination but his stomach could determine the route. When he sniffed, nostrils flaring, he could smell a change in the weather, a coldness coming. His bear instincts told him he needed to bulk up and that he'd been neglecting his preparation for – the word came to him from his schooldays – winter.

What's winter? wondered Jannlou. He stood on his hind legs better to look around but the wisps of white turned trees into hooded mages with grasping hands or tangles of snakes and crocodiles. He scented the air again, grunted and dropped back down on four paws in a fast lope, following the odour of fresh kill.

Here. The scent burst raw and bloody on his nose. At the same instant a wolf materialised, golden-eyed and grey in the gloom, as he stopped his feasting to stare at the intruder. The wolf hesitated but his protruding ribs showed how much he needed the buck's meat and he returned to his meal. A luckier stag's rutting bark could be heard echoing oddly in the gloom. No doubt the dead deer had been so weakened in the fight between males that even this lone wolf could bring him down.

Lone wolf, thought Jannlou, knowing that he could chase off this competitor as easily as open his mouth. But why should he? A bear knew all about being *lone* and there was plenty of food for two. He ambled towards the carcass, ears relaxed, not looking at the wolf, who had the courtesy to make space at their dining table.

Jannlou tucked in. There was a kind of companionship, with no words needed. He'd had enough of words. Enough promises. Not because he didn't mean them but because they tore you apart, whether in the keeping or the breaking. He'd promised Mielitta he would control his nature but was that what he wanted? The wolf beside him didn't worry about getting blood on his maw.

Jannlou ripped shreds of meat with his claws and devoured them, messily. Even as a bear, he preferred to use his paws to grab food rather than mouth everything as the wolf did.

I haven't broken any promises! he told an invisible accuser, Bastien of course. *We took the blood oath to be friends, to keep each other's secrets: my lack of magecraft, the beatings and pressure from our fathers. And I never told! You don't have to be a mage to have honour. You don't have to be forced by magecraft to keep an oath.*

He knew what Bastien would say. *But you fought in her war, against me, against the Citadel. How is that friendship? How is that loyalty?*

Jannlou had no answer because *that* was the betrayal. And he could never regret it. What there was between Mielitta and him was born in the Citadel but part of the Forest and needed no words.

The wolf had been taking liberties while Jannlou was

distracted, edging close to some of the choicer morsels. A growl and a cuff served as a reminder of their relative status as predators and order was restored.

Don't think, Jannlou told himself. *No words. Just be bear.*

When he'd eaten his fill, he grunted at the wolf. Whether it was taken to mean, 'Think yourself lucky this time,' or 'It's all yours now,' or even 'Good hunting, friend,' Jannlou neither knew nor cared. A bear didn't worry what other Forest creatures did or thought.

The mist drifted low among the trees, blanching out all trace of sun or even clouds above the canopy. Treetops wavered into view like the scribbled remnant of a prophecy in green ink, then disappeared again.

Meat was heavy eating and Jannlou relished the prospect of roots, seeds and flower-heads. Now he knew he was supposed to gorge and fatten up, he could combine business with pleasure. He scented gopher and a stash of whitebark pine nuts, another creature's preparation for winter. He dug fast and scooped up fistfuls. The gopher was either absent or wise enough to stay hidden. But in truth, Jannlou had eaten enough meat and preferred the crunch of nuts. No need to be too fussy as his body would take what was useful and expel what wasn't. The whitebark seeds would be none the worse for their journey through his body and the Forest would be renewed.

A hollow in the roots of a great cedar attracted his attention and, after some further digging, he had a den suitable for a nap. Just a brief daytime shut-eye, not the long winter sleep that was coming.

What's winter? he wondered again but felt full and drowsy so he let himself drift away, cosy in the dried needles and leaves.

He had no idea how long he'd slept because the same timeless white ghosted among the trees. T was still daytime, though, so he'd follow the trail all the way to the Citadel, stopping at the sunflowers for more snacking. Satiating his appetite was as good a purpose in life as any other, Jannlou decided. Simple.

Then he scented bear and life grew complicated again. His hackles rose at the thought of meeting a mature male and the inevitable fight that would follow. He remembered Mielitta climbing a tree to escape the tiger, his own defiance of the beast and the bear that came as if summoned to their aid. How would that bear react to meeting Jannlou now, in the form that had been born that day? Could it be as it was with the wolf? Tolerance if not friendship? After all, that bear had come to his aid.

He sniffed again and realised this bear was female, not brown like him but a black bear with cubs.

Jannlou walked on, left paws moving, right paws moving, seeming slow and clumsy but covering the ground far faster than he could in human form. A swirl of mist revealed the mother, watching as her three cubs played cuff-and-run or king-of-the-tree. Then she saw Jannlou and in a second she'd chivvied her cubs up a tree, which she guarded, ears back, eyes defiant, ready to fight but hoping not to. The air reeked of fear.

Jannlou looked up. Three pairs of beady black eyes peeked at him through mist and branches. The wise mother had treed her cubs at his approach, teaching them fear of adult males and also how to escape. He could kill the black bear, climb after the cubs, if he chose. The lower bear would always have the advantage in a tree, even if fighting an equal. He wasn't as good at climbing as a black bear but the branches here were spaced just right for him. He shook off the thought. He had no desire to kill other bears. Most of the time, most bears weren't interested in a fight.

Being king of the Forest meant you ate when hungry, fought when angry, slept and played in between, like three happy cubs watched by their mother. Playtime. Jannlou suddenly longed for play as much as for sunflowers. He walked past the black bear, massive and indifferent, eyes on the trail ahead, where it vanished into the mist. How strange that indifference could be a form of mercy.

The ground underfoot became soggy and dipped steeply down on one side, empty of trees in a swathe of churned earth.

The work of woodcutters, perhaps, or boar in their perennial quest for acorns, fungi and roots in damp soil. Jannlou smelled the stagnant water at the bottom, dank rotting plants and a fly-infested miasma.

He was king of this forest so he ran at the slope, threw himself onto his furry behind and skidded his way down the mud-slope on his backside to land with a gentle slurp and suck in the bog below. He thought it a reasonable first attempt but one that could be refined for greater enjoyment. So he scrambled to the top, taking a roundabout route that allowed some purchase on roots and tree stumps. Then he did it again. And again, with a great bear whoop. By his final run he'd stirred up so much activity among the moths living in the bog that he could gulp them in mouthfuls on landing.

Who said you couldn't have fun on your own?

Jannlou performed rudimentary ablutions in the bog water before climbing up to the trail again and continuing to the edge of the Forest, his heart lighter and sunflowers in view.

The subtle scent of oil suggested the seeds were ripe and although the flower heads drooped, they too still had flavour so the bear helped himself to all that was on offer.

Water babbled nearby on its way from the Forest through the water gate into the Citadel and Jannlou lifted his head occasionally, looked across the gloaming to the wall and canopy that had once been his home. By tracing the path of the stream, he could just make out where the water gate must be but it was as grey and impenetrable as the walls and canopy.

What was he hoping for? That Bastien himself would come out of the Citadel, that Jannlou could make things right, that they could be friends again? *Better keep chewing sunflower seeds*, he told himself. He was supposed to be learning self-control so this was a start. He was in control of eating sunflower seeds. And of stopping.

He was due another snooze so he went back to the den he'd made, snug under the cedar roots. He'd sleep until total darkness then enjoy a night hunt. The combination of his sensitive ursine nose with night vision promised ever new discoveries and he was going to enjoy them all to the full.

He woke to the moon slipping in and out of mist veils, like a dancing-girl in the Citadel. But that wasn't what had woken him. Something sharp prodded him in the ribs again. Clearly, he hadn't eaten enough yet to cover those ribs with the protection they needed.

'You want to prove yourself? Come on then. Or are you too fat to get out of bed?'

Is fat supposed to be an insult? the bear wondered lazily but Jannlou knew the human answer and his hackles rose.

He stared through the tree roots at the strange youth above him, carrying a basket and poking him with a knitting needle as long as a lance.

CHAPTER THIRTY-ONE

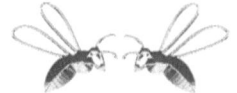

Jannlou charged out of his den, smashing tree roots as he went. He stopped short of the youth, who skipped around in front of him like a suicidal chipmunk. His instinct was to lash out with claws but the roar died in his throat and he held back. He knew how easily he could shred a man's flesh to gore, what fatal weapons his claws and teeth could be. His nightmares reminded him, forcing him to re-live the moment he'd killed Rinduran, over and over.

'Afraid you aren't up to it any more?' The taunt was accompanied with another physical jab, equally pointed.

The assault brought back to mind neither tigers nor mage-warfare but training bouts in the Citadel, Bastien and himself against the other would-be warriors, fighting with sword and shield. Preparing for a bout like this one, against a weak but persistent opponent.

This was no fight for a bear but a lesson in manners to be delivered by a knight. Jannlou resumed his human form, ducked another prod of the knitting needle and laid his hand on his sword-hilt. Stones be thanked that he retained all he'd been wearing as a human when he shifted back, weapons included.

Despite feeling nothing but contempt for this jackanapes, he made the formal bow of respect before a duel, raising the hilt of his sword to touch his forehead. The old ritual carried its own discipline and physical memories, embedded in every muscle and sinew over years of training.

Arven's eyes were white as the mists, his gesture a mockery as he mimicked Jannlou's gesture. A smile tilting the refined bow of his lips, he raised the blunt end of the knitting needle to his forehead before assuming an *en garde* position, as if he were wielding a sword.

He tutted. 'That wouldn't be fair, would it?' he said to himself and the needle shrank to sword-length, gleaming silver now.

Jannlou had not forgotten the prick of blood from Drianne's skin, drawn by this very weapon and he would not make the mistake of underestimating the damage it could do. Nor could he rely on a fair fight against this mage. But he too had some skill in trading insults. Gamesmanship had figured in the Citadel training and Bastien had been a master of the art. What would his friend have said to rile this boy?

'Fair isn't something I expect from your kind.' Jannlou put the same sneer into his tone as Arven had used. Two could play at that game. He made an experimental lunge, slow and clumsy, easily avoided by his opponent. Let Arven think him lumbering.

Jannlou's next stroke was swift, an upwards thrust that caught the needle and carried it away in a sideways follow-through that would have broken Arven's wrist if he had stayed still and kept hold. Instead, he followed the movement with his whole body, leaping impossibly sideways and up onto a tree branch, allowing the momentum to slow gently before he came to a standstill.

Perched on a branch like a mocking-bird, he sang out, 'Every branch, every rock in the Forest is *my* terrain from childhood and the ground's my friend. How well do *you* know the Forest, little bear? Whoops-a-daisy, watch that root.'

Having overreached with his sword, Jannlou was looking up at his target as he tripped over a tree root, which he was sure had not been there seconds earlier. He had to steady himself with his sword or he'd have fallen over.

Like an old man who needs a walking-stick, thought Jannlou, his neck flushing in a wave of embarrassment that spread to his face.

'If you were only a bear, you could climb after me,' taunted Arven, sweeping the needle down in arc below him, then flitting up to a higher branch.

Dark skin was not enough to hide Jannlou's humiliation and he felt the heat of shame hardening to a fireball of rage in his guts. However fleet and acrobatic, Arven would have no chance against a bear, reaching up to claw the light and laughter out of that irritating human frame.

Nobody would know what had happened. Jannlou could tell the truth, that Arven had attacked him, unprovoked and he'd killed in self-defence. Just like when he'd killed Rinduran. And Mielitta thought that was heroic. He should use his second nature, be heroic again.

He growled, looked up into the swirl of mist, reflected in eyes that expressed no fear, no emotion at all, cold as fate.

Jannlou did not shift into bear form.

'You fight like a girl,' he yelled up. 'Come down and fight like a man. Then we'll see who wins.'

The irritating grin grew wider, floating in the mist, disembodied. 'Happy to fight like a girl,' Arven crowed. 'Granny always said I'd thank her one day. But have it your way.' He swung down from the tree and was on a rocky outcrop before Jannlou had time to predict where he'd land.

'Watch your feet,' Arven called but Jannlou did not make the mistake of looking down. He wasn't going to make the same mistake twice and he'd scanned his path for roots and stones before rushing towards the outcrop. So he saw Arven launch himself in the air, not flying but jumping. This time his landing platform was Jannlou himself, who would have missed the move if he'd been studying his feet.

'Whoops,' said Arven cheerfully as he grabbed Jannlou round

the shoulders, twined his legs around his waist. This time the 'whoops' was aimed at his own miscalculation, for Jannlou was not in the least bit off-balance but stood solid as a bear with a spider on its fur. One shake and the annoying insect would be under his foot and stamped upon.

Arven smiled and kissed Jannlou on the cheek; in the Citadel, that would have been a criminal act.

Jannlou instinctively recoiled, too shocked to move. His opponent disengaged, brushed himself down and stood far enough away not to get a sword through his chest. Then he raised the knitting needle to his lips, bowed, this time with respect and threw the needle to the ground.

'You win,' he told a bemused Jannlou.

'You really do fight like a girl,' observed Jannlou once his breathing had calmed and he could trust his voice. He remembered Mielitta hurling herself at him in much the same way. 'Like a girl who's a trick archer.'

'I take that as a compliment!' the strange youth responded. 'Mielitta and I had the same training.'

'But she never met your Granny till now.' Jannlou was confused. 'And how can you say I've won?' Suddenly he didn't want to fight any more. He sat down, weary of enigmas, weary of enemies.

'Who were you fighting?' asked Arven.

Not more tricky words.

'You,' Jannlou replied gruffly, reluctant to enter into this philosophical nonsense.

'And what was your target in the Forest?'

Jannlou just grunted but he knew what Arven was getting at. He'd promised Mielitta he'd learn self-control. There'd been a moment in the duel when he could have lost his temper and he hadn't. Some kind of test. He scowled at Arven, who'd retrieved his basket and both needles, normal size and dull beige, harmless.

'You have no right!' Jannlou was half-minded to resume their duel with a few well-deserved jabs of his own.

Knitting steadily, Arven asked, 'Did you have the right to kill Rinduran?'

Jannlou had never asked himself such a question. He knew how he felt, in nightmares and out of them and whatever Mielitta said about his acts as a bee, he was afraid of his brutal nature. She'd told him often enough that he'd saved them, her, Drianne, Kermon, the bees, the Forest itself – that none of them could have defeated Rinduran. Or done what he had done.

But had it been his right? What did that mean anyway? How odd to be asked such questions by a stranger. Yet how much easier to talk to a stranger than to somebody whose judgement he valued and who would condemn him. In the forgiving mists of the Forest, where all could be shrouded and shifting, Jannlou's self-imposed silence lifted.

Reluctant but curious, he said, 'He killed my father.'

Arven's face was like carved stone and for the first time he hesitated before speaking. 'That does give some rights,' he acknowledged. Then he looked steadily at Jannlou, his black eyes darker than mage-robes, not hiding his pain. 'Your father killed mine,' he said. 'Crimvert.'

The word 'traitor' came automatically to Jannlou's lips, as it always had when anybody in school criticised his powerful father's discipline of citizens. But, as he'd controlled his bear nature, so he held back judgement.

'That does give some rights,' he acknowledged.

'And you killed Bastien's father.' Arven merely stated the fact but Jannlou could see the knitted fabric growing, misty white.

'Where does it end?' asked Jannlou heavily.

'With a kiss.'

There was silence, then Arven laughed. 'I was just needling you.' He looked up, met Jannlou's outraged stare with eyes that danced, growing blacker by the second, mists banished.

'That was my choice, my right.' Arven's tone dropped all laughter, flashing in and out of moods like sunlight through the mists. 'This wasn't just about you. It's my story too. And

Bastien's.' He held up his knitting. If there was a pattern, Jannlou could not see it.

'I will go to the Citadel, find out who killed my mother,' Arven said.

Suddenly, Jannlou felt pity, an emotion he'd forgotten. Pity for all of them and for all they could not put right.

'You can't,' he said. 'I looked, I wanted to, but we are barred and the gate is locked.'

'For now.'

Jannlou had no answer to that. Instead he had his own question. 'What is winter?'

Arven made an airy gesture, embracing the monochrome Forest scenery, swathed in mist. 'The dragon's breath is just a hint of what is to come,' he said. 'Cold whiteness and a great sleep.'

Yes, thought Jannlou. *Eat now and then sleep. That's what it is, winter. Time for me to leave the world to its own devices. But – dragon's breath?*

'What's a dragon?' he asked.

Arven laughed, packed his knitting into the basket. 'Let's go back to the others,' he said.

Which was a win for Jannlou, of sorts. He hoped Mielitta would see it that way. Which of course depended on what they both told her.

'I wouldn't want to upset Mielitta,' he began cautiously.

'She has enough on her mind,' agreed Arven.

So that was settled. Neither of them would speak of what had happened in the mist or of what had been said.

CHAPTER THIRTY-TWO

Bastien smiled at himself in the mirror, experimenting with a slight sneer that made him look even more like a younger version of his father. He felt he had come fully into his inheritance at last: Chief Mage, accepted as Rinduran's successor in every way. He'd even achieved this without magecraft, on which he imagined his father congratulating him. 'Hide your power as much as you can and then use it without mercy when you must.' Too busy with politics, he'd slackened off when it came to training as a mage and a warrior. Now he must put that right. After the next Council meeting.

He flexed his muscles. He was lean and built more for speed than physical power. That had always been Jannlou's forte. When they were friends. He faced the thought rather than banish it as he usually did. The man was a traitor, had chosen the freak over his childhood friend, evil over Perfection. There was no friendship any longer and any memories of past closeness were sullied by Jannlou's betrayal. What would Rinduran have said regarding Jannlou?

As clearly as if his father were in the room, Bastien heard his opinion, voiced so many times. 'You've spent too much time with Jannlou. He's not at your level. And he is his father's son as you are mine. He has served his purpose. It's time for you to distance yourself.' Of course Bastien had been loyal to his friend, kept his secrets. What would his father have done if he'd known Jannlou was a fraud with no magecraft? Suppressed him, no doubt and then perhaps the Battle of the Forest would have gone the Citadel's way. How right his father had been.

Every precious word of his father's advice came back to Bastien now and was all the support he needed for the role he must play. Recently, he'd felt like his father was back beside him, advising him, steadying his resolve.

'You're too kind-hearted, especially towards women. If they're not Perfect, they can't be rescued!' His father had been right about that too. After all he'd done to protect Drianne, to offer her the kind of future as his wife that most ladies would have swooned for, she too had followed the freak. Another traitor.

Well, no more! He was stuck with females around the council table – his hand twinged in memory of his blood oath – but there was nothing to stop him curtailing their influence. Even his little sister had grown too big for her boots and was turning the blacksmith into some kind of mage henchman. Once, she'd been so sure he was a traitor, nagging Bastien all the time on the subject. And now look at them together – thick as thieves. No doubt the smith's muscles were as much the attraction as his magecraft.

Little Vivi had grown out of childhood in the sickroom and now she needed a husband who'd keep her in check. The obvious choice to consolidate the siblings' control of the council was Hamel. Bastien could sense his father's approval. Marriage to Verity would keep both Hamel and Verity in check. The green-hued mage was perhaps not the man of a girl's dreams but Verity would understand the importance of such an alliance. She'd benefited from Rinduran's advice too. He would give the matter further thought. The forthcoming Courtship Dance would be the Perfect opportunity for Hamel to woo the girl and a touch of magecraft could compensate for many shortcomings.

Bastien smiled at himself again in the mirror, satisfied with his start to the day's work. The Courtship Dance was already a pleasing prospect as he'd invited a partner himself, a very pretty girl who never stuttered. He must remember her name before the event. He felt in Perfect condition despite the lack of training and her eyes had conveyed the appreciation he deserved. Before long he'd be commissioning two new badges to add to his belt: engagement and marriage trophies. This time, he would leave no time in between the two events so nothing could go wrong.

His good mood was such that Bastien even nodded to the various servants who flattened themselves against the wall as he stalked the corridors en route to the Mage's Tower. Gone were the days when he and Jannlou chased the freak through the castle or cornered her stuttering follower in the archery yard. The Forest could keep all three of them! The whole castle was his now. He skipped two at a time up the spiral steps to the Council Chamber and was still smiling when he entered. Until he took in the scene.

All the seats were occupied but in a different arrangement and with a new councillor present. Bastien felt his stomach knot at the double insult. A councillor had died and been replaced without him knowing? Then he realised that there was no new councillor, merely Lady Puggy in her old avatar. Lank mousy hair, dumpling-faced and oozing danger.

Merely in her old avatar? His stomach knotted again. How and why had she changed back? Had she regained her mind? And her magecraft? She had Hamel fixed in a Medusa stare and the green mage was clawing the table as if he wished the surface were her skin.

Beside her were the other female mages, Fabrisse and Yacinthe, glaring at the wife-Councillor opposite them, who looked nervous and held her husband's hand.

If Bastien read his sister's expression aright, she was dispensing contempt evenly to all the other women around the table, with Mage-Smith Kermon at her side. The sooner he put a stop to *that*, the better, thought Bastien. At least they weren't holding hands.

There was a flutter of acknowledgement that the Chief Mage had joined them, more a change in the quality of the silence than anything, then the councillors resumed their silent war of attrition.

'Session commenced,' Bastien announced for the record, which wrote itself in the Council's Red Book. The record could also be unwritten and rewritten but until that happened, it provided a useful aide-memoire for the Chief Mage.

'Agenda items are: a report on the progress of the Adulthood Test; plans for the Courtship Dance; and of course any other business.' No councillor was ever foolhardy enough to raise an item under A.O.B. and risk alienating everyone at the table, who would have to respond to who-knew-what with no warning.

And now Bastien had to respond to who-knew-what without prior warning. He'd rather do that to begin with or he'd never concentrate on the rest of the meeting. His day was spoiled anyway so he dived in. 'Lady Puggy, we've not seen you in this form for some time so if there's some good news we should hear, let's start with that before proceeding to business.'

Bastien was awarded a benevolent smile of approval from the Mage-Smith, whose patronage he did not appreciate. He would have added a glare of his own to the general ambience but he controlled himself.

'Why assume it's good news for you, Lord Bastien?' came Puggy's reply, in those harsh northern vowels that made him wince. 'And that's *Mage* Puggy, if you please. It was always Mage Puggy, even when I was – ill. And yes, I'm back, with a vengeance.' Her sincerity in her last words was clear as her gaze lingered on Hamel, then on Bastien.

For the stones' sake, thought Bastien, irritated. He was only being polite and now he'd have to put up with that thing women did, where every word you said was turned against you. Council meetings would take forever if some kind of female agenda took over.

'That's wonderful,' he said. 'Shall we get to business?'

'Yes,' said Hamel, at the same time as Puggy spoke.

'This *is* business,' she said and the two female mages nodded their heads vigorously.

'We were wrong,' said Mage Fabrisse. 'We should never have accepted a non-mage at the Council table.' She pointed at the woman opposite. 'How can she possibly decide Perfect policy when she has no talents? When she's been,' her mouth formed a moue of distaste as she dropped the word like a turd on the table, 'forged. As a lady.' She shook her head and Zora clutched her husband's hand more tightly.

Mage Yacinthe took up the argument. '*She* never gave up husbands and children for her calling. We earned the right to be here. She didn't.'

'I'm sorry to say this,' Mage Puggy's expression made it clear that she wasn't. 'But Lady Verity has no place at this table either. She's not a mage and shouldn't be a Councillor, never mind a *leader*.' The spit from her vehemence reached one of the wives, who surreptitiously wiped her face.

Verity's cream skin flushed in hectic spots as if allergy-ridden as she waited for a male mage to defend her. Bastien said nothing. After all, they had a point. He agreed with them but could say nothing without triggering the blood oath.

Kermon's face contorted as if he were wrestling with himself. Sweating profusely, he gasped, 'Lady Verity was never forged and has a mind every bit as sharp as her sainted father's, may the stones praise his name.' Then his eyes glazed over and his mouth clamped shut.

Truly, there's madness in the air today, thought Bastien, drumming his fingers on the table with the irritating rhythm he'd caught from Hamel, who spoke next, his voice at the same pitch as the squeaking nails. But people listened.

'Mage Puggy makes a very good point,' he began, which meant he despised her and her opinion but could turn it against her. 'And I think we should respect her views. No, more than respect. We should act upon them. I suggest we have two councils. One for female mages and one for the rest of us.'

Uproar broke out, with everyone except Bastien and Zora shouting at once. Suggestions of a female-only council vied with suggestions that there be an election for replacement of all the councillors. The thought of involving ordinary citizens in a vote was so shocking to all that there was a temporary halt to the rumpus.

Broken by Puggy. 'The Council is quite capable of coming to an agreement by voting here, in the Chamber.'

'Just so long as we're clear what we're voting on and why,' challenged Hamel. 'I don't remember anybody nominating you as Chief Mage. Perhaps your husband should remind you of your place on the Council.

All eyes turned to Kermon but none as full of loathing as his wife's.

'I preferred my wife as she was before,' he responded. Nobody knew whether he meant before this new change or before the change before that, or whether that was support for her opinions or not.

Puggy laughed. 'You see. Even my husband, who could be said to be responsible for my change.'

Which one? Bastien wondered.

'Even my husband is at a loss to explain how this Council has moved so far from Perfection.'

Verity had stood up, crimson-faced. She was trying to speak but unable to get a word in edgeways as the mages all shouted over each other to make their points. Not that anybody was listening but points had to be made, all the same.

In one of the lulls, Puggy managed a full-volume interjection. 'I want all my magecraft back. I thought I was dying or I'd never have given it away. Where's that girl, the one who went into the walls as a witness, so I can take it back?'

'The girl?' Hamel's glee was tangible, turning the chamber a ghostly green as he turned the knife. 'You mean the girl who was *forged* with you? The one who was going to marry Lord Bastien?'

The others flinched at his lack of tact but no lightning forked from the head of the table. Before he exercised his authority, Bastien needed to know what this was all about; how much power had Puggy regained and whether he could turn her request to his own purpose.

'Yes. Where is she?' Puggy asked, unable to hide her desperation. Which told Bastien that she'd not been aware of all that had gone on while she was in her more attractive form. He must remember not to say that aloud. She'd also made clear how little magecraft she had left. Enough to maintain a form she was accustomed to, certainly. But any more than that? She was probably more dazzle than delivery.

'The Forest.' Hamel delivered the *coup de grâce* with enthusiasm. 'Playing handmaiden to the Queen of the Warrior Bees.'

'Then we'll wage war on the Forest!' declared Puggy, with all the fervour of ignorance, provoking spiteful laughter from Hamel.

This sparked a hubbub of enraged questions from Puggy and explanations from the kinder mages. Verity was still trying to make herself heard.

Under the row going on across the table, the very quietness of a male voice near him caught Bastien's attention.

'You shouldn't be here, my dear,' Kermon told Verity. 'It's too distressing for you. Go to your chamber where it's quiet and let your brother deal with this. You're only making his life more difficult and he can't protect you at the same time as managing the Council. I'm sure he'll talk to you later, tell you all about it and you'll be a great help to him.'

Bastien couldn't believe he'd heard the Mage-Smith speak so reasonably. Maybe he'd misjudged him, as Verity had initially.

She didn't look kindly on Kermon now but thrust her chair back so hard it toppled. Ignoring the chair, the noise and the general chaos, she ran out of the Chamber, looking as if she would burst into tears.

'It's for the best,' the Mage-Smith told Bastien, letting his quiet voice carry across the empty space between them. 'Now, you can concentrate. Time for a little magecraft demonstration, I think.'

Bastien ignored the somewhat patronising tone of the encouragement and acted upon it; for the first time in the Council Chamber he unleashed the full force of his powers. Every Councillor but Kermon was frozen in a position of ugly shouting, muted.

'Please record this,' Bastien ordered. An artist's impression joined the written notes in the Red Book.

'Now, while you are listening, this is what will happen.'

Kermon nodded his approval.

CHAPTER THIRTY-THREE

Kermon looked at the final year students, squirming in their seats, affected by their teacher's nerves and his own presence. Should he try to be friendly, put them at ease? No. That would be dishonest when he was here to test their readiness for Adulthood. Not like in the old days, when Shenagra would stalk the rows of all the classes with children older than eleven, seeking out the rebels, marking them for suppression during the Maturity Test.

The new Test would be for the oldest students only, all of them. He was not going to fail any but if he entered their minds, knew their strengths and weaknesses, he could partner them up for mutual support.

Maybe some New Adults could help them practise before they gave their presentations in the Great Hall.

Pathetic! If you keep the failures, Perfection will grow weaker and weaker. Bastien understands this now. His inner critic rarely left Kermon in peace these days and he felt the counterweight dragging down his every attempt to fulfil his mission with the children. Even while he was making an inspirational speech about their future contributions to Perfection and the Citadel, Kermon could hear the nagging.

Do your job. Find the mages and the freaks. Let the female mages see how much better their lives will be as Ladies, cherished and fulfilled in their natures. Suppress the freaks.

Kermon was shocked by the word as much as the thought. How could he even *think* the word *freak*? What would Mielitta think of him? But she was so far away, leading a different life. And he was here, with real children in front of him.

'He won't hurt you,' Janette whispered to a girl sitting beside her, whose frizzy plaits stuck out sideways like rope handles on a bucket. Kermon brushed her mind, read her colours. Not a mage, not a – not a rebel.

Maybe he could be honest and less of an authority figure. He took his cue from Janette. 'I'm not going to hurt you but I would like you to open your minds to me so I know how to help you when we visit the walls.'

Janette's face was glowing with the enthusiasm he recognised from her work in the forge and he kicked himself for creating the wrong expectation. 'The boys will visit the walls with me and the girls will be their partners, their anchors. This is a vital role because it's easy for an adult to become lost in the walls and an anchor will keep you safe. Without girls and women, we could become lost.'

Perhaps he hadn't properly conveyed the terrors of being lost because Janette looked at him with big-eyed disappointment. A mage and a rebel, he realised, watching her colours flare rainbow. Trouble in the making.

Suppress her, the voice hissed. *Do it now before she causes a man's death or worse.*

Kermon's gift did not include reading the future and his training focused on the present so he was able to ignore the insistent advice without too much difficulty. Sometimes he felt like he'd stepped into a little stream, aiming merely to cross it, but the opposite bank moved ever further away, leaving him stuck in the mud, sinking deeper. Without help. Without an anchor.

An anchor drags you down deeper.

He couldn't even shape his own metaphors! As for Janette, he looked at her with irritation now. What right did she have to be disappointed in him? She was a child, with no idea of the responsibilities a mage carried. Typical female, wanting more all the time while suffering none of the pressure men carried. How could she begin to comprehend an ordinary mage's work, never mind a Councillor's or a Chief Mage's? What would Bastien do with the freaks among these children, when they were adults?

Then Kermon remembered the pact between Forest and Citadel, Mielitta's terms. Anyone who did not fit in Perfection had the right to leave, to choose the Forest and exile. For one glorious moment, he wondered whether he could go back, leave this double life, rediscover sunlight and birdsong.

Then the mud sucked him down again. He'd be a self-confessed spy and traitor, everything Verity had once believed about him. He'd never be allowed to leave – or even live. There was no way out of his situation and he must continue to play the part he'd assumed. *All* the parts he'd assumed.

Some youngsters were more open than others but none of them resisted Kermon's exploration of their minds, child by child, and he was soon too full of their fears, hopes and memories to have room for self-doubts. A mother's warmth, a cut knee, a friend's hand in yours. Horrors lurking under the bed, fear of being left out, shame at letting your father down. Kermon duly consigned to his own memory each individual's collection of moments.

'Now, boys, your teacher tells me you've each chosen one item of food and done your research in the library, ready to go into the walls with me.'

There were nods in response from the more open-minded.

Lady Amity interjected, 'The girls have done the research too. I thought it would be good for them all to work independently; each of them chose something different and kept it secret, so as not to influence each other. I hope I didn't do wrong. This is all so new...' She tailed off.

'No, that's Perfect.' Kermon wondered how he could find out what they'd all chosen, without seeming to put them on the spot or praise some more than others. This was so complicated! Luckily, the teacher had that organised too.

'Get your pens out, everybody.'

Classroom routine hadn't changed since Kermon had sat here and paper appeared as if by magecraft on each desk. Not that any schoolteacher was a mage. That would be a waste of talented citizens. But good organisation did sometimes seem like magic.

'Now, write down your name and the food topic you chose, then fold up your paper and pass it to the end of the row.' Eight youngsters brought the papers out to the front, where Lady Amity unfolded them all so she could present them to Kermon. As she read them, her face grew ashen.

'I-I-I'm sorry, Mage-Smith Kermon, I don't know what's got into them. I've never known them be so insolent.' She turned to the students, her expression fierce. 'If this is some kind of prank, there will be repercussions and I will find out who the ringleaders are.'

Kermon read the first few papers. There was no need to read any more. He remembered their day out in the Forest, the bees giving individual attention to each of these hostages. The outing which must not be mentioned, on which all of Mielitta's hopes rested.

The teenagers looked at each other in unfeigned confusion.

'I don't understand,' said one of the bolder ones. 'I chose honey and that's what I wrote down.'

'Me too,' chimed in another. And another. And another, until they realised they'd all chosen honey. Their bewilderment was so genuine that even the teacher looked for somebody else to blame.

Her face darkened. 'The Librarian Mage,' she said. 'She must have made some kind of suggestion. They don't even know that their minds have been influenced! That's not–' Then she remembered she was speaking to a mage and whatever observation she'd been about to make on the right uses of power went unspoken.

Mielitta would be delighted at this proof that the children remembered their taste of Forest. But what should he do? He could hardly encourage forty speeches on the same topic. The audience would be asleep before the third! And he didn't want the teacher to know the truth behind their choice of topic. Or how *he* knew.

Dealing with the practical aspect first, and giving the teacher something to occupy her mind, Kermon said, 'This is exactly the sort of teamwork that will help us in the walls, so we can all research honey. But each pair needs a second topic to present to the Great Hall so Lady Amity,' he nodded to her, a clear instruction, 'will write twenty topics on pieces of paper.'

'Each girl will dip into the hat,' he continued. That would compensate the girls for their passive role in the Adulthood Test. A rather severe black hat appeared, upside-down, waiting for the papers on which Lady Amity was madly scribbling, sucking the end of her pen from time to time in an endearing way as she sought inspiration.

Kermon ended, 'And I will write down the names of your pairs so you can talk about the new topic and plan some more research.'

That should cover it. If there gaps in the organisation, he could rely on Lady Amity to fill them. He smiled at her, then let his own mind open to his deep thinking while his magecraft worked on all the information he'd gathered that morning.

Suddenly aware that all eyes in the room were on him, Kermon wondered whether that was because they were waiting to know their partners' names or because he looked so strange. He staggered, drained, then summoned the strength to set his conclusions down on paper. He sat down while the pen filled the unscrolling paper with neat duos of names.

'Lady Amity, if you will? Then they should do library research as soon as possible. We will meet at the walls in two days' time.'

With a nod that probably seemed curt, Kermon left the schoolroom. He needed rest before his next appointment, one he'd been putting off. He had to speak to Verity.

Lady Verity to you, his inner critic corrected.

He had no idea what he'd said or done to annoy her but she'd clearly been upset after the Council meeting and they'd had no chance to talk since they'd liberated Mage Puggy.

Lady Puggy. She's barely got the magecraft to maintain her ugliness.

And then, later, he could at last contact Mielitta with good news. The children had been affected by their taste of honey. There was hope for the Future. Maybe he wouldn't be trapped in the Citadel forever.

Freaks. Suppress them now or you'll regret it. Especially the girls.

Where did such thoughts come from? Sometimes he thought his most deadly enemy was inside his own head. The now-familiar pain struck him and he held his breath, counted to four. Gone again. He shook his head to clear it and rehearsed what he was going to say to Verity.

CHAPTER THIRTY-FOUR

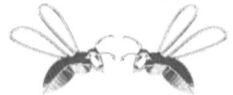

Verity had the same expression on her face that Kermon had last seen on a disappointed fourteen-year-old in the schoolroom. He suddenly realised that Verity was probably the same age as or younger than Janette, despite her striped robe and air of maturity. When had he forgotten how young she was? And yet, her youth was all that excused his lack of propriety.

She'd replied to his message, saying that she would come to the forge. That too was a reminder for him that such meetings had become clandestine. The only places they should meet were in the Council or in the Great Hall and in company. Even if he'd been more sensitive to her reputation before their meeting, he could hardly ask Mage Puggy to act as chaperone. This would have to be the last such meeting. He could not afford to draw Bastien's anger over a perceived insult to his sister.

About time you realised that, observed the cynical voice in his head.

Now she was here, her mood seemed no better. She should be grateful to him for getting her out of the unpleasant shouting in the Council Chamber, so unfit for delicate ears. He looked at her soft white skin in the light from the spheres, unblemished.

Knowing that Verity would come, Kermon had not lit the fires so the forge was dull, almost ordinary in the greylight. His young apprentices were undoubtedly busy in frantic library research and would not trouble them. The Adult Assistants were at work sanding handles, polishing badges and blades, all the menial tasks that Kermon could delegate without any supervision being required. They still had ears though and this conversation required privacy. He'd rather be reported to Bastien for being alone with Lady Verity than for plotting treason with her.

Whether it *was* treason, he wasn't sure, but he was certain it could be reported as such.

'Lady Verity, what a surprise,' he said and she raised an eyebrow but accepted the game.

'I have a commission from my brother,' she informed him, high-handed. 'A new badge for his belt, a betrothal symbol. He wants a marriage trophy at the same time.'

It was Kermon's turn to raise an eyebrow. He suppressed the urge to enquire whether the two badges concerned the same or different women and merely picked up the ledger and pen to note the details.

The clatter of the assistants at work gave him an idea. 'Perhaps you'd like to step outside with me where there is less noise,' he suggested, indicating the small back door which led to the greensward in front of the Maturity Barn.

'It is noisy,' she agreed and followed him meekly outside, to the enclosed area that had witnessed so many Maturity Celebrations. Her air of gentility vanished the moment she'd shut the door behind her.

'This is ridiculous!' she exploded. 'People talk over me in the Council Meeting so I can't get a word in and now you–' her glance made it clear that 'you' was short for 'lowest life-form not fit to grovel at my feet.' She continued, 'You dare waste my time bringing me here in order to talk rubbish. I don't want to hear your apologies.'

That was a relief. Kermon hadn't even thought of apologising because he couldn't remember doing anything wrong. He opened his mouth to speak but Verity hadn't finished and he thought it impolitic to interrupt.

'And another thing. I might not be a mage or a man but I have more understanding of this Citadel and everyone who lives in it than all the mages at that table combined.' She reflected a second. 'Except Bastien,' she added hastily.

Kermon opened his mouth again.

'And another thing. I might not be a man but that's the whole point of me being there. I represent a different point of view. And I'm not going to be silenced and sidelined.'

Kermon waited.

'You should have told them to be quiet and let me speak.'

Ah. That's what he'd done wrong. As had Bastien, but he was not going to use that defence.

No need for a defence. She's turning into a woman. Irrational, governed by her emotions. Just pay her a compliment and get on with what you have to say. Time she was married.

'You don't look at all ill these days.' Kermon dropped the words into the first available pause.

You call that a compliment? Why am I stuck with such an imbecile?

'No,' Verity agreed. 'I'm not.'

Kermon got to the point. 'Have you spoken to Mage Puggy? Since we … you know?'

Verity's expression turned brooding. 'I'm beneath her now. I preferred her the way she was before, beautiful, stupid and admiring. Now she's bitter and sneers at non-mages, at men too. Was she always like that? Did we do the wrong thing bringing her back?'

Yes.

'No,' said Kermon. 'Forging people is wrong, even if they're not how you want them to be. I mean, even if they don't fit into Perfection. Everybody has a right to his or her deep thinking, even if they're horrible people.'

She looked at him, eyes narrowed. Had he gone too far?

'She is, isn't she,' Verity stated. 'Truly horrible. But we might be able to use her.'

Startled, Kermon asked, 'How?'

'She wants to find the girl, get her powers back. And so do we, to get rid of them all. Puggy can help us. And we have leverage on her.'

Kermon couldn't believe his ears. No wonder he always forgot how young Verity was.

'She told us she loved women, in some unnatural way,' Verity explained, as if telling him the time of day. 'I think there is one special woman, so that is Mage Puggy's weakness. Also, she has little magecraft and she has an enemy on the Council, so we can make the most of that too.'

'Hamel,' Kermon said, just to show he was keeping up.

'Exactly. So what I want you to do is to make contact with those freaks in the Forest. I'm sure you know how, if you haven't done so already.' She waved her hands airily. 'Oh, don't worry. I trust you. I know everything you've done with the children and I would know if you'd betrayed me. So, make contact and tell them everything. Tell them you've married Puggy and got her back from the forging – partly – and that she'd love to meet up with that girl again. They have so much in common and everything, blah blah blah. It should be easy because you don't have to lie one bit. We'll just make the connection, little by little until everybody wants to meet up and then–' Her eyes flashed.

Kermon didn't need to be told what was to happen next.

Verity took his assent for granted. 'Speaking of Hamel, there is something you should know. I'm afraid this must be our last meeting in this manner, unless there is something of major importance and then I will summon you.'

What did it have to do with Hamel? The meeting was whirling out of Kermon's control. He felt aggrieved, despite the fact he'd planned to tell Verity this was the last time they'd meet alone. Or perhaps because of that.

Verity looked at him with that candour he'd thought childish and now knew wasn't. Whether it was the years she'd spent in a solitary sickroom or her innate nature, she was not like the other Ladies.

She's not a freak!

Kermon had spent the morning evaluating the minds of students and he had total confidence in his judgement. Verity was different. Not a mage, not a rebel, but different. And she didn't know it – yet.

'Speaking of Hamel,' she continued, 'Chief Mage Bastien has suggested to me that an alliance with Mage Hamel would be favourable to the equilibrium of the Council.'

Kermon couldn't take it in.

'You're going to marry Hamel?'

'Yes,' she said, quite composed but with a warning light in her eye. Neither of them was supposed to mention Hamel's repulsive physique or the age difference or his vile habits or …

'You're sure?' asked Kermon, trying to sneak a surreptitious glimpse of her real thoughts.

'It is a good match for the stability of the Citadel,' she declared. 'Which is my dearest wish. And,' she looked at him darkly, 'nobody will cut across me in Council when I speak, not when I'm Hamel's wife as well as Bastien's sister. That will never happen again or there will be magecraft spilling across the table on my behalf.'

Kermon bowed his understanding.

A woman's trade. Marriage for power. Her father's daughter crowed his inner voice. *Excellent choices, my children.*

'We shall make the betrothal public at the Courtship Dance and marry shortly after, as will Bastien and his bride.'

Kermon had forgotten all about the badge Bastien wanted but before he could ask the details and note them in the ledger, Verity gulped and said, 'I want a favour from you. A wedding gift, if you will. Please.'

'That depends on what it is,' he replied cautiously and earned another withering glance.

'I wouldn't ask if it were impossible, silly. I can't have an Adulthood Test because of who I am and it's too late now but I want you to take me into the walls. Pretend I'm your student, let me do the whole visit just like the boys will. I don't want to be just an anchor. I want the whole experience like my father had.'

Tell her no!

'We could both get into serious trouble,' warned Kermon, his heart thumping. 'And I don't just mean in the walls but that too! We won't have an anchor.'

'We won't need one. I can find my way back. It's in my blood, I'm sure it is. And if anybody finds out, they'll forgive me anything because I'm marrying Hamel. It's not as if we're doing something against Perfection. I only want to find out about some food.' She laughed.

Kermon's stomach flipped. He knew what she was going to choose as her topic. She'd been with the other children in the Forest, witnessed the bees delivering honey to their designated boy or girl. She'd seen the beehive where the honey came from. She too must have been affected by her experience in the Forest, even though she hadn't tasted the honey – she'd killed the bee who brought it to her and been stung. Maybe the sting had changed her like it changed Mielitta.

Maybe Verity would be the link between the Citadel and the Forest. The bees could persuade her not to pursue her vendetta with Mielitta and Kermon would be free of this double life. He could be loyal to everyone he cared about.

'I think I know what topic you want to research,' he said slowly.

She clapped her hands, childish again. 'I knew you would. Chocolate torte.' She beamed at him triumphantly.

'Of course,' he told her but he couldn't find an answering smile. He was doomed.

'Will you try to rescue more forged citizens?' she asked him.

'I think not,' he replied, his thoughts scattered.

'You can contact *them* now,' she told him. 'You have *lots* they will want to know.'

Long after Verity had gone, Kermon gazed at the grassette, seeing nothing.

At last, Verity is coming into the walls to join me. Such a pity it's not Bastien but it's a start.

CHAPTER THIRTY-FIVE

What did Mielitta see when she looked at him through her arrowhead? Fire, steel and a liar?

Kermon had forgotten how she affected him. When he didn't see her, he could pretend he no longer felt anything but absence merely intensified the kick in the guts when he saw her again. He clutched Perfection Unfinished, the patterned steel a cold reminder of reality, but he was still transported into the Forest as he looked at the wavering image. Her long red hair danced with bees as she shook her head, imperious, unique, beautiful. Like the forest, she dazzled. And she cared about him.

'Where have you been?' she asked, without waiting for a reply. 'I've been so worried. *We've* been so worried. The bees told me what it's like to be stranded overnight when the hive entrance is closed by the beekeeper. And you've been shut up so long, too long, away from us. And then I saw you marrying Puggy. That's insane. We've decided to get you out.'

Then she paused.

'I don't think–' began Kermon but she cut him off, her eyes flashing, decisive.

It's easier when women aren't on the Council. Either they complain about being talked over or they never stop. But you carry on as always, a nice little errand boy for both of them. I'll just keep quiet. For now.

Kermon ignored the unhelpful contribution from his inner critic and listened. He could make his point more forcefully if he knew what he was arguing against. After all, he'd won the argument as to who should go back to the citadel with the children – more's the pity. Looking back at how nobly he'd sacrificed his life was like watching the children in the schoolroom.

'One of the mages used to take a party of lumberjacks out of the Citadel to get wood for all the special uses still allowed; handles, bows and so on,' Mielitta was explaining. 'You can say you need wood and then they're bound to send out a party. You can go with them and escape to us. If that's not possible, let us know when they're coming into the Forest. We'll find them. follow them back to the Citadel, break in after them and get you. We're not leaving you stranded. Something's wrong, I know it is.'

'Crimvert,' said Kermon, buying time so he could think. 'Crimvert was the mage who used to leave the Citadel. Nobody does now. And the water gate's sealed. There's no way in or out any more.'

Somebody behind Mielitta reacted to Crimvert's name and she turned to say something.

'Who's *we?*' asked Kermon, realising there were strangers present and that Mielitta was in a room, not a tree in sight. 'Where are you? What's been going on?'

He felt even more distant from the others as he listened to some tale of a beekeeper and her grandson, Crimvert's son, who had taught Drianne and Jannlou to control their powers. He took in the facts and would process the information later. The conversation was becoming more and more difficult, overburdened with information. Meanwhile, his own time to speak was diminishing to nothing.

What should he say? What was his target? To stop their rescue plans, obviously.

To tell Drianne about Puggy, as Verity had suggested.

Well, it wouldn't do any harm, and would fit both his conflicting loyalties. 'No, there's no problem.' He made his voice light and cheerful. 'In fact, I've been busy working on your plans and I have good news,' he told Mielitta and anybody else who could hear him. 'The children *have* been changed by the Forest.'

He told Mielitta what had happened in the schoolroom and all the plans for the new Adulthood Test, approved by Council.

'So I can't leave now,' he finished. 'My work's only just beginning. And I have support from Verity.' He corrected himself quickly. 'Lady Verity.'

The red hair stilled and the bees vanished from sight as they usually did when Mielitta was irritated.

'That insipid whiner. What do you mean *support?*'

Kermon fought his instinct to give an impassioned defence of Verity's character and potential. That would not have gone down well and, anyway, he excused himself, he was short of time. 'You made Lady Verity an equal leader with Bastien,' he reminded her. 'So I have been cultivating them both.' He liked the sound of that. *Cultivating* was a good word, avoided the suggestion of friendship. 'You know what Citadel politics is like. And Lady Verity is a huge asset to our Maturity programme. She's changing.'

'Well, just be careful. Don't trust her.' A few scout bees reappeared, checked on Mielitta's mood and presumably buzzed an all-clear to the others, judging by the increased numbers flying around.

'Mage Puggy. You married her?' Mielitta's tone posed more than one question.

Kermon delivered his prepared speech. 'It's a marriage of convenience. She was to be given to Hamel as if she was a toy. I wanted to save her from that and also try to get her back, undo the forging. What she did saved Drianne and she deserved better.'

All true. No need to mention Verity's involvement.

'They haven't gone back on their word, have they? Started forging again? Bastien's blood oath should kill him if he breaks it but I don't trust the mages. They'll find a way round our treaty if they can. And is it possible, unforging?'

'It was possible with Puggy but dangerous.' Mostly to him and Verity. 'She has regained her previous choice of avatar and her personality seems to be much as it used to be.' If Mielitta thought Verity vindictive, she should face Puggy across the Council table.

'I remember,' said Mielitta. 'When I was a servant in the Council Chamber. She smelled of roses, thorns and blood.'

'She played her role in Perfection. As Maturity Mage she carried out the Test as ruthlessly as it was later done to her.'

Should he tell the truth about Tannlei's murder? About her preference for women? If he did, too many emotions would be unleashed. Mielitta had worshipped her teacher as much as Drianne did Mielitta. And talking about Puggy's nature would lead too easily to her allegation about Drianne, hardly something to reveal with others present.

He remembered what he was supposed to say. 'But she did save Drianne. She wants to meet her, to see that her sacrifice was worthwhile.' He should have added 'and to get her powers back' but he didn't. Why give a warning when such a meeting would never happen? He'd be able to report to Verity with a clear conscience, telling no lies.

'She's not all bad,' he added. Nobody was, he told himself.

Mielitta had that look of concentration which meant she was communing either with her bees or with Drianne.

'Maybe in the future,' she said. 'Drianne *would* like to thank her.'

Not if Kermon could help it.

'I'm taking the Maturity Candidates into the walls tomorrow.' Then he remembered. 'I'll keep looking for clues, about your parents, but…' The day after that he'd promised to take Verity in search of chocolate torte. 'And then after that comes the Courtship Dance. Oh and Lady Verity is going to marry Hamel.'

'What!' Mielitta wasn't the only one gasping. 'She's only a little girl and he's—'

Kermon knew all too well what Hamel was so there was no point saying anything.

'Is this another marriage of convenience?' asked Mielitta, an edge to her voice.

'It's an alliance,' explained Kermon. Somehow the word made less sense when spoken to the Queen of the Warrior Bees than when the co-ruler of the Council had justified her actions.

'It's an abomination!' said Mielitta. 'But I suppose you can't marry every woman in the Citadel you take pity on so she must live out her own doom.'

Kermon flushed. He felt exposed at the mention of him marrying Verity. These Forest dwellers talked too freely about his private life and had lost touch with what Perfection required, if you were to live there and survive.

Something moved on Mielitta's shoulder, half-masked by her hair. Jannlou's hand, stroking the curve of her bare neck, reassuring her. *Don't listen to their words: watch their hands,* he told himself.

Mesmerised, he watched the large brown hand's rhythmic motion, the way the fingernails curved into claws, denting but not breaking the golden skin, then retracting as the hand – paw? – moved back out of sight.

Bear. Jannlou. Kermon struggled to make sense of what he saw while Mielitta seemed to notice nothing unusual.

That's because she doesn't think it's unusual. Two freaks.

Kermon tasted bile. 'I'll have to go,' he said, teeth gritted. 'Don't worry if you don't hear from me for a while. I'll be fine.'

He broke off the connection but could still see the warrior's hand, strong but gentle, asking no permission to claim the love of Kermon's life, in front of him. And then the same hand metamorphosing into something animal. There were marriages of convenience and alliances – and then there was what lay between Jannlou and Mielitta. What was the word she used? An abomination. Yes, that was it. An abomination. Kermon hated them both, the bee and the bear, sub-humans. He set to work with a hammer.

Well into the night, dripping with sweat, the Mage-Smith watched the fire die down in the forge. He held the arrowhead and turned the conversation over and over in his mind. Having wrung all the pain he could out of every aspect of his contact with the Forest, he pondered the information he'd collected.

Why had Drianne and Jannlou needed to learn self-control from this Arven person Mielitta had mentioned? Because Drianne had misused her magecraft. Why? She was usually so gentle, compassionate, a softening influence on Mielitta. Like Kermon, she'd give up her life for Mielitta in a heartbeat. He mused on that for a minute, let all he knew about Drianne swirl into a pattern that made sense.

Why had Jannlou needed to learn self-control? He had no magecraft. But he had his massive strength, warrior's skills – and claws. He was the saviour of the Battle of the Forest, Bastien's nightmare, Rinduran's murderer.

Kermon began to shake, fury and fear blending into a fever.

'Do you love him?' he asked Mielitta. To that question, he did know the answer. He'd always known. He was tired and his inner voice was no longer a critic but a comfort with its clear advice, its promise.

Bring Verity into the walls. Everything will be Perfect again.

CHAPTER THIRTY-SIX

'We shouldn't be doing this,' Kermon told Verity, as they stood facing the wall at the bottom of the spiral staircase in the Mages' Tower.

Her confidence was unshakeable. 'Everything went well yesterday. You told me the children behaved Perfectly.'

'They did.' Even Janette had fulfilled her role of anchor for Nathan, with no sign of resentment. The boys had entered the walls as a group, found their bearings and Kermon had tested the agreed signal, a mental summons they'd practised in class. Then they'd followed their individual research paths until Kermon recalled them. They'd followed Kermon's instructions to the letter and his own control over wall time had been faultless.

There was no reason to think anything would go wrong for Verity, who was so much more mature than those she called children. Unless they were caught. Kermon could only imagine how Bastien would react if he knew his beloved sister had been on an illicit, unchaperoned jaunt into the walls.

Promising himself that she would not be out of his sight for one second, he took her hand. He steeled himself against the jolt that went through him, then enjoyed the clarity of thinking that followed, his inner critic silenced.

The previous day, they'd entered the walls as an anxious human chain, all holding hands, leaving the girls to wait and watch in the stairwell. They'd returned in the same manner, bubbling with excitement at what they'd discovered. The pairs had disappeared to various nooks and alcoves in the castle to turn the boys' research into notes and prepared speeches. Verity had no such pressure on her but she'd insisted to Kermon that he be as rigorous with her as with the boys.

He prepared mentally. 'Now,' he said softly and they stepped in unison across the boundary that was no longer a barrier.

Verity swayed and gasped in the onslaught of a million trillion past lives, an avalanche of alien people, animals and objects. Then she steadied and looked around. What did all these layers of history look like to a girl who'd been confined to a sickroom most of her life and was only just discovering the greater area of the Citadel? Kermon used his skills to see through her eyes, without intruding on her thoughts.

Their landing-point was the one he always used now. Familiarity made it easier for him to find his way here and also to acclimatise to wall life. More recent history was stronger and showed this place as a public park, its people walking, running, playing with balls, in pairs or family groups. Impossible to tell men from women, girls from boys. Around the perimeter of the park whizzed motor-carriages, loud as a Citadel full of angry bees and dulling his nose with noxious fumes.

'Can you hear their thoughts?' he asked Verity, indicating two runners who would have passed through him if he hadn't moved. 'It feels too strange when they do that so I act as if they were corporeal and move out of their way if I can.'

She shook her head, concentrated. 'I can hear them faintly,' she said finally.

'That's what you have to improve,' he told her, 'if you want to taste what they do, that connection. Remember your focus or you will be snowed under with new experiences, trivial distractions.'

'Snowed under,' she repeated and he kicked himself for introducing one of the distractions he'd warned her against. 'That's what the girl was thinking. She's snowed under with work.' She thought some more. 'It's a weather word. They speak in pictures all the time, pictures from their world, their experiences. Like we say stones or grassette. If you don't know their world, you don't really understand what they mean.'

She was more open than he'd expected from a girl raised in such narrow Perfection. As if sensory deprivation had left an immense hunger, waiting for a banquet.

'And I knew it was a girl,' she continued, 'because of the way she thought. You can't tell from those britches. They're like Assistant Smith clothes!' Her obvious disapproval showed that her Perfect upbringing had not been entirely discarded.

'You need to watch out for time shifts,' he warned her. She wouldn't need to be as careful as him in keeping a distance from people's minds. 'Look at that fountain and keep looking. Then tell me what you see.'

'It's stone with some kind of statue, a fish with water coming out of its mouth into the basin.'

'Keep looking.'

'Oh! It's getting fainter, disappearing and so are the park people. So is the park! We're dropping down below the ground only now it *is* the ground. And we're in a sort of Citadel, with people all dressed a bit like mages in robes.'

'Can you hear any thoughts?'

Verity took on a strained expression. 'That man's heading to a meeting about the barbarians,' she said finally. 'And he's late.' Carrying a scroll, a robed man hurried across what was now an open square arcaded with columns. 'A Council meeting, I suppose, to fight the Forest.'

Kermon nodded. 'Further back in time than the park. Every place has layers of history built one above the other.'

'Like the layers of a chocolate torte,' said Verity, smiling. 'You want me to focus – I'm focusing!'

'Impressive.' Kermon couldn't help smiling back.

'So,' Verity summed up, 'I need to stay at the historical level that suits my research as well as locating where I can find out everything I want to know about chocolate tortes.'

'Or places, plural,' Kermon pointed out. 'And people. Don't forget the people. What is your target?' Would any of them ever ask that question without remembering Tannlei, her wisdom and skills?

'To find out about chocolate torte.'

Kermon waited as Tannlei would have done, letting Verity ask herself why, the deeper target. Another layer. He looked around him, at the children running races on vast expanses of real grass, a dog fetching a ball. Old-style normal, so different from Perfection.

Apart, that is, from two figures ducking behind a tree, who looked as if they were wearing britches and jerkins. Someone in what looked like a mage's robe walked right through a family sitting on a plaid blanket, laughing together. Citadel clothes. He blinked and looked again but they were gone. Maybe a time-slip to earlier modes. Verity reclaimed his attention.

'To taste it the way people in the walls would, to understand why Puggy made it sound important,' she said slowly.

The only judge of such an answer was the person answering.

'Where do you want to start?' Kermon asked, prepared to give more direction if needed. It wasn't.

'Chocolate, of course. What makes a cake into a torte. How it's made. Then we need to find somewhere we can be with people tasting it. Simple.'

But of course it wasn't. 'Chocolate' led to manual harvests of purple pods, husked to reveal cacao beans, the food of the gods. A time-shift tempted them with the prospect of feathered headdresses and rituals, spiced cacao drink and a full moon but Verity resisted, kept to her plan.

'Torte,' she declared firmly and they found more trees, whiteblossomed in spring and nut-bearing in summer. From seed to tree to nuts, Verity watched the history of ground almonds.

Flour interested her less as the pattern of seed, growth and harvest, then grinding, was repeated.

'What tree does butter grow on?' she asked, having listed all the ingredients from a recipe in someone's kitchen. Kermon let her find out for herself and her shock at discovering the animal origin was only equalled by the enthusiasm of her search for eggs and her discovery of chickens.

By the time they found a café where they could linger and wait for customers to choose chocolate torte from the glass counter, they knew the variety of soils in which the evergreen cacao tree grew and the difference between dried and roasted beans. They knew the origins of every ingredient from vanilla pods to eggs. Above all, they knew all the work that lay behind one cake, glistening almost black beside the other baked goods, displayed like treasures in a wall-time museum.

'Baked,' murmured Verity. 'Put in forge fires.'

The café was part of the bakery and the aromas of fresh bread and cakes reached Kermon through customers' sensual responses. *Wonderful!* He began to relax and enjoy himself.

He glanced towards the sign engraved on the glass door, reversed from where they stood inside. Two short people who'd been peering in, turned their backs and walked off quickly. Others were bolder and the bell on the door tinkled as customers came in.

Strange. Kermon had the feeling that some people in wall-time were less – transparent – more like themselves. His unease about visiting the walls returned. And yet nothing had gone wrong, either yesterday or today. Or during his solitary visits, as far as he knew. Premonition was not among his gifts so he shrugged off the feeling and focused on tasting chocolate.

Chattering about books or jobs, love affairs or children, those customers who chose chocolate torte paid little attention to what they ate but their palates appreciated each bite.

'Crumbly,' said Verity, tuning in to their senses as best she could, finding words to take back to the Citadel. 'Caramel with dark undertones.' Her eyes opened wide. 'Very melting dark.'

And then, 'It's as if you can taste where each ingredient came from. Because you know. I can *see* the hen that laid the eggs, the cow that gave some milk for butter. It's all there in the taste.'

Then she frowned. 'It's not Perfect to take food from animals. It's cruel.'

'There are no animals in Perfection, so there's no cruelty,' Kermon pointed out. *But it's different in the Forest. Creatures roam free, kill and eat each other.* 'Keep the experience in your deep thinking. So you can find it again in the Great Hall and have chocolate torte whenever you want, with any of the flavours and associations you want. Nobody can control your imagination.'

She gave him a suspicious look. Had he gone too far? Challenged Perfection?

'That would be boring,' she said. 'Chocolate torte all the time. I need to come back for more flavours.'

Oh, stones. 'But you promised,' he reminded her. 'And when you're Hamel's wife, this won't do.'

She was getting that stubborn look in her eye that he knew well and was clearly about to launch into some convincing argument when Kermon saw two people bob up from the ground outside, peer through a window and duck back down quickly. This time he was sure. And he knew exactly who they were. The cone of black hair was unmistakable.

CHAPTER THIRTY-SEVEN

'Sorry,' Kermon told Verity. 'Wait here.'

He envisioned himself outside, standing behind the two miscreants. They were still bobbing up and down, slow to take in that their target had disappeared, when he grabbed them both by the collars of their jerkins.

'Nathan! What on earth are you doing, bringing Janette into the walls? Dressed up as a boy too!'

He couldn't leave Verity on her own and it would show no respect to summon her in front of these youngsters so there was no option. 'Come inside and tell me exactly what you're doing!' he told them. Not that he gave them any choice. They were certainly corporeal enough to drag into the bakery, where an astonished Verity looked them up and down.

'Well?' Kermon demanded.

'It was my idea.' Nathan was flushed but defiant, shoulders squared for the punishment that must surely come. 'Janette is a better student than I am, with more powerful magecraft, so I didn't think it was fair that she couldn't visit the walls. I did exactly what you taught us yesterday and we were very careful.'

'Yesterday was with permission.' Kermon couldn't find the words to make this stripling understand what he'd done: jeopardised not only two lives but the whole Adulthood Test, the future of the Citadel. He was conscious of Verity listening and had to be careful what he said.

'Today you put a lady's life at risk and broke the rules which allowed you to visit the walls.'

Janette was staring at him in a very unladylike manner. 'It's all right, Nathan,' she said, not looking at her partner. 'You don't need to protect me. It was all my idea, Mage-Smith Kermon. It *isn't* fair and I don't see why there's any harm me coming here. I wanted to do my own research, not just support Nathan. And I don't care what you do to me because it was worth it.'

Her chin jutted out and her whole demeanour reminded Kermon so much of Mielitta in attitude, if not appearance, that he almost forgave her. How could he not forgive Nathan when he'd have done likewise? He'd have done anything Mielitta asked, *had* done everything she asked. How could he have thought her or Jannlou repulsive when they were part of the Forest he loved too? His head felt clear of the horrible doubts that usually tormented him as he looked at his two students, rebels and rule-breakers. And he admired them for it.

Before he could pronounce sentence, the incorrigible Janette came to a judgement of her own. 'And anyway,' she said sweetly, 'Lady Verity is here in the walls. With you.' The implied accusation hung in the air.

Stones! This grew worse by the second. While Kermon thrashed around for a responsible way out of this mess, that would uphold Perfection, punish his erring students and avoid his own execution by the Council, Verity yawned.

In her most imperious voice, she said, 'This is wasting my valuable time. Just send these children back and make them promise not to do it again. Then we can get on with monitoring the Adulthood Test so I can report back to the Council from a woman's perspective.'

She frowned at Janette. 'Some girls clearly need a reminder of their role as women in the Citadel. You do *wish* to attend the ceremony and the Courtship Dance, don't you?'

The question dented Janette's confidence and her gaze dropped. 'Yes,' she said quietly.

'Then I'm sure Mage-Smith Kermon will forgive you this once. We don't want anything to mar yesterday's success, or Nathan's prospects, so we'll pretend your transgression never happened.'

And ours, thought Kermon, embarrassed at the implicit blackmail taking place.

'I understand, Lady Verity.' Janette stopped short of insolence but only just, and Kermon wondered for a moment who was blackmailing whom. So much for women's roles in Perfection! But he understood his well enough and he pontificated on respecting rules, concluding, 'So we'll say no more this time.'

A thought struck him. 'Your research, Janette. What was the topic?'

Her whole face came alive with the passion she showed in studies of any kind. 'Honey,' she said, 'and I discovered something, a scene many layers back in the past that I think is important.'

'No doubt,' Kermon said, cutting her off. He did not want any discussion of honey with Verity present. That would definitely be pushing her too far. 'No doubt. Write it all down for me and I'll read it when I get time. But you need to work on Nathan's research, for the presentation. That takes priority.'

'Can I write mine as a story?' she asked.

What a strange question.

'She's found her mage specialism,' explained Nathan. 'She's a storyteller.'

How bizarre. Was there such a specialism in the Citadel? If so, there hadn't been a Story Mage for centuries.

'I don't see why not,' said Kermon as Verity yawned again, pointedly. 'Now go straight to the park and back home. Can you do that?' He should escort them but he didn't want his students to see the surreptitious manner in which he and Verity would have to return. Nor could he leave Verity here.

Nathan looked very serious. 'I will look after her, Mage Kermon. I promise.

Janette gave him a scornful look but took his proffered hand; the two of them faded from view.

The bell over the door tinkled as customers went out and came in.

'We should go back too,' Kermon said.

'I shall report on the Test, you know,' Verity told him, 'from a woman's perspective. So I didn't lie. I just shan't say I went into the walls.'

'Neither will Janette,' he said drily.

He meant to reach out for her hand, as Nathan had done for Janette's, but his arm wouldn't move. Had he been in the walls too long? He focused all his deep thinking and magecraft on himself, on his own mind and body.

So good to be back, that sarcastic voice mocked him. He felt cold, frozen. All his initial fear of the walls paralysed him.

'Daddy,' yelled Verity and threw herself into the arms of the robed mage who'd appeared beside them in the bakery.

'You've come at last. I knew you would.' Rinduran stroked his daughter's hair as she nestled into his warmth.

He looked at Kermon over Verity's shining golden head, his smile more venomous than his deadened eye, still pierced by the bee's sting that Mielitta had injected.

'I would have been here sooner but something blocked my connection with this oaf and I needed it to find you. But everything seems to be working now.'

Kermon could not speak or move. *Nothing* was working. And the voice which had been destroying him from the inside was now here. It had never been his voice, his thoughts. It had been Rinduran all the time, possessing him more each time he entered the walls, destroying the memory and returning to the Citadel with Kermon.

Everything made sense now. The paternal feelings towards Verity and Bastien, the vicious lust towards Puggy, repulsion at Mielitta's and Jannlou's second natures. His self-contempt, his despair. They came from outside, from this leech on his emotions, channelling all his worst possible selves. Rinduran's dark magecraft had been destroying his mind.

And I will finish the work I've started, exulted the voice in his head. Even though he knew what was happening, Kermon had no defences left. Rinduran had been in his head for too long. Whatever this wall-remnant of the dead Chief Mage might be, he still had power. And Kermon could only watch the loving reunion in front of him, helpless.

CHAPTER THIRTY-EIGHT

'How are you here? asked Verity, her eyes glistening. We thought you were dead. That the bear–'

'Yes, in your world.' Rinduran's anger flared, a blinding red halo that sizzled and faded. 'But I experimented. Made an avatar that lives in the walls, has power here. I might be incorporeal in your world but here…'

'I don't understand.' Verity frowned. 'You're real, here, in the walls? Not like them?'

A woman passed straight through Kermon as she chatted to her friend about tired feet and election day. He identified the food choice on their tray: carrot cake and coffee, wondered whether Verity's fascination with cakes would expand. Wondered whether he was losing his mind completely, in a bakery where past people flitted in and out of his consciousness. Where he was trapped in his own motionless body listening to this revenant who could squeeze his mind into a black knot of despair, one he couldn't cut through.

A pulse of power jerked his thoughts back to the conversation.

Concentrate, weakling, the voice in his head ordered. From his deepest core, a scream rose, ripping his throat raw, expressing all that had been done to him.

The bustling café should have been filled with his scream. Every pane of glass should have shattered and every human within earshot should have rushed to his aid, to defend him against the criminal. But he made no sound, no movement. Nobody came to his aid.

'You aren't capable of understanding, sweetheart. You're not a mage.'

Verity stiffened slightly then relaxed as her father explained, 'The walls are real and not real or you wouldn't be here. Even I still have much to learn. In the walls, I'm real too, as you put it.'

'I've missed you so much,' Verity told Rinduran, snuggling up to him.

'I've missed you too, little one.'

How could she not notice? Kermon was dying, losing what was left of himself little by little and she had eyes only for his killer.

Harsh thoughts, weakling. Not all of you will die. I need your body, your perception, your knowledge of the events that happened after this version of me stayed in the walls. You have my undying gratitude. Without you, I wouldn't have known about the bear, nor who he is, underneath the pelt. I wouldn't be able to contact the freaks without you, so don't worry: I'll keep the parts of you I need. Flavouring, like salt in a stew. See? I can talk about food too. You like that, don't you?'

The last words were spoken as if a caress, more repulsive to Kermon than any overt hatred.

We've cohabited for some time now and you've adjusted. This is just a shift of who's in charge. It's very frustrating, you know, to be in Council and listen to your mealy-mouthed proposals. And treachery. But of course I can't confess your sins or I lose the mouth that speaks them. Your secrets are safe with me.

Vanilla latte and Americano coffee. Kermon read the menu behind the counter as if it were a magecraft exercise to focus his mind. Cream tea with scones. Earl Grey, Bitter Orange Pekoe, Darjeeling, English Breakfast.

He heard mocking laughter in his mind but kept reading the café menu as if it was a mantra.

'My, but you've changed.' Rinduran held Verity away from him to study her better. 'Almost a woman now.'

Verity stepped back so she could twirl in her striped Council Leader's robe, to impress her father.

Instead he frowned. 'I approve of you marrying Hamel. Good alliance. And then you can dress as a lady, properly. There will be no need to attend Council meetings. You can further Perfection in other, more appropriate ways.'

Verity stopped twirling. 'I want to be on the Council,' she stated. 'It's good for women's viewpoints to be represented.'

'Of *course*, women should be represented. They always have been! You don't think we men underestimate the importance of women? No, indeed. You are the reason we work to keep Perfection as it should be. To make sure that you can fulfil your role as we do ours. I was quite upset at how you were treated in the last meeting, everybody shouting and talking over you. I don't want that for my daughter! You must listen to me on that, Verity. I only want what's best for you. A life in politics leaves you open to unpleasantness, threats you couldn't even imagine. Most unsuitable for a woman.'

For a moment, Kermon thought Verity would argue but she said, 'You're right. I won't put myself in a situation where I'm talked over like that ever again.'

A politician's answer, thought Kermon. Agreeing in a way so ambiguous it committed to nothing. And if he knew Verity, she had no intention of giving up her place on the Council.

Rinduran seemed oblivious to any reservations she might have, continued to treat her as the little girl he remembered. The sick little girl.

'Have you been taking your medication?' he asked, concern in the eye that still showed expression.

A soul-reader could always observe and learn, draw deep on

that talent while he still could, however constrained. Kermon studied the damaged eye, the shaft of a bee-sting protruding, its black barb embedded in the pupil. Like a bull's eye on an archery target, a poisoned circle had spread around the barb, fixed and lifeless in the milky sea of blindness. Poisoned, fixed and lifeless, reducing Kermon to the same state.

No, some part of him deeper than Rinduran could reach kept on thinking. *Drianne too has only one part of her face mobile. Her appearance is more damaged than Rinduran's. Yet, where he absorbs light and hope, she emits both. Perception is more than sight.* Why didn't Verity see Rinduran as he was? Could he really be a loving father to Verity while being loathsome in Kermon's eyes?

'No,' she said. 'I've stopped taking the pills. But you don't need to worry. I'm fine.'

And clearly, she was. When Kermon had carried her into the Forest, she'd looked ashen and gaunt. She had been racked by coughing fits. Now, he couldn't remember the last time he'd heard her cough and she seemed to have grown taller as well as filling out in a young woman's curves. So quickly, it seemed like a glamour. Kermon wondered if the bee-sting in her hand had something to do with it but he knew Verity would hear no good of any Forest creature.

For all his compliments, Rinduran presumably saw a different Verity. His frown deepened. 'I was warned about this, that there might be a remission, an illusion of health, if ever you stopped taking the medication. I should have known they couldn't be trusted to look after you without me there. I should have checked on your care when I was visiting the Citadel in the weakling's body. I knew there was something wrong when I saw you in Council but I thought you were just growing up, lacking guidance. Now I see your health was neglected.

'You must return to your sickroom, my child, start up the medication again. Postpone your wedding until you're stabilised once more. I thought there must be something wrong. This isn't like you at all. It's a reaction to withdrawing from medication.'

Verity's face paled. 'I'm fine,' she repeated. 'I went without medication for a day when I was kidnapped.' She glanced at Kermon, her kidnapper.

See me, he pleaded silently. *See what he's doing to me.*

But she carried on trying to reassure her father. 'And then you weren't there, the Citadel was in confusion, everybody forgot and I felt fine, so I didn't say anything.' She shrugged. 'I don't just feel fine. I feel better than I've ever done in my life.'

There was no accusation in her voice but Rinduran reacted as if there had been. 'You don't understand,' he said. 'I watched your mother die from allergy. I knew you would be the same. I consulted the best doctors, consulted the walls, changed doctors until I found one who would give you what you needed. It was so hard to keep your chamber sterile, to keep you untouched, but at least you had your mother's company.'

'My dying mother's company,' Verity observed quietly, 'through the veil that separated our two chambers.'

'And I kept you alive! It will all be for nothing if you don't take care of yourself now. If you take your medication, you can still get married, even have children. The doctor said it was possible, if you take it step by step, with not too much time out of the sickroom at first.'

'It's too late, father. I've left the sickroom for good.' Verity thought for a minute, looked at Kermon again. 'What did you mean, when you said you should have used the weakling to check on my care?'

'It's not important, child. Just that I can travel back to the Citadel, in a manner of speaking, through his body, keep an eye on things there, catch up on news. What matters is that you are safe and well. Please listen to me.'

'You went into his mind,' said Verity slowly.

'Yes and very unpleasant it is there. You have no idea of the stupidity I've had to put up with. And inappropriate feelings towards you. Which you should have put a stop to, straight away. But of course I wanted to see you so I *had* to put up with it all.

From now on, I'll be able to control all that so you won't be bothered.'

Verity's cheeks had two pinks spots in them that Kermon recognised.

'Like forging,' she observed. 'You've been trying to forge the Mage-Smith.' Kermon remembered the Maturity Barn, Puggy's account of being forged and Verity's reaction, realising that would have been her fate had she been healthier.

'In a way,' agreed Rinduran with pride. 'And I've nearly succeeded so from now on I will be able to return to the Citadel and contribute more. But never in my own body or with my own magecraft. I'll have to make do with *his*.'

Please, Kermon prayed, with no optimism.

'There is no forging in the Citadel now,' Verity told Rinduran.

'We can bring it back,' he told her eagerly. 'It's not too late for you to be forged, to become a woman. You would be so much happier with a Perfect Maturity Test.'

'I'm sure I would,' said Verity.

Rinduran smiled. 'I knew you would see things my way.'

Kermon thought back to the Maturity Barn. Had he felt that inner voice then? The torment of conflicting impulses? He thought not. Maybe Rinduran had not been there, didn't know that Verity was no innocent regarding the Maturity Test, the suppressions, what had been done to Puggy.

Rinduran's little girl weighed her words. 'No, I don't see things your way. Forging is wrong and Perfection is changing. Banning women from the Council is wrong. Discriminating against non-mages is wrong. And when you interfered with Mage-Smith's Kermon's thoughts, his feelings for me, you crossed a boundary. I can never forgive you for that!'

Her self-control broke and she resorted to the tone of any girl shouting at her father for invading her privacy.

But Rinduran was not just any father. Alive, he had been the most powerful Chief Mage the Citadel had ever known. Kermon felt the storm gathering inside him, an echo of the magecraft whirling around its summoner in lethal shafts of red. This fire was beyond the Mage-Smith's control. First his head, then his core spasmed and burned. His chest tightened and each breath was a struggle.

'A pot of tea for two, please.' Customers ordered and the cashier rang up their bills, in the unbroken rhythm of the cosy bakery, oblivious to the power amidst them.

Then the trivial transactions of the bakery disappeared from Kermon's perception in the maelstrom unleashed by Rinduran.

'You will do as I say!' roared Rinduran, using the words that have ended many father-daughter relationships. He had the power to make it so and no qualms about what would be lost between them.

Kermon's heart sank. Although he was not the target, his body crawled with a million insidious worms, sizzling through his arteries to seek his heart, his reason, writing 'Submit!' over and over again as they passed through his body. If he could die and save Verity from a life in a sickroom, subjugated by this monster, he would so he struggled. One lapse in his enemy's concentration would free him to fight, even though he was sure to lose.

Verity stood as still as Kermon while the blackness targeted her, showered red sparks in its whirling rage.

She'd been brought up in Perfection, brought up to obey and her moment of rebellion was short-lived. Fists clenched, as ashen-faced as when she'd been ill, she stammered, 'I will do as you say, father.'

Kermon didn't blame her. No human could stand up to the pressure, outside and within, when Rinduran unleashed his powers. Stones only knew what he was doing to Verity's mind. Kermon struggled again but nothing budged. He was imprisoned as securely as ever.

The whirlwind changed colour, grey rather than black, its fires quietening.

'That's a good girl. Go home now and get your brother.'

'Why do you want Bastien?' asked Verity, shaking from the onslaught but still wanting to know more.

'To talk about Perfection, men's matters,' Rinduran did her the courtesy of replying. 'The weakling would never have brought Bastien here so I needed you and now you can go and get Bastien. Run along now.'

'You wanted to see me so I could get my brother. So you can talk about the future of the Citadel.' Verity's voice held no emotion at all but Kermon read her soul easily, not needing to enter her mind. He feared for her, for what she would do next.

'Then I will go back to the Citadel,' Verity said. 'But you can whistle for Bastien. I'm not your errand girl. Come on, Kermon.'

To his horror, she reached out and took his hand, as if this was a normal wall visit and they were heading back home, just as Janette and Nathan had done. She held on so tight, he couldn't drop her hand but Kermon twisted in front of her, to take the blast that must surely follow such a speech.

The reprisal was swift. The bakery turned black in choking fog, from which a murderous streak of power flamed at Verity and Kermon hit instead. He saw the lethal strike reach him in all its malign venom but he felt nothing. It was as if Rinduran's magecraft was no more than a thrown tray of cakes and tea for two.

The Wall Mage staggered, spent and shocked.

At Verity's touch, Rinduran had vanished from Kermon's mind and body. It was *his* turn to grip *her* tightly.

'How? gasped Rinduran, eyeing his daughter.

'I have something better than magecraft,' she said. 'It seems I'm immune to it.'

She raised her hand, joined to Kermon's. 'And so is the person of my choice.'

The bee sting, thought Kermon. Interacting with Verity's essence.

'Home,' he said and she nodded. Then they were in the park

and out through the walls. They looked at each other in the stairwell.

He wanted to speak, to acknowledge what had happened but Verity cut off his stammered thanks and shook her head.

'I'm tired,' she said and left him there, staring after her.

CHAPTER THIRTY-NINE

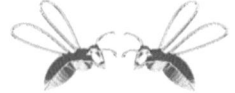

Not even the prospect of Council tensions could dampen the spring in Kermon's step as he headed towards the Mages' Tower. His steelwork that morning had contained the finest patterns he'd ever created, his reward the awe in Janette's and Nathan's eyes. They'd repaid his patient explanations with the priceless gift of respect. No snide references to wall visits although they must have realised that Kermon's presence with Verity was no more sanctioned than their own, however much she'd covered it up.

This would be the first time he'd seen Verity since – since *that* happened – but he refused to worry. Every particle of his body and mind was at his service. If he wanted to fly to the Council Chamber he could, so free he felt to be Kermon, without his inner enemy.

His elation was not daunted by the hostile mages around the table. He'd been forged in a different fire and found true, his patterns fixed to the core, not superficial etchings by a fraudster. Nobody could unmake him now, certainly not those who clung to Perfection's past.

Verity and Bastien entered close on his heels, their expressions difficult to read. Not one glance in Kermon's direction as they took their seats. Kermon barely had time to ask himself what, if anything, Verity had told her brother, when Bastien started the meeting with what was clearly a prepared speech.

'In the last meeting, members of Council expressed conflicting views on membership and on Perfection itself. As some members are new–' a nod to Garth, Zora, Fabrisse and Yacinthe – 'and others are recovering from serious illness–' a nod to Puggy.

Hamel snorted and received a withering glance from Bastien. The Chief Mage was in no-nonsense mood and his listeners held their peace.

For now, thought Kermon. If Bastien had half Rinduran's power, he would be invincible in a duel. Unless he was fighting more than one and there was no sign of the dissidents banding together. As yet.

'I want to recap the terms of the treaty we negotiated after the Battle of the Forest,' Bastien continued. 'They are written in blood, my blood, and while I am Chief Mage, the terms will be upheld.'

This time, the silence was full of the unspoken thought that if the blood oath was broken, Bastien would die. How sad. Then somebody else could become Chief Mage. How interesting.

The table's surface suddenly seemed to fascinate all seated there. Eyes down. Especially Puggy and Hamel, thought Kermon, as he sneaked a glance around. He felt no fear. Not after what he'd been through. And it was unlikely that anybody saw him as a contender to replace Bastien. He would have smiled but he was not quite that reckless.

'However, as your leaders, Lady Verity and I have discussed your evident concerns.' Bastien no longer looked as enthusiastic about what he was saying and Kermon guessed at Verity's input behind the scenes. How had she influenced her brother? She could be very persuasive but even so, Kermon couldn't see Bastien taking advice from his little sister, even good advice. What hold did anyone have over Bastien? Then it came to him.

Of course. The same hold they all had over him. The blood oath. Mielitta still controlled the composition of the Council, as long as Bastien lived. What if Verity had used that as, what was the word she'd used? Leverage. Yes, she was becoming an expert in leverage. As were his own students, he thought ruefully.

'However,' continued Bastien, 'neither of us is content to rule over such discord.'

The Council held its collective breath. Would they abdicate power? Surely not. Bastien could not do so without breaking the blood oath and calling down certain death on himself. Kermon could not imagine Bastien sacrificing himself for his mages' idea of Perfection. And the mages didn't agree with each other.

'Lady Verity has a solution to this impasse,' Bastien announced and sat down, clearly disgruntled at having his hand forced. Or more than disgruntled. He couldn't control a tic under his left eye.

This time, Verity had no problem making herself heard. 'Let us leave aside the treaty which Chief Mage Bastien swore on our behalf by blood oath and let the Council itself resolve the disagreement.'

There was a gasp. Open up the possibility of Bastien's death? Merely by voting? Greedy dreams flickered in lowered eyes.

Straight-backed, white-faced, Verity's voice was clear as the bell on a bakery door. 'I am particularly affected by the assertions that women and non-mages have no place at this table. As your leader, as a woman and as a non-mage, I refute this and I am willing to prove it in a duel against the leading proponent of this view. I challenge Mage Hamel to a duel now, in this Chamber. He may use the full power of his magecraft to make me do anything; he may mute me, force me to sing, walk around the room, whatever he chooses. If he succeeds, the Council will vote on its members and leadership. If he fails, then my leadership is proved beyond question, as is the right of women and non-mages to representation here.'

No wonder Bastien was afraid! But Kermon wasn't. He still felt that inner calm as he looked at Hamel, whose mouth twitched. Torn between greed and suspicion, no doubt. How could anything be so easy?

'My Lady Verity, wife-to-be,' Hamel reminded her. 'This is an unseemly exhibition. Please think again.'

'If you turn down my challenge, then, according to the tradition of Perfection which you hold so dear, you accept defeat,' Verity announced calmly. 'And nobody is to interfere in the duel,' she announced. 'You are all witnesses.'

'So be it.' Barely had Hamel accepted the challenge than Kermon felt the wisp of power sneaking around the table to mute Verity.

'Do tell me what weapons you will use, my dear. That is tradition too.' Hamel was smug, knowing that Verity would try to speak and be unable to.

'Yours,' said Verity, without a tremor in her voice.

Green frown lines deepened down Hamel's face and his irritation made grooves in the table, where he clawed rhythmically. Then he clenched his fist, the grooves smoothed out, disappeared, and he hurled power at Verity's unlined face. The deep fissures he'd scored in the table disfigured Verity's face for a second, then trickled away like water drops from glass. Despite the vicious intent, not one wrinkle aged the young skin. The mages shifted uncomfortably at Hamel's choice of outcome but nobody remonstrated. Verity stood unmoved.

There was no mistaking Hamel's frustration. He was livid green, crackling with all the power he could draw on and the blast he aimed at Verity shook the room and everyone in it, discharging its lethal venom for aeons it seemed. Even as Hamel's strike ebbed with his power, green smoke hung thick and, for a second, Kermon doubted.

Then the air cleared. Hamel had flopped over the table, unconscious and transparent, drained of all power.

And Verity stood untouched. 'Can you revive him?' she asked Bastien, dispassionately.

He sent some of his own power towards the vulnerable mage, in what seemed a gentle movement compared with the previous storm.

Hamel's pallor greened slightly. He lifted his head, regained focus, looked at Verity with open hatred. 'You may withdraw from our marriage contract if you so wish,' he squeaked. 'As my wife, you would have to obey me.' The threat was clear enough.

Everyone knew that he was bound by blood oath to his fiancée. He must marry her or pay with his death unless she should choose to end the contract. In such a manner did careful male relatives like Bastien protect their women.

Verity paused long enough to show she knew this too and was weighing up the pros and cons. 'I do not think we are well-suited,' she said finally. 'I withdraw from our marriage contract.'

Hamel slumped back wearily over the table, his head on his arms, irrelevant.

Bastien stood up and stated the obvious. 'Lady Verity has won the duel. She has successfully asserted her right to leadership and that of women and non-mages to be Council members.' A mix of frowns and smiles could be seen at the table. Zora didn't seem sure what expression was more appropriate and Kermon suspected she'd be far happier if Verity had lost.

'I prefer to be called Chief Councillor,' Verity announced. 'Or by my new title. She nodded at Bastien, giving him encouragement to continue. Or permission.

'Now that is established, there will be changes to Council procedure.' Bastien's relief at being alive added confidence to his voice. 'Nobody will speak out of turn. To ensure that, Lady Verity–' He corrected himself between gritted teeth, 'Chief Councillor Verity will take on the new role of Speaker. She will ensure that business is conducted in a proper and polite fashion. She will choose who has permission to speak. Magecraft in this Chamber is now forbidden, except to me as leader if discipline needs to be established or to the Right Hand of the Speaker, who will be a mage of her choice.'

As she had vowed to her father, nobody *would* talk over Verity ever again, thought Kermon with admiration, as all eyes turned to him. There was no need to announce which mage was the Right

Hand of the Speaker. He'd been seated there for several meetings now. What had she said? *I want you to be my knight.*

'Perfection is changing,' Verity announced. 'Mage Puggy has taught me that a woman has more choices than I realised. I hereby renounce marriage and children so I can dedicate myself to the good of this Citadel. That does not mean I forsake the support of a man, of a mage, at my side. Without him I would be unequal to the task.'

All eyes were on Kermon, questioning, sarcastic, suggestive.

Verity turned to her brother and put her hand on his arm. 'Chief Mage Bastien is my partner, my support.' All eyes dutifully switched to her brother.

'And,' she continued, slipping a little out of her imperial role. 'I'm going to be much happier that way.'

Then she sat down in a rush. The attack by Hamel had taken more out of her than she wanted to show.

Bastien wisely brought the meeting to an end and the mages escaped as quickly as they could.

Amid the hubbub, Kermon heard Bastien murmur, 'I miss our father. Do you think he would approve of these changes?'

'I'm sure his spirit is safe in the walls and watching over us.' Verity's reply was even lower but Kermon was attuned to her voice. 'I think he would be proud of both of us.'

So she hadn't told him, thought Kermon. And he had a year before the next Adulthood Test before he had to go into the walls again and face Rinduran. Unless he was going to take Verity with him, he must think of a way to deal with the revenant.

But not today. His heart lighter than it had been since he came back to the Citadel, Kermon couldn't wait to get back to his Chamber and contact Mielitta. So much good news to tell her. Once there, he held Perfection Unfinished, its patterns glowing silver-blue as he reached out to his friends. He would never betray them, nor the Forest. He would tell them he was glad for them, for their love of each other and their concern for him.

In losing that inner enemy, he'd remembered who he was and

that he should be proud of himself. His new inner voice was his best friend, himself.

Buoyant, he reached out through the arrowhead, felt the connection with Steelwing, with Mielitta. He could feel her presence but saw nothing, only whirling thick white. Like a blind eye, he thought in sudden panic.

No, said his new inner voice. *Soul-reader, concentrate on what is there, not on what you fear.*

Kermon looked into the white, still saw nothing. But he heard calm breathing, felt a sense of repose.

They're there, he told himself. *They're all right.* Just in case he could be heard, he said everything that was in his heart, so they would know. He felt a sense of peace as he finished with the best news of all.

'Perfection is changing. Verity said so in Council. Imagine that! Your bees, the honey, the children – something is happening, just as you hoped, just as we hoped.' And it was because of him. He'd been wrong. His sacrifice had not been for nothing. And he could live without the Forest as long as it took to do his work in the Citadel. He was needed here.

'I'll be fine,' he told his friends in the Forest. 'Don't worry about me.' And this time he meant it.

CHAPTER FORTY

The familiar sounds of the farmhouse seemed louder now that the newcomers had departed, gone to look for somewhere they could live in the Forest, where Jannlou could spend nights as well as days. Hui purred. A clock ticked its comforting double rhythm, like a heartbeat, although its hands never moved. His grandmother had stopped them when she felt his mother die. Arven's needles clacked and he sat in his usual, wingless chair, unreeling the yarn from its basket, knitting in beige, the pattern yet to take shape.

Before the visitors left, they had all walked around the farm, its pastures and orchards, gentle woodland hidden within the wilderness of the Forest. As Arven had foreseen, the reaction to what they discovered at the northern boundary was extreme.

Mielitta was the first to ask what the object was, wooden and wheeled, with a canvas top, but Jannlou was quicker to realise the implications.

'It's a wagon. We hitch up a horse and go to market,' Qingzhao had told them.

Wonder and curiosity in his eyes, his bear nature rising up, Jannlou realised, 'If there is a market, there are people, outside the Citadel, outside the Forest.'

'The world is always bigger than the one you were born into. The further you explore, the more connections you will find.' Qingzhao had saved these words for this moment. 'If you live your best life, the world in which you die is beautiful and you will always be part of it.'

They had not known what to say, those intruders to the world Arven had known from babyhood. They had not even explored their own second natures, let alone a greater world. But the words had been meant for him too so he'd replied for all of them.

'I will try, grandmother.'

She'd smiled and he'd known then. They'd talked of this moment but he'd always hoped it would never come. The nearer he knew it must be, the more impossible it seemed.

Now he sat in his chair, knitting, his eyes on his grandmother rocking gently in her chair. Another double rhythm like a heartbeat.

Hui jumped onto Qingzhao's lap and his purr grew louder, startling her awake.

Her gaze went straight to Arven and she nodded, as if pleased with what she saw. Her love for him filled the room, a warmth without words.

'I've played my part,' she said softly. 'Forgive me for leaving you.' Her eyes spoke the rest.

'It is time,' he told her, playing *his* part, the strange boy with his ancient knowledge of what mattered. But tears fell on his knitting, a rainbow in each transparent drop. All the colours combined and the fabric turned snow-white, his memories of his grandmother making patterns as he worked. On the windowpanes, tears froze into ice-gardens, bouquets of winter flowers. The sky cried white, a flurry of sparkling flakes that moulded a magical landscape.

Arven knitted six-sided shapes into white fabric flecked with silver and watched his grandmother's sleeping face, listened to the double-rhythm of the rocker. So like a heartbeat.

He remembered running away when he was seven, hiding

high in a giant tree from breakfast until nightfall because Qingzhao said needles were his weapon, not arrows or a sword like his noble parents had used. Needles were toys for grannies. Tired and hungry, he'd come down from the tree to find his grandmother sitting at the base, with her needles and basket of wool.

She'd handed him a pair of needles, told him he could stay in the tree until he'd earned her tuition by fighting his way past her. He'd laughed, told her he was too tired for joking, then realised she was serious. She'd taken up a readiness stance, wielding her own needles as if they really were weapons. Suddenly, they looked very sharp.

He'd made some pathetic little jabs, been disarmed at once. Tried again with more concentration. Been disarmed again. She had no weaknesses and was equally adept with right and left hand, moving as if part of the Forest.

'How did you do that?' he asked her as she flicked his right needle up to land in her own hand, with its twin.

Then she smiled and put all the needles back in the basket. 'That is how to defeat me,' she said. 'Ask me the right questions. Day by day, I will show you how. I will teach you everything I know, just as I taught your mother. Always ask yourself, *What is the target?*'

'And what was *your* target?' little Arven had asked, as he slipped his arm through his grandmother's, the counterweight to her basket of knitting as they trod the path back to the farmhouse.

'To steal a tiger's tea,' his grandmother had told him, squeezing his hand.

'But–' Arven objected, then he understood her target. To show how much she loved him.

He knitted the memory in sparkling white snowflakes, along with a lifetime – his lifetime – of warmth and work, meals together at the scrubbed table in the kitchen, the ritual of tea and cakes.

Her eyes were closed and as he watched, the lines eased from her face and her skin smoothed into peace, more and more transparent. Her form shimmered in the rocking-chair and was gone. Too like a heartbeat, the double rhythm of the rocker stilled, leaving only the tick of the clock.

Hui meowed his loss, curling into a corner of the empty chair as if trying to cling to the lost lap.

Arven cast off, left the needles and basket by his chair and took the white snowflake fabric to the rocking-chair. He sat down in it himself, lifted the protesting cat gently onto his own lap and he carefully tucked the white pall around them both as a comfort blanket.

'I will tell the bees,' Arven told his grandmother. 'In springtime. No need to do anything else, until springtime.'

Then he curled up in hibernation, spreading the deep sleep of grief to the world around the farmhouse, alone with his cat and his stopped clock as the snow kept falling.

CHAPTER FORTY-ONE

Drianne was silent, the silver tracery on her face blending into that on the leaves around them.

Dewdrops, thought Mielitta. They glittered silver in the mist that still clung in wisps around them. She reached out and brushed a leaf as she passed but the glitter was solid, icy. Her backpack slipped and she adjusted the weight of bow and provisions on her shoulders. Qingzhao had insisted that they take food and blankets.

'You can ask the beekeeper,' she told Jannlou. 'But I think we have a more immediate problem. We need to find somewhere to live, now.' She shivered. 'It's grown too cold for sleeping in trees.'

'I could dig a den, for all of us, said Jannlou.

Mielitta imagined being cocooned in an earth burrow, underground, relying on her friends to keep her warm. For how long, she wondered. This time, it was her bees who shivered.

Winter, they told her.

'For the winter,' said Jannlou. 'I knew it was coming. I should have eaten more.'

Silly bear, tinkled the bees. *We need our winter stocks of honey so we can stay warm in the tree hollow and eat when we are hungry. Until spring comes.*

'We can't live in a tree hollow, nor in a bear den!' Mielitta snapped, wondering how long their provisions would last and how they'd hunt in a frozen forest. 'We're humans.'

You don't have to be human... insinuated a bee. Mielitta ignored her.

Drianne's voice slipped into her mind. *Bears don't just live in earth dens. If we could find a cave...*

Mielitta translated for Jannlou, added, 'Have you found any caves, when you were on your own?'

He shook his head.

'What about other bears?'

'Only one with cubs, nowhere near her den, I don't think. I'd have smelled it.'

The earth crackled under their feet, whitening.

'It's as if the mist is freezing around us.'

Drianne's clothes were covered with frosty spider-webs as if her face tracery were spreading. The distinction between her form and the Forest was diminishing with every step they took.

'Stay close, Drianne,' Mielitta told her, suddenly afraid that they would lose each other in this weird whiteness.

'There was another bear,' Jannlou remembered, 'by the waterfall. Remember?'

How could she not? Mielitta was glad of the gloom to hide her expression.

'Maybe there's a hideaway, a cave if we're lucky.'

'What if he's still there?' Mielitta asked.

'I will fight him,' said Jannlou quietly.

None of them liked the idea of chasing another creature out into the cold – or of Jannlou losing the fight – but they didn't have a better idea.

Mielitta pictured the waterfall, danced it to the bees and confirmed the directions they should follow, unphased by the diminished visibility. Seeing one tree ahead instead of three made no difference to bee-sight.

Let the bear brag about his nose!

Leading the way and keeping Drianne between her and Jannlou so there was no chance of losing the young mage, Mielitta couldn't help marvelling at the change coming over the Forest.

Dressing in sparkles, as if for the Courtship Dance, she thought. Kermon had said there would be a second one. He could be dancing at this very moment. She held her arrowhead, tried to see the Mage-Smith, whether to reassure him or herself, she didn't know. An ice crystal brushed her cheek and broke with a tinkle as she passed.

She squeezed Steelwing, felt the chill of the patterned waves, denying the fire of their birth. 'Kermon,' she called.

She saw nothing but whiteness and trees looming. But like a voice in the mist, she heard a faint echo, felt a vibration in the arrowhead.

I'm fine, I'm fine, I'm fine. Then nothing more. But Steelwing warmed in her hand for a moment, in a reminder of its fiery birth, and she knew the connection was true. That it was truer than she'd felt for some time.

'What is it?' asked Jannlou.

She must have slowed down. 'Kermon,' she said. 'A flicker, not a proper connection, but I'm sure he's all right, better than he's been. I've been worried,' she confessed.

We all have, said Drianne.

Jannlou gave a huge sigh. 'It should have been me. In the Citadel.'

They walked on in the eerie white silence. Mielitta was so accustomed to ice drops shaken from leaves and melting on her skin as they landed, that at first she didn't realise the change. The drops were softer, falling faster, not translucent but white. Rocks were shifting into ghosts, sharp edges rounding, softening. The muffling of sounds was not just in the air but from below where whiteness settled.

'Snow,' said Mielitta, walking faster. Beautiful and treacherous. They must find shelter.

Nearly there, the bees encouraged. *Hurry. A bee who steps on snow dies. We should be in the hive.*

They led her in as straight a beeline as they could manage, allowing for the clumsy human mode of travel. The rush of water on stone grew ever louder and Mielitta took the last steps carefully, not wanting to tumble over a snowy ledge by mistake. She let her bees guide her until it was Jannlou's turn to lead.

'Can you smell anywhere to go?' she asked him, a little peeved that her bee senses were no use for the task, however finely tuned they were to flowers, honey and hive smells.

He scented the air, nodded, took the lead.

'Old scent,' he told them. 'The bear's gone.'

They filed carefully up beside the fall, then away from it among rocks until Jannlou stopped, sniffed, nodded. He moved aside a curtain of branches to reveal a dark opening, big enough for a large bear to enter on all fours, or for a man who stooped.

'Go in and have a look,' he told Mielitta. 'See what you think.'

A fringe of leaves shook snow down the back of her neck as she entered the cave and blinked in the darkness.

The narrow entry was good defensively.

'You're blocking the light,' she called back to the others. 'I'll just look around then I'll report back. Give me a minute. It's better if you wait there with all our things.'

The cave itself was surprisingly large and when Mielitta felt the dark walls at the back, she came across two tunnels. There could be further caves beyond the main cavern.

A current of air and some flakes of snow caught her as she felt her way around the side wall. If they lit a fire here, the crack above might serve as a chimney. It couldn't be very big or there would be light. Maybe there was a bend.

She returned to the cave mouth.

'It's dark,' she told them. 'This is the only light source. But it's perfect for shelter and sleep. I think we could light a fire here where there's a draught and the smoke would draw. I'll show you. Come and see what you think.'

Just right, was Drianne's verdict.

Jannlou said, 'Bears chose it in the past.' Which presumably meant he approved.

They dropped their packs of provisions onto the sandy floor, in a small, inadequate heap. What they needed and what they could get were likely to be two very different matters with snow falling faster and lying deeper.

Water was a few careful steps away but what about food and dry firewood?

'We should clear the cave entrance. And forage before nightfall,' said Mielitta reluctantly. The safety of the cave reminded her of her chamber in the Citadel, somewhere you could let your guard down. She was so tired.

In what little light reached them from the entrance, she could see Jannlou blinking and yawning. Drianne was as white as the snow, obviously exhausted beyond magecraft, so Mielitta didn't ask.

Sleep buzzed her bees. *Winter.* But they didn't sound worried. *Throw out the drones,* they advised her.

Jannlou looked outside, brushed off the snow and came away from the entrance. At that moment a wild wind whipped up the snow and blew it into the cave, where it formed a growing pile of glittering white crystals.

'We'll go out to find food when it stops,' Jannlou said.

What if it doesn't? wondered Mielitta. She had to go back out there and get firewood, see if she could shoot some game. Otherwise they would end here, their lives drifting into oblivion.

Look! said Drianne.

The pile of snow reflected light into the darkest corners of the cave, illuminating two chests, three mattresses, a pile of furs and a table. They had not been there before, when Mielitta had explored. She was sure of that. Something had changed.

Mielitta could smell the food before she saw it, piles of fresh-baked bread, a tureen of venison stew, cheese, yoghurt and honey.

There was also a scroll pinned to the table. When Mielitta

unrolled it, she recognised the same green scrawl she'd first seen in her chamber on her birthday morning, what seemed a lifetime ago. This time there was a second section.

She read aloud,

'When the bottle is empty, you will be full.
No life ends while The One lives.
In the year of the prophecy, choose well.

Eat and drink your fill,
then sleep the winter through,
till Bee, Bear and Flower are
knit in spring.
The Forest thanks you.
The Beekeeper.'

'You know what it means, don't you,' Jannlou's voice held a note of accusation.

Tell us, Drianne demanded.

'I had a note like this, before, in the Citadel,' admitted Mielitta, 'and when I saw writing like this in the beekeeper's house, I asked her about it. Drianne heard what she said.'

'And you didn't tell me?' Jannlou's voice held a hint of a growl.

'There was so much going on and you were both so upset...' Mielitta felt the weight of his glare even in the semi-dark.

'All right!' she said. 'I should have told you. But it was only about me and I thought it was finished. Then I forgot about it. Qingzhao said she just followed Arven's instructions. You know the way he has feelings about what should happen? So she wrote a note and the walls took it from her, brought it into my chamber for my eighteenth birthday, with the perfume that made the bees sting me.' She shrugged. 'And you know the rest. But the second part is new to me too. And all this.' She gestured to the riches around them.

'What does that mean? She said the walls took the note. And how did it end up in your chamber? How did it end up here?'

'I don't know.' Mielitta shrugged again. 'The walls are strange. Maybe Kermon can tell us more about them.' She didn't feel ready yet to talk about just how strange the walls had been, how they'd given birth to her and rescued her. Not yet.

We can ask the beekeeper, suggested Drianne.

'Yes, we'll ask Qingzhao. She'll know.'

'Can we trust Arven? Can we trust all of this?' asked Jannlou.

'I have no idea,' repeated Mielitta, 'but the bees seem happy. Or asleep. And I don't think we have many options. Besides, I'm starving and this tastes wonderful!' She spooned honey into a bowl of yoghurt and licked her fingers. 'I would know if there was something wrong with the honey. And there isn't. So if you don't eat anything else, eat the honey.'

She took another lick, pronounced, 'Thyme, summer savory and a hint of lemon balm.'

The mention of honey seemed to have calmed Jannlou's fears and he scooped so much of it into a bowl there was no room for yoghurt.

The bear and the flower, repeated Drianne. *I suppose we are.* She helped herself to some food, with rather more delicacy than the other two.

When they'd glutted themselves, without any apparent ill consequence, they investigated the chests, in the light of the snow-pillar formed by the wind. Leather jerkins and britches, fleece coats and cotton shirts. Chainmail, swords and daggers. Goblets, plates and platters.

'Real leather, wool, fleece, silverware.' Mielitta's hands shook as she smelled the origins of each treasure. Priceless and practical gifts from the past, from the cave, these walls outside the Citadel.

Furs, murmured Drianne, wrapping herself in soft cream.

Jannlou held up a dark brown pelt. 'Bear?' he asked, his voice faltering.

'A gift from the Forest.' Mielitta was firm. 'We are not going back to the Citadel so we have to learn new ways. Sustenance, leatherette, greylight and fake grass are not Forest. If the new ways hold danger and death, that we give and that we risk, so be it.' She grabbed a couple of furs from the pile and dragged a mattress to a corner.

Jannlou followed suit, placing his mattress by hers and throwing carefully-selected furs over them both. Any colour of fur except dark brown. They were soon asleep in each other's arms.

Sitting alone on her mattress in a pile of furs, Drianne watched them for a while. She shivered although she wasn't cold. The frog on her knitted scarf glowed in rainbow colours and opened her mouth to sing. But she was a female frog, her vocal sac small and her voice barely audible.

We sing in different ways, Drianne told her frog, who hopped around her neck in warm rainbows and then settled back into her place in the pattern.

We all have a place in the pattern.

One by one, forest creatures slipped through the entrance hole, past the snow pillar into the cave.

Come little brothers and sisters, she invited them, and they skipped, hopped, scurried or bounded to join her. Two rabbits, three squirrels, a pine-marten, a white wolf and a goat kid let her smooth their living fur as they stretched out, safe and peaceful by her side. A spider traced its silver nets in her hair, beautiful as the lines on her face, then they all snuggled up in winter's soft truce of falling snow and sleep. Until spring should come.

EPILOGUE

Down below the castle, where the walls ran wet near the water gate, two old boots had disintegrated, merging with the moss they contained. They were hidden under a pile of leaves dropped by a dozen young saplings, planted too close together, which were shooting up from the boots towards the incoming water and the light they sensed was there, beyond the water gate.

Their roots were embedded firmly in moss, boot fragments and mud on the ledge above the purified stream-water entering the Citadel. Or rather, what had been purified stream water but which was now tainted with a taste of the Forest.

Seeking light and home, the saplings twined around the wrought-iron water gate, forcing their way through, out, over and under, as is Nature's way. Uncurling fresh leaves, their tips explored the barrier between the Citadel to the Forest. They destroyed the magecraft wards like water drops wearing stone, by persistence and infinitesimal pressure points until they reached the other side of the boundary.

Growing, questing, calling to their own kind in plant fashion, the saplings multiplied their branches and leaves in a joyous response to sunlight, formed a thin canopy under the open sky, their roots well-nourished by the Citadel moss below.

But things look different from the other side of a boundary and the chill of snowflakes hit them. Winter had come. Their leaves fell and their sap stopped rising. They must wait for spring to make further progress.

Somebody walking down the path inside the Citadel to the water gate would have only seen the lower half of the plants, ending in a shimmering rainbow at the place where the water gate had been.

But nobody was there to see that Perfection had been Unfinished.

MATURITY ASSIGNMENT

THE HONEY HUNTER

By Apprentice Storymage Janette
Witness and Anchor: Apprentice Mage Nathan
Tutor: Mage-Smith Kermon
Sources: Wall location: Sub-layer 15, tribal

He wasn't there. Qwian scanned the gathered villagers again while the Headman spoke the words of blessing for the honey hunt. The familiar ritual brought her no comfort and she barely listened until mention of her own name burst into her self-doubts.

'Qwian was chosen by her father, whose passing we grieve. And she has been visited by the dream so she must lead the honey hunt in his place. Her shoulders are slight, with much resting on them. Today the bees will make their own choice, confirming or rejecting.' Gurratan's voice was clear and sharp as the diamond he was named after.

Qwian shivered in the dawn chill and her heart hammered like a war drum. Where was he? Surely, he would not let her go on the hunt without one gesture to wish her well? He knew she might die this day, falling like her father had, one year ago, to death below the cliffs. What if the bees slashed the bamboo ties of her rope ladder, as they had done to his?

When they argued last night, she'd told Tau that she must walk her own path and if she died hunting honey, then this was her fate, like her father's. Of course he retorted that death would find her more easily halfway down a cliff, attacked by giant bees, than if she sat cross-legged, weaving in her family hut, like the other women.

'I am not like other women,' she'd told him and his eyes gleamed like stones wet with river-water but he had not kissed her to make up. He'd turned away, stoking his fears to a blaze of resentment. He could not even come with her. The Headman's son was too precious to the tribe's future to be allowed to hunt honey. He could only wait to know if all who set out returned and waiting was a humiliation fit for women, not warriors. So he'd told her.

What if she did die today? Her thumping heart told her that she would. Her father had said she must have the honey hunter's dream to follow in his footsteps so she'd told the Shaman of the one where she climbed down a rainbow in pursuit of a dark red monkey. This satisfied everybody although Qwian was sceptical about the way men's interpretations of dreams suited their plans.

Maybe she had never had the honey hunter's dream. Tau was not here because all the omens were bad and she would die. Gurratan would be forced to buy a honey hunter from another tribe and the bees would be angry at such disrespect. She did indeed carry a heavy burden on her slight shoulders.

Gurratan brought the rite of well-wishing to an end but it meant nothing to her if Tau was not here. The Headman handed her the two long bamboo spears with square wooden ends that she would need for her work. Her father's spears, recovered undamaged from the shrubs around his broken body, by the bees' will. She had been there, his apprentice, when he fell to his death and now the spears were hers. In such a manner did a child become an adult. She bowed her head in acceptance as she took them.

'Do not taste the honey,' hissed Gurratan, for her ears only. 'You are still only a woman even if the bees accept you as our honey hunter. If your father had been blessed with sons, we would not have come to *this*.'

As she raised her head, she felt some shift in the scene, the presence of the newcomer, before she saw him, coming out of the shadows at the back of the gathering. Dawn sunlight bronzed hair that hung straight as weighted threads on a loom. Tau. His face granted her no smile but he raised one arm slowly, put his hand on his heart and offered it to her in mime.

Qwian's open palm caught his invisible heart and placed it on her own, in a gesture that could have been acceptance of Gurratan's words. But was not. Her heartbeat steadied and now she was ready. She would not die this day because she was born for bees.

Now she could smile and so she did. 'The day begins well,' she told her team of twelve hunters and she turned her back on the village to lead the way with her spears through the surrounding jungle to the place of preparation.

On the previous day, the honey hunters had carried bamboo ropes, slats of wood and a wicker basket to the sacred clearing above the high cliffs. They'd braved the freezing river, helping each other across on the slippery stones. Leeches had latched onto two of the men; their wounds were still bleeding. This time they knew all the danger spots and could move more quickly without their burdens, chanting songs to bring courage.

When they reached the place of preparation, they needed no word from Qwian to set about their tasks. The ropes and slats were assembled as ladders and the bamboo-shoot joints were double-checked. Nobody spoke of the death of Qwian's father but she knew they all carried the blackness of it, like the rage of bees. This day's harvest would be in homage to him.

With nods and whistles, their work at the top of the cliff was done and the group split in two as the May sunshine grew stronger. One team took the pathway down to the base of the cliffs, avoiding the bees.

Last year, Qwian had been among them. She'd gathered wood and saplings for the fires, secured the rope sent down from the top. She'd shinned up the rope, carrying leafy brushwood and lodged it in crevices, just below the huge scallops of honeycomb, so that the smoke would reach the bees without hurting them. The roar of the giant bees drew her, spoke to her in a language she did not yet understand.

'Be patient,' her father had said, before he fell to his death.

She'd been fanning flames upwards, proud of her work with the brushwood, when he reached out with his spear to dislodge more comb. The cliff was black with giant bees, clouded with smoke, but she saw him stretch, saw the ladder tilt impossibly as a slat gave way. He should have been held by two security ropes.

Had he slipped them to reach that tempting honeycomb, just out of reach? Had the jerk on the two security ropes been too much for the trees they were attached to, on the top of the cliff? Had the knots come loose? In the confusion of smoke and fire, fall and death, cause was irrelevant. The bees had decided.

When the first whistle came from below, Qwian looked over the edge. She saw the first wisps of smoke and the first black clouds of bees swarming in panic two hundred ladder-steps below. She could glimpse the team of fire-starters, like ants scurrying in and out of flames another hundred ladder-steps or so further down the cliff.

Her stomach filled with wings. Tau was right. A woman could be safe weaving in her hut.

The men beside her gestured, whistled back to those below. All was ready. It was time.

She donned the honey hunter's veil, her only protection.

Anything more would show disrespect to the bees, deny the bond they shared. She murmured the words due to the gods, attached the two security ropes and started to climb down the ladder into the smoke and black buzz, into the heart of bees.

Then Qwian was lost, choking in fumes, her entire body vibrating in the wrath of bees that bounced off her veil, her arms. They were almost weightless but there were so many she was suffocating in bees. Thousands of them in contagious panic. She must fly! She pulled on one of the security ropes, the signal to lift her up again, get her to safety. She could not do this!

Nothing changed. Was this how her father died? Wondering why he'd been abandoned?

A rope whistled down beside her, snaking through the blinding white, dangling an empty basket that stopped close enough for her to hook it with a spear. The men were good at their jobs. They'd interpreted her jerk of panic as a sign to send down the basket and they'd guessed where she was on the cliff face. They'd guessed well.

Already she was adapting to short breaths, closed mouth, listening to bees and echoes, marking the position of the honeycomb each time she had a clear view of the glistening hives. She made a tentative stab, swung a little on the ladder, stabbed again. She *would* do this. She grew used to the swing of the ladder as she stretched more, became braver, determined to dislodge the first comb.

Nearly severed, Qwian thought. She used one spear to position the basket and then gave a last jab with the other. Stretching the last sticky dollop of dark red honey as it ripped free, the comb dropped into the waiting basket, which jerked with the weight. Immediately, the basket was lowered by the top team to those on the ground.

Qwian swung on her ladder, waiting for the empty basket to come back up, so she could fill it again. She was a honey hunter surrounded by her bees. Her mouth opened in laughter and at that moment a breeze of bees lifted her veil and smacked her mouth with a morsel of honeycomb. She licked it instinctively, the mad honey made from rhododendron nectar. Aphrodisiac honey, that made men crazy or healed them. Forbidden honey that she should not taste.

Fly, the bees told her. *Fire! Dangerous!*

She understood them in their language but it did not seem strange. Their voices were in her head.

'We are not robbers but guests in your home. Thank you for the gift of honey,' she told them politely, licking the last bit from a corner of her mouth as blackness zoomed around her, too fast to be more than fuzzy shapes.

We will need you, they told her. *Your hive and ours. Never forget our gifts and your promise.*

Her head swimming, Qwian saw the smoke curl into the image of a girl's face surrounded by bees. Then the girl was running through a forest. A bee tattoo glittered on her thigh, came to life, took flight. The smoke blanked white and the vision was gone, broken by an empty basket, returning from below.

Remember, the bees buzzed. Then they stung her so she would not forget but she just laughed. The stings did not hurt her. Qwian shook her head to clear her thoughts of honey madness.

She heard the bees say, *We must protect our queen. We must protect you...* and then all she heard was humming. She set to work once more, careful to take only outer honeycomb, leave the heart of the beehive safe, where the new brood was in capped wax cells. Where the queen was at work, laying eggs. *Protect the queen.*

After four heaped basketfuls of comb, Qwian's work was done and she jerked on both ropes to show she was coming up. The ascent was slow, her limbs suddenly stiff with fatigue, and she let the men help her onto firm ground. Her legs shook as if she was still swaying on the ladder and she disguised her weakness by sitting.

Someone passed her the leather bottle and she eased her throat with freezing river-water. *Waiting is women's work,* she thought. On the ground below, the men were mashing comb and straining the precious honey into their containers. On the top, ropes and ladders were untethered and dismantled. Qwian had earned her moment resting.

When the honey harvest arrived on the cliff top, each man saluted Qwian, kissing her spears in reverence.

'The bees have recognised your father's daughter,' they said.

More could not be said without transgressing the mystery of bees and Qwian had no desire to ask questions. She too was reluctant to talk about her experience. And of course she could not say she had tasted the honey. She merely looked on, indulgent, while each man took his allotted gulp of honey and became talkative, foolish or quarrelsome, as was his nature.

Although each felt the urge, nobody returned to the honeypot for more. Nobody wished to go home in the shame of drunken sickness, remembered only in jokes. This harvest was their triumph, worth a fat year for the village.

The trek homeward was lighter in spirit than the outward journey, not just because of the honey's effect. Now the men could tell stories of past hunts and talk of Qwian's father. She felt his approval like a warm blanket on a cold night.

They called out as they approached the village, to let all know they were returning. This time, Qwian did not need to search for the one person who mattered. Tau, in front of the other villagers, did not wait for her to reach him but rushed towards her, heedless of custom.

'You came back,' he said.

'I will always come back,' she replied, losing words in a kiss that tasted of mad honey. 'For the honey,' she murmured, kissing him again. 'And you.'

If you enjoyed this book, please share your thoughts in a review, however short. Reviews help other readers find my books.

Anyone who reviews one of my books can have his/her dog featured in the Readers' Dogs Hall of Fame on my website

Contact me at jeangill.com

I love to hear from readers.

Acknowledgements

Many thanks to:
my editor Lorna Fergusson of *Fictionfire Literary Consultancy* for believing in my bees and for sterling work (you have to read *The Troubadours Quartet* to fully appreciate the word 'sterling');

Kristin and Jane for your continued input to my books and for your creative genius;

all my writer friends for your support and help;

and my readers, especially those prepared to follow me to new genres, from sustenance to chocolate torte.

Tannlei's archery teaching owes much to the most famous philosopher-archer: Confucius.

Selected reference works:
The Buzz About Bees – Jürgen Tautz
Honeybee Democracy – Thomas D. Seeley
Grizzly Heart – Charlie Russell and Maureen Enns
When Bears Whisper, Do You Listen? – Stephen F. Stringham
Great Bear Almanac – Gary Brown
L'Apiculteur – a monthly French journal for beekeepers

ABOUT THE AUTHOR

I'm a Welsh writer and photographer living in the south of France with two scruffy dogs, a beehive named 'Endeavour', a Nikon D750 and a man. I taught English in Wales for many years and my claim to fame is that I was the first woman to be a secondary headteacher in Carmarthenshire. I'm mother or stepmother to five children so life has been pretty hectic.

I've published all kinds of books, both with traditional publishers and self-published. You'll find everything under my name from prize-winning poetry and novels, military history, translated books on dog training, to a cookery book on goat cheese. My work with top dog-trainer Michel Hasbrouck has taken me deep into the world of dogs with problems, and inspired one of my novels. With Scottish parents, an English birthplace and French residence, I can usually support the winning team on most sporting occasions.

www.jeangill.com

facebook.com/writerjeangill
twitter.com/writerjeangill
instagram.com/writerjeangill
goodreads.com/JeanGill

If you enjoyed *Arrows Tipped with Honey*, don't miss the new challenges facing Mielitta, Drianne, Jannlou and Kermon

in *The World Beyond the Walls*

'*The most original book I've read this year,*' Anna Castle

'Fabulous world-building and spellbinding intrigue,' Karen Inglis

Bee-shifter, bear-shifter, Forest spy and woman-lover: what's second nature to four unlikely friends is a death sentence in the Citadel. The climax to an award-winning series. Royal Dragonfly Award winner. 2020 Kindle Book Award Fantasy Finalist and Wishing Shelf Finalist.

Block Nature out and she'll force her way in.

'Beautiful yet tense… continually surprising and exciting. Jean Gill's *Natural Forces* series offers a rich and alluring adventure that buzzes with intrigue and nature.' *The Booklife Prize*

SAMPLE CHAPTER

'Evil lurks in the walls,' they said.

Nobody would listen to her, so why should she listen to them? If she was too young, too stupid *and* a girl, then they were too old, too blind *and* men, so how could they see the truth that was so obvious to her? Arguing with herself, Janette hopped from one foot to the other in front of a stone wall, in the gloomiest corner at the base of the spiral staircase in the Mages' Tower.

She was really arguing with Nathan, who was not there. Usually he was as unobjectionable as a boy could be and he was her only sure way of returning from an excursion into the walls. And he'd said no.

His black spike of hair nodding in agreement, he'd responded to all her irresistible logic with that one word. And she'd let him think he'd won.

Her cheeks grew warm at the memory of his relief, his offer to help her in apprentice work in the forge, which he hated, or in binding her stories into books, which he hated even more. But she had not lied to him. She'd never said she wouldn't go. He'd just assumed she wouldn't dare go without him. And if he'd let her down, then she had no choice but to go alone, did she?

The more she thought about it, the more she realised this was all Nathan's fault. He didn't appreciate how important her work was. He didn't appreciate her gift. He didn't appreciate *her*. He was just like the adult mages who still wouldn't allow girls into the walls. Now they'd even banned *all* apprentices from entering the walls unless under mages' orders and then only one at a time, in the company of Councillor Verity.

She mimicked the pompous tones they used. 'Because evil lurks in the walls.'

Janette had seen Councillor Verity often enough, a girl barely older than her, as waif-like as Janette was solid, as pale-skinned and golden-haired as Janette was dark and haloed in frizz. The Councillor didn't even have any magecraft whereas Janette could levitate Nathan with just a thought-beam. He objected to that, as did their tutor. Mage-Smith Kermon said it was a very clever trick but not respectful to a fellow-mage.

He could talk! Her teacher hadn't even looked at her story, however often she reminded him and said how important it was. Janette didn't need any of them. She'd been into the walls before and she could stand up for herself. She could balance on one leg too: it helped her concentrate.

The story. Telling stories was her special mage gift, just as Mage Kermon was a smith and a soul-reader. But it was as if her gift was cursed. Nobody believed her stories mattered. And this one could shake the Citadel to its foundations.

Was that what she wanted? Oh yes, that was *definitely* what she wanted. When she'd sneaked into the walls with Nathan, back when he'd been a true friend, she'd seen the honey hunter and she'd known in her bones how important the girl was. And she'd *known* she had to go back, to get the whole story. She'd imagined discussing the implications in Council, being a hero for what she'd discovered. Instead the story was languishing on a shelf. Read and dismissed. Or maybe not even read at all.

Calm now, in the ageless certainty of her gift, Janette stepped forward and walked smoothly into the walls.

A shimmering, a shift of the light and, instead of stone walls, stairs and darkness all around, she was now in a leafy green space. Not grassette like in the Citadel but real grass. Dozens of people ran, walked, played ball and not one of them could see her. Nor was she interested in them.

Janette's paces were regular as her heartbeat. She walked through people as if they weren't real – or as if she wasn't. She shivered and continued to picture the honey hunter in her mind's eye until the scene shifted to a village in the mountains, the inhabitants outside their huts, watching a girl argue her cause.

Qwian. Long black hair, flashing eyes and her father's two long bamboo spears in her hands. No woman had ever been a honey hunter and at first the Headman denied her passionate claim. She insisted that her dreams had named her the honey hunter, that her father's sacred role had been passed on to her when he died. Only when the village Shaman spoke on her behalf was Qwian given the chance to prove herself worthy, as judged by the bees themselves.

Janette's story lived and breathed in front of her. Qwian's team of twelve hunters carried bamboo ropes, slats of wood and a wicker basket through the jungle, across the leech-infested river to the sacred clearing above the high cliffs.

When the men at the top lowered her down those sheer cliffs in a basket, Qwian was almost flying herself among the giant bees that streamed out to protect their comb. Vast, glistening slabs of their treasure filled every crevice in the rock face.

Qwian's only protection was a veil around her head as she speared huge chunks of comb through black clouds of enraged insects, sent the severed pieces down the dizzying drop to the men waiting with baskets below. The rhododendron honey so prized in the village was its trading lifeblood. Men craved the heady rush, akin to madness, offered by a single teaspoonful. Those who risked a second helping, learned of its dangers.

As she swung in her basket, amid smoke and bees, doubts and stings, Qwian was smacked in the face by a morsel of comb, before it fell into the waiting basket below. She automatically licked her lips and then deliberately licked again. Qwian tasted the honey as she'd been warned not to do.

Hah! thought Janette, watching her story again. *Someone like me.*

And what Qwian saw during the honey madness was what had brought Janette back here. Not the boy and the kiss waiting in the village. Not the celebration for the first woman honey hunter, at the moment when she came back to the village, victorious.

In that honey-mad moment, swaying in a basket, dizzy from bee-stings and vertigo, Qwian spoke to the bees, thanked them.

And they replied.

We will need you, they told her. *Your hive and ours. Never forget our gifts.*

Through Qwian's eyes, Janette saw the smoke curl into the soft lines of a girl's face, surrounded by bees. The girl running through a forest. A tattoo glittering on her thigh, a queen bee coming alive, flying.

Never forget, the bees buzzed. *We protect our queen. We protect you.*

Born and bred in the Citadel, like generations before her, Janette had never seen living beings that weren't human until she'd made her illicit trip with Nathan into the walls. She knew of such creatures from books in the library and had been brought up to give thanks they'd been exterminated. The Citadel was indeed free of infestation but rumour populated the nearby Forest with all manner of monster, including the defectives in exile from the Citadel.

Like every citizen, Janette had heard the terrifying story of the Citadel freak who'd been infected with Forest. Who communed with bees, could even become one. And who'd been defeated – the stones be thanked! – in the Battle of the Forest, where she now lived in exile.

And then, in the mysterious world through the walls, where the past existed in layers of time, Janette had found the honey hunter and the bees. *What if?* Janette had asked herself ever since she shared Qwian's vision through smoke and the blackness of bees. *What if* the vision had come to pass? What if the girl running through the Forest was the Citadel's enemy, the Queen of the Warrior Bees?

Conquered but alive, she was held as a threat over naughty children by Citadel parents. Bees instead of hair, black eyes filling her face. 'She'll take you off to the Forest if you don't behave. And if you don't obey her every wish, she'll have you stung until you're more full of holes than a hairnet.'

Not that Janette believed such stories any more. Given the number of times she'd misbehaved, she should have been whisked off to the Forest long ago.

What if this was where it began? This communion with bees, a promise and a prophecy? Were Qwian and the boy who loved her parents to the freak? And if the running girl was the Queen of the Warrior Bees, Janette knew something about her that would end her reign. Their queen would not be protected, however many bees were with her, if she was suppressed before her life began, here in the walls.

First, Janette had to follow the story, find out how it led from here to the Citadel side of the wall. Then she could go to the Council of Ten and impress them. Mage-Smith Kermon would be sorry he hadn't taken her story seriously.

'Show me the honey hunter returning with her harvest,' she instructed and, in the manner of the world within the walls, her focus created a destination and the scene shifted around her, until she was once more among the huts of the village, watching Qwian lauded by the Headman, returning triumphant with her two spears and precious baskets of mad honey.

By refining her search terms, she navigated the stages of Qwian's life, willing time to pass ever faster so she watched only key scenes. She saw Qwian and her young man grow older, their children playing hunt-the-honey with wooden sticks. Until the year came when one of the boys knelt in front of the Headman and received his mother's spears as pride lit her eyes.

SAMPLE CHAPTER

Not a girl-child, thought Janette. And the other children showed no interest in bees. So the running girl was still in the future. Janette must walk through time, following the story of the bees' promise. Once she was on the scent of a story, she was oblivious to all else and she was happy on the honey trail.

But her presence in the walls had not gone unnoticed and a great evil awoke. Finally, its time had come. And it laughed.

You might also like

SONG AT DAWN

Book 1 in the award-winning *Troubadours Quartet*.

FREE *to members of Jean Gill's Special Readers' Group. Sign up at jeangill.com*

'*Historical Fiction at its best.*' Karen Charlton, *the Detective Lavender Mysteries*

Four Discovered Diamonds Awards

Historical Novel Society Editor's Choice

Winner of the Global Ebooks Award for Best Historical Fiction

Finalist in the Wishing Shelf Awards and the Chaucer Awards

Set in the period following the Second Crusade, Jean Gill's spellbinding romantic thrillers evoke medieval France with breathtaking accuracy. The characters leap off the page and include amazing women like Eleanor of Aquitaine and Ermengarda of Narbonne, who shaped history in battles and in bedchambers.

LEFT OUT

If you like Young Adult books that are enjoyed by adults too; if you're left-handed or know a leftie, try *Left Out*

"A compelling story about friendship, its strength, and the unusual ways it develops." Rebecca P. McCray, The Journey of the Marked

Being different isn't easy but it can be exciting!

How well do you know your friends? Are they left-handed or right-handed? Are they left-brained or right-brained? And what difference does it make?

Shocked at discovering how left-handers are persecuted, Jamie ties her hand behind her back for a public protest in school. This does not go down well with the teachers. Her best friend Ryan joins in but just when their campaign is working, Ryan's mother drops a bombshell. She's whisking him off from Wales UK to live back in America.

There he faces bullying at its most deadly.

FORTUNE KOOKIE

Can dreams take over your life? Although it is Book 2 of the series *Looking for Normal,* the book stands alone.

Shortlisted for the Cinnamon Press Novella Award

"Jean Gill brings her magical storytelling skills to teens, to weave compelling and thought-provoking stories that will linger on in their minds well after the last page is read."

Kristin Gleeson, author and children's librarian

Jamie's mother is hooked on fortune-tellers, and running the family into debt. To cure her, Jamie decides to investigate the psychic world. Their research causes havoc in school and they are drawn deeper into the very world they are investigating.

Jamie's dreams of walking a medieval battlefield are so vivid that she feels compelled to resolve a historical mystery that starts at Kidwelly Castle in South Wales, where Princess Gwenllian once lived.

Jean Gill's Publications

Novels

Natural Forces

Book 2 Arrows Tipped with Honey *(The 13th Sign)* 2020

Book 1 Queen of the Warrior Bees *(The 13th Sign)* 2019

The Troubadours Quartet

Book 5 Nici's Christmas Tale: A Troubadours Short Story *(The 13th Sign)* 2018

Book 4 Song Hereafter *(The 13th Sign)* 2017

Book 3 Plaint for Provence *(The 13th Sign)* 2015

Book 2 Bladesong *(The 13th Sign)* 2015

Book 1 Song at Dawn *(The 13th Sign)* 2015

Someone to Look Up To: a dog's search for love and understanding *(The 13th Sign)* 2016

Love Heals

Book 2 More Than One Kind *(The 13th Sign)* 2016

Book 1 No Bed of Roses *(The 13th Sign)* 2016

Looking for Normal (teen fiction/fact)

Book 1 Left Out *(The 13th Sign)* 2017

Book 2 Fortune Kookie *(The 13th Sign)* 2017

Non-fiction/Memoir/Travel

How Blue is my Valley *(The 13th Sign)* 2016

A Small Cheese in Provence *(The 13th Sign)* 2016

Faithful through Hard Times *(The 13th Sign)* 2018

4.5 Years – war memoir by David Taylor *(The 13th Sign)* 2017

Short Stories and Poetry

One Sixth of a Gill *(The 13th Sign)* 2014

From Bedtime On *(The 13th Sign)* 2018 (2nd edition)

With Double Blade *(The 13th Sign)* 2018 (2nd edition)

Translation (from French)

The Last Love of Edith Piaf – Christie Laume *(Archipel)* 2014

A Pup in Your Life – Michel Hasbrouck 2008

Gentle Dog Training – Michel Hasbrouck *(Souvenir Press)* 2008

www.ingramcontent.com/pod-product-compliance
Ingram Content Group UK Ltd.
Pitfield, Milton Keynes, MK11 3LW, UK
UKHW042002230426
12048UKWH00009B/500